His expressi excitement to som deep and dark and- ...

He repeated my name, and before I could blink, a pair of strong arms wrapped around my waist and a torso I knew was as solid and defined as a redwood tree flattened against the front of me.

He dipped his head, those dreamy eyes dark now with desire, and zeroed in on my own like a laser pointer. Hypnotized by the naked need facing me, I took a breath—a physical and a mental one—and pushed up on my unshod toes until my lips pressed against his.

For a nanosecond, Frayne stilled. The notion that he didn't want this blew across my mind. A beat later and the thought died as his arms tightened and he pulled me fully against his body.

And then kissed me back.

Praise for Peggy Jaeger

Today, Tomorrow, Always

by

Peggy Jaeger

A Match Made in Heaven, Book 2

Today, Tomorrow, Always

Contact Information: info@thewildrosepress.com

Cover Art by *Diana Carlile*

The Wild Rose Press, Inc.
PO Box 708
Adams Basin, NY 14410-0708
Visit us at www.thewildrosepress.com

Publishing History
First Champagne Rose Edition, 2019
Print ISBN 978-1-5092-2934-5
Digital ISBN 978-1-5092-2935-2

A Match Made in Heaven, Book 2
Published in the United States of America

Dedication

To Jane Rokes ~
Thanks for all the insights into what it takes
to be a wedding officiant.
Now I know why you've been voted "Best of the Best"
so many times by your happy couples.

Chapter 1

"Cathy, don't forget you've got the historical society luncheon today," my secretary-slash-office-be-all-end-all Martha told me as she placed a client brief on my desk.

"How could I forget? Clara Johnson's called me once a day for the past week to remind me."

Martha chuckled.

"Was she the same way with Dad?" Martha had been my father's paralegal and office manager back in the day. He'd told me more than once he couldn't have survived without her and joked she knew where all the bodies were buried.

"Nope. Whenever she was around your father, be it at a meeting or even if she happened to see him on Main Street, she'd smile and keep quiet as a dormouse." Martha executed an eye roll a teenager fifty years younger would have been impressed with. "Clara was raised in a household where the menfolk ruled the roost and the women nodded, listened, and cooked."

"That explains a lot."

Martha left me alone to finish some preliminary paperwork I needed for an upcoming court appearance. At the door to my office, she turned. "Oh, I forgot. Fiona called."

"On the office line? She didn't use Instagran?" My ninety-three-year-old grandmother never called my office, or those of my sisters, if she wanted to speak with one of us. Instead, she used our cell phones, knowing we were never without them, and therefore available at any time. She called the speed dial we'd all assigned as her Instagran number.

"It went straight to voice mail. She thought you might be in court because that's the only time you don't pick up."

I opened my desk drawer and pulled out my phone. "I forgot to take it off Do Not Disturb after yesterday's court session." I turned it back on. "Did she say what she wanted?"

"A reminder"—Martha's lips twisted into a wry grin—"that she needs a ride to the doctor tomorrow. Her exact words were, 'Tell Number One I'll be ready to go at nine, and I'd appreciate it if she managed to get here on time and not be late like the last time.' "

"Two minutes." I shook my head and held up my first two fingers. "I was two minutes late because I got stuck behind a school bus."

"Don't shoot the messenger. I already made sure your first appointment doesn't start until after lunch. You've got the entire morning free in case she goes overtime with the doctor."

My grandmother had broken her arm a few months ago and required casting and then a temporary move to an adult-care facility while she recuperated. Up until then, she'd been living in our family home with my middle sister, Colleen.

"Thanks. Nanny's no doubt got a laundry list of questions for the doctor, plus another one filled with 'suggestions.' "

"Should I cancel your afternoon?"

I knew she wasn't serious.

Well, maybe a smidge.

"No. I'll be back by one even if I have to clamp her mouth shut with my fingers like she used to do to us to keep us quiet in church."

"I'd pay to see that."

"Keep your money."

Once she was back at her desk, I concentrated on the brief in front of me until it was time to leave for the meeting.

My father had practiced general law in our hometown of Heaven, New Hampshire, for over thirty-five years, and most people in the area knew, or knew of, him. My love of arguing and always wanting to be proven right no matter what the subject matter had led me to follow in my father's well-heeled footsteps. With his retirement and my parents' move south, I'd inherited his practice, his role as justice of the peace, and his position on several town boards and committees. Not to mention a third share in my elderly grandmother's care and keeping.

And believe me, there was a lot involved in her care and keeping. A community activism gene ran deep in my family's bloodline. Keeping Nanny out of jail when she was the ringleader of a protest march, boycott, or sit-in, was a full-time job. My lawyer status made me her de facto one call, and no matter what time of the day or night, I was available to bail her out.

At about fifteen minutes before twelve, Martha called out she was leaving to get lunch. A glance in my office bathroom mirror showed I needed to run a quick brush through my hair and reapply the lipstick I'd eaten off.

The historical society was a quick walk up the street from my office. Our New England winter temperatures had been mild the past week, but experience as a lifelong New Hampshirite had taught me never to be caught without warm gloves, a hat, and a scarf any day after Halloween. The weather today had decided to stick to its temperate forecast, and I made it to my meeting without the need to pull on my gloves.

Heaven's historical society was housed in a two-century-old building as famous for its archives as it was for its Victorian Gothic architecture. The building had been designed by the great-grandson of the town's founder, Josiah Heaven, and had been gifted to the town in the early twentieth century by the family on the condition it be turned into a museum.

As I jogged up the sixteen marble steps of the front entrance portico and pushed through the massive oak doors to the foyer, the warmth of the interior smacked me square in the face. I'd forgotten how hot it stayed in winter due to its twelve-inch-thick walls. The opposite was true in summer. The interior remained cool on all floors except the top, due to the marble flooring and tempered glass windows.

"Right on time," Clara Johnson announced as I entered the dining room. "I don't know why I was worried you'd forget about the meeting. You're as punctual as your dear father always was."

It was on the tip of my tongue to say there was no way I could have forgotten about the luncheon since she'd called me numerous times to remind me of it. If Nanny had taught me one thing in my thirty-nine years, though, it was to respect my elders.

Clara grabbed me into a bone-crushing hug. For a

woman in her seventh decade, she was surprisingly strong.

I smiled at the society members taking their seats around the large table and found my own chair.

There were nine members present and ten places set for lunch.

"Is someone joining us?" I asked Davison Clarkson, my ninth-grade history teacher, seated to my right.

He tugged at his goatee—a habit he'd had even when I'd been his student—and said, "Writer fellow, what's his name? The one who wrote that Emily Dickinson book a few years back? Frey?"

"Frayne?" I said. "McLachlan Frayne?"

"A-ya. 'At's the one."

"Mr. Frayne has requested to meet with us," Clara said, butting into the conversation, "so I invited him to join us for lunch."

"Do we know why?"

"Maybe he's writing a new book," Eloise Cruckshank said. She clapped her palms together like a tiny bird flapping its wings, a wide, childlike smile gracing her chubby cheeks.

"No one for him to write about 'round here. No one famous hails from Heaven." Peter Gunderson's booming voice startled me. I was wondering if he'd forgotten to turn on his hearing aids just when Olaf Tewksburry chastised him.

"Fer Cris'sake, Gunny. Turn your damn ears on. They can hear ya screamin' in Concord."

Peter's hand flew to his ears. A second later, the air around us shattered with a shrill whistle.

"You're gonna deafen us all!" Olaf clamped both

his palms over his ears.

Clara thwacked her gavel against a book she'd placed next to her luncheon plate in an attempt to protect the antique table, and called us to order. "Let's get started. We can get some work done before Mr. Frayne arrives."

For the next several minutes, Eloise read the long-winded minutes from our last meeting in her singsong, high-pitched voice. My mind began to wander before she got to page two. For more than the first time since I'd become a member of the society, I wished I hadn't been invited. For his last act as board president, my father had put my name in for consideration and knew, because I was his daughter, I'd be voted in unanimously. I was the youngest person in the room by at least thirty-five years, the only one who worked full time, and one of three females.

Nanny Fee likened my position as a board member to the Pope's. Namely, I was stuck with it unless I moved at least one hundred miles away, was kicked off for a major offense like criminal malfeasance, or died, whichever of those three came first.

Since I was an officer of the court, I wasn't getting voted off the island anytime soon for a crime, and I had no intention of leaving Heaven. Ever. It appeared I was stuck until my funeral mass was conducted at my parish church.

Clara banged her gavel against the book again, and I was yanked out of my mental meanderings.

"Any discussion on the minutes before we vote to approve?"

I crossed my fingers and prayed no one issued a challenge.

"Good." Clara smiled and rang the one-hundred-year-old dinner bell sitting at her right to call for the staff to serve lunch. And just in time, thank you, Jesus. Forget growling, my stomach was literally howling with hunger.

A knock on the door sounded at the same time it was pushed open.

"Ah, wonderful," Clara said.

"Looks like the writer fella is here," Davison said. "Right on time to eat, too."

I had a vague idea of what McLachlan Frayne looked like from his last book jacket photo—a book I'd devoured in bed one Saturday night, because Emily Dickinson was my favorite poet. He was in his late thirties maybe, with a serious, authorial air only a black and white headshot gave justice to. His eyes were light hued since the photo was devoid of color, his hair a generic dark, cut military-like. If I'd had him for an English professor in college, I might not have chosen law and instead opted into literature. Not that it would ever have happened. Not if my parents had anything to say about it.

Clara jumped up and trotted to greet our visitor. An impressive set of wide shoulders filled the doorframe. Gone was the chopped crew cut of the book jacket photo, replaced by a longish mop of wavy, salt and pepper hair, heavy-handed on the salt. Clara pumped his hand, and I could imagine the jaw-wide smile she graced him with. My secretary hadn't been exaggerating when she'd told me the head of the historical society was deferential to the male population.

With Frayne's hand still clasped in her own, Clara

turned to the group. Yup. Her maniacal smile was front and center. "Everyone, Mr. Frayne is here."

"We got eyes in our heads, Clara." Olaf's mouth pursed into a decided sour pucker as he shook his head. Under his breath he added, "Fool woman. Thinks we're all blind."

I bit back a grin and lowered my head to hide it. These two had known one another since the cradle, gone all through school together, and even—old gossip had it—been involved romantically for a while when both their spouses died.

When I was sure my amusement was no longer noticeable, I lifted my head as Clara arrived at the table with our guest.

Any remnants of a grin remaining on my face died the moment my gaze lit on McLachlan Frayne.

On the book jacket, he'd given off an air of commanding arrogance as he'd stared into the camera's lens. In the flesh, that description flew out the window.

He was tall, so I had to lift my head to view him properly. Those wide shoulders were covered in a dark sports jacket a size or two too big for his frame. Under it, a black V-neck sweater sat over the same color T-shirt, the collar peeking through the jagged neck of the vee. Yards of leg were covered by faded jeans, white from wear in all the regular stress places. Black Converse sneakers adorned his feet and looked so soft and comfortable, I grew a little jealous.

Shaggy hair a good time past a trim framed a face that could have been a tourism board ad for Ireland. Eyes the same color as frozen Arctic ice were deer-caught-in-the-headlights wide as a twin set of commas indented the corners of his mouth. The notion he was in some kind of pain shot through me, and for the briefest of moments, I wanted to reach up and run a finger along those grooves to smooth away whatever anguish had caused them.

Clara introduced us all in turn, Frayne reaching out to shake each hand as it was offered. When I slipped my hand into his, his wide eyes narrowed, tiny lines fanning out from the corners to his temples.

His gaze swept over my face and confusion drifted over his features as if he recognized me but couldn't place from where.

A moment later he tugged his hand from mine.

"We were about to have lunch, Mr. Frayne. Please, join us." She indicated the chair next to hers, which put him directly across from me. As everyone around me started in on what I knew were delicious crab cakes, I took my time opening my napkin and placing it in my lap. Time spent in a feeble attempt to get the unusual sensations circling through me under control.

"I'll admit," Clara said, her bright smile aimed at Frayne, "we're all excited to hear why you wanted to meet with us today."

"The man's a writer, Clara." Olaf shoved half his crab cake into his mouth. "Obviously he's here to write 'bout something," he added, speaking around the food.

Frayne opened his mouth, but Eloise spoke before he could.

"Or someone," she twittered. "Someone famous."

"Nobody famous 'round these parts," Gunny said, loudly, preventing Frayne from answering again.

"Wasn't that gal on the TV singing-competition show from Rutland?" Olaf asked. "You know, the one where you vote the lousy ones off each week?" A sea of bobbing heads circled the table. "Rutland's only thirty miles away. You writing about her?" he asked Frayne.

"Why would he be writing about someone who lost, you old coot?" Finlay Mayhew, who'd been unusually silent up until now, asked.

Once again, Frayne open his mouth to answer, then shut it when Finlay started laying into his brother-in-law.

This started a loud discussion between the two, each vying to be heard over the other. Unfortunately, this wasn't an uncommon occurrence at these meetings.

Clara's inability to scold anyone who possessed a Y chromosome had rendered her useless to halt these two once they got started. Since I spent my days dealing with argumentative clients, I stood, grabbed my filled water glass, and rapped it a few times with my knife.

I rapped harder when they ignored me.

"Gentlemen." I used my firm, loud, lawyer voice cultivated over years spent in the county courthouse. "Why don't we let Mr. Frayne explain why he's here instead of getting all riled up with unnecessary speculation?"

Their bickering came to a stuttering stop. Both octogenarians looked first at me, then one another, the rest of the room, and then back to me, mouths agape.

"He is, after all, our guest."

Olaf was the first to capitulate. With a determined shake of his hairless, billiard-ball head, his mouth closed, the corners of it pulling upward. He winked at me, then at Finlay. "Smart. Same as her pa."

"But prettier," Finlay, who always wanted the last word, added.

With a smile for both of them, I then turned my attention to Frayne. His gaze hadn't left my face since I'd stood and commandeered the situation. The comma in one corner of his mouth grew and a dimple appeared deep enough to shove a button into.

A moment after the darling curl appeared, it flew, and once again Frayne's expression grew serious.

"Mr. Frayne? You've got the floor."

I sat back down, and he stood.

With one hand, he swiped the hair tumbling across his brow straight back on his head, only to have it fall forward again the moment he let go. "Thank you, Ms. Mulvaney."

I have to admit I was impressed he'd remembered my name. I was good at names—a factor of my job— but I don't think I could have had the immediate recall he had after being introduced to nine new people all at the same time.

"And thank you all for letting me intrude on your lunch today."

"Oh, it's no intrusion at all," Eloise piped up. "We're all excited to meet such a famous writer." She probably more than any of us, evidenced by the way she fidgeted in her chair.

"Eloise." Clara made a zip-it motion with her hand across her lips.

Frayne took a breath and then ran his gaze down the table, briefly touching on each of us. Because I was the last one he lit on, he addressed me. "I'm writing a new biography, and I need access to your historical archives for research. Frequent access, in fact."

"Who's the book about?" Clara asked.

"Your town founder, Josiah Heaven."

"Oh, goodness." One of Clara's hands flew to her throat as her eyes popped wide open. "What an—"

"*Honor*," Eloise gushed, clapping her hands together again.

"Don't know it's much of an honor, Weezy," Olaf said, his lips twisting. He turned his attention to Frayne. "Why'd anyone outside of Heaven want to read about ol' Josiah? Man's been dead a couple hundred years. I can't see much interest in him in this day and age."

Peter and Finley started defending the town founder, both of their sonorous voices rising against the other to be heard.

I shot a quick glance at Frayne. The furrows in his brow deepened as his gaze ping-ponged between the two—now three—men who were all vying for attention. The notion the poor man was out of his league blew through me. Once again I rose, dinged my water glass with a knife, and called for the trio of city elders to quiet.

With reluctance, all three did, but not after I shot each of them what my sister Colleen called my *lawyer death stare*. She claimed she'd seen me use it on trial witnesses when I didn't like an answer I'd been given and the witness tended to disintegrate under its power. She also claimed I used it on family members when I was being *pissy*—her word—about something.

Once the room was again quiet, I said, "Please continue, Mr. Frayne."

He lifted his water glass to his lips and, after taking a large draft, said, "Thank you. Well, as I was saying. The biography is of the reverend. There have been one or two books written about him over the years, though none have presented a sense of the real man behind the

12

legend. For instance, what brought him to New Hampshire? I've never been able to find the answer in any research I've done. The man doesn't exist on paper before he showed up here one day, built a homestead, and then a town. No birth certificate on record, no background material at all."

Heads bobbed around the table. This was information we'd all been weaned on.

"And why did he insist all the streets and businesses have Biblical associations? I understand the town charter still requires any new enterprises to use a city-council-approved name whether it fits the business or not."

"That's the truth." Davison nodded. "It's written in perpetuity in the town charter."

"Why? Why did he want to ensure the town continued on the same way generations after his death?"

"Some folks think he was a bit of kook," Olaf offered.

"I've read that." Frayne nodded. "It's also been theorized he had a God complex, a mental fixation on Heaven and Hell, perhaps even, that he suffered from delusions."

The table grew quiet for a moment.

"The reverend was a complicated man," Clara said.

Frayne cocked his head to one side. "Correct me if I'm wrong, but this society has never allowed any writers into the Heaven archives, the personal ones I mean, of Josiah, his sons, or grandsons, have you?"

"No." Clara shook her head. "Not the personal annals. We've had people conduct research through the town charters and the county historical records. Never

Josiah's personal ones, though."

"Why not?"

All committee members turned to me. Since I was the sole lawyer at the table, it was my duty to answer what they collectively viewed as a legal matter.

Frayne's attention lit on me as well. I could tell from the question in his eyes he didn't understand why they'd all zeroed in on me to provide an answer.

"The Heaven family," I explained, "viewed the private documents as personal property, which legally, they were, and which weren't, therefore, included in the museum's archives. They kept a tight hold over those documents. Whenever someone wanted access to them, we needed to ask, formally, in writing, for permission to show them. It was always denied."

"Why?"

"We never asked," Clara said.

"As I've said, the documents were ruled over by a family member who was placed in charge of their caretaking. I believe the society asked for decades for the public to be allowed access to them."

"And they were always told no," Eloise said.

"Are there any descendants I could ask now for permission?"

"No. Josiah's line ran its course two decades ago with the death of his four-times-great grandson. He left no children when he died, and no other direct blood relatives exist."

"So, there's no one to seek authorization from to view those files or documents but this committee, then?"

All eyes settled on me again. I took a silent breath. "Correct.

With a hopeful expression on his face and in his eyes, Frayne bent forward and leaned his knuckles on the table, all the while keeping his gaze on me. "So." He took a breath. "What do I have to sign to be allowed access?"

Chapter 2

"Why are the personal papers so important to you, young fella?" Olaf asked, his bushy, snowcap white eyebrows lifting up to his bald head.

Frayne's expression blanked and then, just as quick, recovered. I don't think anyone else noticed because it happened in an eye blink, but my lawyer spidey-sense went on hyperalert.

"Yes, what do you think they contain that the other biographers haven't already made note of?" Clara said.

"The other books have skimmed the surface, stating the facts of the reverend's life as much as is known. I'd like to dig deeper, get to the man himself, his thoughts, his motivations, if I can. Try to give a more balanced view of his life and history. That's kind of my specialty."

"You sound like one of them investigative reporters, digging up dirt anywhere they can." Finlay Mayhew's thin lips bent down at the corners, deepening the grooves in his face into dermal crevasses.

"You're not working for one of them slander rags with enquiring minds, are you, boy?" Olaf asked. " 'Cause we ain't gonna let anyone sully the name of our town founder."

I don't know if it was the reference to a salacious weekly tabloid or the fact he'd been called a boy, but Frayne's entire face changed in a nanosecond. The guarded cast in his gaze flew, replaced by a quiet mirth. His lips twisted up, and two delicious dimples developed at their corners.

Holy Christmas.

Frayne's gaze met mine, and I swear his charming grin grew before it moved to his accuser.

"No, sir. I'm not. I can assure you I'm not a tabloid journalist, and I have no intention of writing anything salacious about the reverend. I simply want to give as accurate a portrayal of the man, the times, and his circumstances as I can. That's the way I approach every biography I write. I want it to be as thorough and balanced a representation as possible."

"You never mentioned who's publishing this book, Frayne," Gunny said. "You got one lined up?"

Frayne rattled off the name of a well-known publisher.

"How wonderful." Clara beamed. She glanced around the table and asked, "Are there any other questions for Mr. Frayne before we vote on his request?"

I had several, but I decided to ask them in private if the opportunity presented itself.

When no one expressed any concerns, Clara said, "All those in favor of allowing Mr. Frayne access to the Heaven family's personal papers and any other historical documentation, please raise your hand."

Eight hands went up, Finlay Mayhew the sole holdout.

No surprise there.

Clara, in a show of uncharacteristic pique, slanted him a squinty-eyed glower, her lips pressed flat together like two squished pancakes. This, from the woman who never missed an opportunity to defer to the man's opinion, was the most heated I'd ever seen her get toward him.

"The motion passes by a clear majority," she announced.

Finlay's response was to fold his arms across his midsection, his flannel shirt tugging across his ample girth with the movement.

"Thank you," Frayne said. "I appreciate it."

"We'll set you up with a schedule to view the documents," Clara told him. "Just give us your time availability."

"All day, any day. I'm staying in town while I do my research. If you tell me where to go, I can get started as soon as possible."

This posed a bit of a problem. I was about to tell him why, when Clara beat me to it.

"You'll need to coordinate with Cathleen—Mrs. Mulvaney," she said, nodding toward me. "Our current curator, Leigh James, is indisposed, otherwise she would be the proper person to help you with your research."

"I don't require any help."

"Yes, well, Cathleen is in charge of the personal archives while Dr. James is on leave, and Cathleen's a very busy woman. You two will need to put your heads together to decide on times she's available to assist you."

"I don't understand." His gaze shot from Clara to me. "All I need is access."

"There are rules involved with viewing the personal archives. Rules you must abide by." Clara directed a very pointed stare at me. "Maybe you should explain it, Cathy, dear."

I nodded. "I need to get back to start my afternoon." I rose and addressed Frayne. "Why don't we go outside, and I'll let you know what needs to be done?"

"Come back and join us for lunch after Cathy leaves," Clara told Frayne.

I grabbed my purse, tossed my fellow society members a quick goodbye, and then moved from the room, Frayne following.

In the foyer, I stopped. "Sorry about that. They're a little much to take when you don't know what to expect."

Frayne shook his head. "I don't think I've been called *boy* for more than twenty years."

I smiled.

"What did Mrs. Johnson mean about rules?"

"It's an archaic regulation passed down from the previous society members. It's never been challenged, and this group isn't going to change anything in their lifetime." I pulled my coat from the closet. "The personal archives are kept locked, and no one is allowed access to them without the curator, or the society board member in charge of overseeing the collection, present."

"That's you?"

"Yes."

"I can't just have the key?"

"Unfortunately, no." With a sigh, I started to shrug into my coat. Frayne slipped behind me to help.

I was surprised by the gesture. It had been a long, long time since a man had done something as chivalrous as hold my coat for me. Standing behind me, he was close enough his warm breath fanned across my neck as I slipped my arms into the sleeves. As soon as my coat was on, I turned around to continue our conversation. The words died on my lips.

Frayne was still standing close to me—so close I could make out the tiny shards of ice blue competing with the light slate in his irises. Long, dark, and thick curled lashes framed his eyes, highlighting the pale colors swimming in them.

"Why unfortunately no?" He slid his hands into his pants pockets and rocked back on his heels.

"Again, it's a society rule. I'm not allowed to give the key to anyone else. It's required to stay in my possession at all times until my term as archive director is over."

"So…" He tilted his head, his brows tugging together in the midline as he examined my face. A ghost of a grin slanted his lips. "You're like, what? The keeper of the keys? Guarding the secrets of the ancient and sacred archives from dark, outside forces, like Cerberus guarding the gates of Hell?"

I laughed, and the sound echoed in the empty space around us.

"Not sacred, I assure you. But the board does regard itself as the historical protector of the past, and the Heaven family in particular. If you want entrée to the private collection and the personal documents, you need to abide by their rules."

After a few moments, he blew out a breath. "Okay. What's your schedule look like, then? Because I'm free, and I want to get started as soon as I can."

"I'm tied up today until about four. I could meet you back here afterward."

I could tell he wasn't happy about having to wait.

"Do you need to stay with me while I do my research?"

"If you dip into the personal files, then yes. If it's the public files, I can arrange to have a docent assist you. The files are all up to date, computerized, and catalogued in the system, but the storage space is a maze and you'll need some guidance finding specific items. The docent can help."

"Okay, well, I guess I'll see you after four."

"You mentioned you're staying in town for the time being?"

"Yeah."

"Where?"

"At the inn."

"Inn Heaven?"

He smiled, and my toes curled inside my boots when those dimples appeared again.

"Yeah. Great name. I need to go check in once I'm done here. I've got a room booked for a month. If it looks like it's gonna take longer, I might rent a place. The inn is good for now."

"Better than good," I said, no small amount of pride in my voice. "You'll get breakfast and lunch every day, and if you want dinner, all you have to do is ask Maureen, the owner. You're in good hands."

"You know her?"

"We share parents."

It took him a moment.

"Sisters." He nodded.

"Got it in one." I shot a finger at him. In doing so, I happened to see my watch again. "Why don't you go have lunch, and I'll see you in a few hours, okay?"

Because it was second nature for me to do so, ground into my manners rulebook by my grandmother, I put out my hand to shake his.

When he took it with his own, I was engulfed in a cauldron of heat so consuming, my entire body stilled, reveling in the sensation.

And not only the warmth, but the actual *feel* of his skin against mine. Little pulses of awareness surged over my wrist and up my arm, spreading warmth to every pore it crossed. I don't know how long we stood there, our hands together, our gazes locked. I do know when the sound of my cell phone penetrated the silent air around us, it was like a booming strike of thunder clapping directly overhead.

We both jumped, Frayne tightening his grip on my hand. I yanked on it, and when he let it go, I reached into my bag.

"It's my office. I'm sorry. I've gotta go."

Without looking back at him, I sprinted through the doors I'd walked through less than an hour before.

****

I wasn't surprised when Frayne was seated in one of the antique sofas lining the perimeter of the marble-floored foyer when I returned hours later.

"Right on time." He shoved his cell phone into the briefcase next to him.

When I'd run from him earlier, I'd tried to convince myself the reason I was out of sorts was because I had a great deal on my mind. Between two court cases on the docket in the next few weeks, concerns about my grandmother, the wedding I was scheduled to officiate at this weekend and for which I hadn't yet written a word, and the thousand other issues that came up daily, it was no wonder I'd been a little unglued around Frayne. I didn't need another responsibility like being at his beck and call when I was this busy. I'd had no say in the matter though. With Leigh James on strict bed rest until her baby arrived, I was duty bound to act on her behalf.

When Frayne stood and swiped a hand across his forehead to push back the shock of hair falling across it, I realized what a poor liar I was. I could argue and debate a cause for someone else ad infinitum, redefine facts, or reinterpret them at will. But I couldn't lie convincingly to myself to save my life.

One look at him and all my girly parts started to tingle, like when your foot is asleep and it's beginning to get some circulation back and waking up. Little shots of nerve-ending sizzles and pops signaling something was going on. And the *something going on* was pure attraction, a sensation I hadn't experienced in a lifetime.

I shrugged out of my coat and slung it over my forearm. "Did you get all checked in?"

He told me he had and then followed me down the marble stairs to the first basement. "I met your sister. She's young to be running an inn all by herself."

"Don't let her age fool you. Maureen is an amazing businesswoman. She's been written up in a half-dozen tourist magazines over the past two years with stellar, glowing reviews of the inn, her food, and her customer service."

"I read a few of them online when I decided to take this job."

At the bottom of the stairs, I reached out to open the door.

Frayne stretched an arm around me and beat me to

it, wrapping his hand around mine on the knob. "Sorry. Old habits. My parents drilled in me from the womb that I should always open a door for a lady." The tops of his cheeks went a little pink with his words. "And I hear how archaic I sound," he said, "so let me apologize again."

I had to smile as he pulled open the door and let me go through first.

The temperature in the basement was kept at a constant sixty-eight degrees, the subbasement under it two degrees warmer since it was placed farther underground.

I explained all this as we walked into a small anteroom strewn with a few computers on worktables. "You'll need to log into the system with a protected password of your choosing," I told him as I tossed my belongings on one of the extra tables.

He sat at a workspace and booted up the computer.

"If you follow the prompts," I said, "they'll guide you through the process."

A few minutes later he was navigating through the system like a pro.

"I think you've done this before."

"The Dickinson Museum uses the same archival system. What are these numbers after each entry?" He pointed to the screen.

"The first one indicates which level the document is housed on," I said as I leaned in closer. "One indicates this floor; two, the subbasement. The next numbers tell you the row the artifact is placed in and the shelf number where it's housed." When I turned, our heads were even, our faces a mere whisper from one another.

Frayne's gaze dropped down to my mouth and lingered for a moment before slowly sweeping back up to my eyes. Awareness bolted through my body, my spine shuddering from neck to thighs with the impact.

The urge to lean in and chase away the sadness in his eyes was surprising.

"For instance—" *Good Lord.* I sounded like I was in dire need of an inhaler.

I cleared my throat and pointed to the screen. "Those numbers, 2-62-9-10, means the document is in the subbasement, row sixty-two, shelf nine, space ten. If you want to see the document, you'll find it there."

"Do I have access to get my own research materials, or do I need to ask the docent to bring them to me?"

I shook my head and stepped away from the table—and him. Where my voice had sounded like I was having an asthma attack, his was composed and smooth, the pitch and tone clear and concise.

"You can get any item from this level by yourself or ask the docent to retrieve it for you. You'll need to log anything out on the computer if you remove it from the storage room and then log it back in again when you return it to its place. Items in the subbasement, the private files, you need me to be here for. Oh, and I should tell you, although you must already know, you can't remove anything from the museum. Every item has to remain here."

"I figured that. Is there a copy machine available if I need it?"

I pointed to the far side of the room.

He stood and slipped his hands into his pockets. "I'd like to get started now."

I glanced down at my watch. "Beverly Carlisle will be here at five. She's got docent duty until seven. The museum closes then, so whatever work you do will need to be finished by then so she can lock up."

"I should be. You said if I want to see anything in the private collection you need to be present, correct?"

"Yes. Do you want to start there?"

With his head cocked to one side again, he said, "Can I click around the files and see what's listed first and then tell you? You don't need to leave right now, do you?

I didn't need to, no, but I wanted to. A nice glass of Merlot and some leftover meatloaf waited for me at home. "I've got some work with me I could do until Bev arrives."

He sat back down and got to it. While he searched, I pulled my laptop from my briefcase to start on the wedding vows I needed to write for the weekend.

In addition to my work as a lawyer, in my justice of the peace role, I officiated at marriages, many of which my wedding-planner sister, Colleen, was in charge of. The three of us, Maureen, Colleen, and I were partners in a boutique wedding business. Colleen planned them, I officiated when called upon, and the receptions were often held at Inn Heaven.

Frayne moved up and down from his computer station several times and disappeared into the storage room. At one point, I found him standing and holding a county record book. From the weathered look of the leather cover, it was one of the older volumes, filled with handwritten accounts of area births and deaths.

He'd slipped on a pair of thick black reading glasses, making him look like a middle-aged Clark

Kent in need of a haircut. They perched halfway down his nose, enabling him to look over the tops to see the distance clearly. He had the record book open and was engrossed in a page as he walked. I'd put his age at late thirties, but now up close and in person, he was a few years older, maybe early to mid-forties.

Footsteps clanged down the stairs.

"Oh, you're here. Good." Beverly Carlisle came through the connecting door. "Dabney said he'd thought he'd seen you two head down here." She introduced herself to Frayne. "Anything I can help with, please don't hesitate to ask. It's what I'm here for."

"Thank you." Frayne turned his attention to me. As soon as I'd heard Bev approaching, I'd started packing up. While I slipped back into my coat, he asked, "You're leaving?"

I nodded.

"What time can I get in here in the morning?"

"The museum opens at ten."

"When will you be available in case I need something from the private collection?"

I blew out a breath and ran through my mental schedule. "Tomorrow is tough. I've got to take care of a family matter first thing, and then my afternoon is booked solid."

"What about lunch? Do you take a break then?"

"Not a long one. I can stop by and see if you need anything, though."

He reached down and pulled his cell phone from his briefcase. "Why don't you give me your number, and I'll text if I need you to be here. It'll save you a trip if I don't."

"Good idea." I tapped my number into his contact

list. "If there's nothing else, I really do need to get going."

"Sure, sure. I don't want to keep you from your family. Thanks for everything."

"Good night. 'Night, Bev."

"Give your darling George a hug from me," she said, with a wink. "I miss seeing him on his walks."

I laughed. "Will do." With one last head bob for Frayne, I headed for home.

Chapter 3

It was full on dark by the time I pulled up to my house. Winters in Heaven could be brutal, with snow accumulations of up to forty inches a common occurrence and daily temperatures hovering just above zero most of the time. Luckily, my garage was attached to the main house, affording me the luxury of staying warm and not having to trudge through the cold. I unlocked the door leading into my huge kitchen and turned on the lights. I'd been leaving the thermostat a little higher than usual to keep the house warm during the day even though I wasn't home. The reason I did this came shuffling out from his usual spot under the kitchen table the moment the lights came up.

I squatted and patted my knees. "Hey, baby. Come to Mama."

George, my fifteen-year-old black Labrador lumbered toward me, his cloudy, rheumy eyes squinting. The stiff, disjointed way he moved told me he'd spent the better part of the day curled up in his dog bed. I waited for him to reach me, silently cursing as his hips swayed rigidly side to side. His back was deeply bowed, his neck hanging from his shoulders like a rag doll's—weak and limp.

I reached out a hand, which he head bumped, then he lifted his nose to nuzzle my fingers. When I slipped my arms around his neck, pulling him closer for a cuddle, George leaned his entire body against mine.

The vet had confirmed my baby was almost blind, certainly deaf, and was living on borrowed time. Arthritis and severe age-related joint atrophy had invaded his once healthy, strong body, leaving him muscle depleted and in continuous pain. Since every movement for him was torture, he spent the better part of his days still. When he did need to move, to eat or to go out, his poor joints screamed against the effort.

The humane thing, the vet advised me, would be to put my closest friend out of his misery. The selfish thing was to keep him alive, making him drag through every day, suffering.

Love, I'd found, made one selfish in ways too deep to fathom.

I sat on the tiled floor, stretched my legs out in front of me, and pulled him onto my lap. In his day, George had weighed in at an impressive hundred and twenty pounds, most of it solid muscle and brawn. When he'd been weighed at the vet's last week, the scale topped at sixty-three.

I wrapped my arms around his once-powerful neck and gently squeezed. This dog had gotten me through some of the worst days I'd ever experienced. If George hadn't been such an integral, important part of my life, I don't know how I would have survived the horrible days after my husband's and my younger sister's deaths. Knowing I had George to come home to every night, to care for, walk, and feed, gave me a purpose to move through each day. Unconditional love met me every night when I walked through the door and greeted me every morning when I slid from my bed.

So, yes, I was guilty of being selfish. When I'd

needed George, he'd been there for me, imparting comfort, love, and loyalty, without ever asking anything in return. Now it was my turn to give him the same.

A thick, throaty moan blew past his mouth followed by a coarse rumble deep in his chest. I've heard it said after many years together pets start resembling their owners. I looked nothing like George—or he me—but after all these years we did have our own private communication system.

"I'm hungry, too," I told him and kissed his muzzle. "Aunt Maureen sent home some boiled chicken and rice for you. Give me a few minutes to heat it up."

I lifted his head from my lap and with it cupped between my hands, rubbed his whiskers back from his face. I swear he smiled at me.

He stood when I did, his legs a little shaky and wobbly, but once he was up, he was sure footed—on all four of them—again.

In a stovetop pot, I reheated the food my sister had sent home for George when I'd stopped by the inn yesterday afternoon. Maureen had a heart bigger than anyone I knew. She understood completely why I wanted George with me for as long as possible and had researched foods that were helpful with nutrition and pain control for aging, infirm dogs. Believe it or not, chicken soup came up more than any other item. Knowing my dog would probably turn his nose up at soup, she'd instead revised her old and favored chicken and dumpling recipe to a chicken and rice one instead. As George gingerly lapped at the stew-like concoction filled with carrots, peas, leeks, and fresh spinach, in addition to brown rice and an entire boiled organic chicken, I sent up a prayer of thanks for having such a wonderful, caring, and nurturing baby sister.

Thinking of Maureen and her inn sparked McLachlan Frayne's face into my head.

The man was intriguing for a variety of reasons from the thatch of thick, unruly hair my fingers had itched a few times to run through to the haunted look in his eyes I was sure had a tragic story behind them. I knew nothing about him other than he'd written an intense, detailed, and well-received biography of my favorite poet and now wanted to do the same for my town's founder and first leader.

I pulled Maureen's meatloaf from the fridge and placed the container in the microwave. She'd given me detailed instructions for heating the dinner in the oven, but I was too hungry and in too much of a rush to eat to waste time waiting for the oven to preheat and then rewarm the food. If my baby sister knew I was nuking her delicious meal, I'd get no further food presents for at least a month.

"What your Aunty Mo doesn't know won't hurt her," I told George, "and will ensure we keep getting leftovers."

I settled down at my kitchen table with a tall glass of Merlot, Maureen's meatloaf, and George under the table, his body settled on my feet.

Another fun-filled, exciting evening in the Mulvaney household.

Three hours later, a cycle of laundry was completed, the kitchen was cleaned and cleared, and I'd finished writing my vows for the weekend ceremony. I settled George in his bed for the night since he wasn't able to climb the stairs to my second-floor bedroom any longer and put a bowl of water next to it. Then, I crawled into bed with my e-reader.

My mind wouldn't concentrate on the new mystery I'd uploaded, though. A thousand thoughts swirled and competed for attention ranging from what Nanny Fee's mood would be in the morning, to my mental notes about my upcoming court cases, and then to a pair of pale eyes filled with secrets and sadness.

Finally, I gave up on the book, shut the bedside light, and snuggled down under the covers.

****

Even though I was five minutes early the next morning, Nanny was already waiting for me in the lobby of the nursing home. She was bundled up in a puffy coat skirting her ankles, a scarf I'd knitted for her last Christmas, a woolen hat and mittens courtesy of Colleen, and winter boots her tiny, dainty feet were lost in. I found her leaning across the check-in desk, blatantly flirting with the twenty-something rent-a-guard stationed there.

I knew she was flirting because the poor boy's face was six different shades of beetroot red.

My ninety-three-year-old grandmother feels her age, social status with the community, and inherent charm (her description) give her the right to say aloud anything and everything that pops into her head whether it be considered appropriate or not. She doesn't possess a self-censor or filter button, or if she does, I'd never known her to use it once in my thirty-nine years.

Her lyrical brogue rang through the lobby when she spotted me. "Ah, Number One. You're right on time, lass. Good girl."

"Actually, I'm five minutes early."

"As long as you're not late like the last time,

you're good."

I wasn't about to debate the two minutes I'd been held up by a school bus.

"Well, Jerald, dear boy"—she addressed the security guard—"it's off to the doctor I am. With any luck, I'll be back long before lunch is served."

"Good luck, Mrs. Scaloppini."

Was it my imagination or did he look relieved she was leaving?

Nanny gave him a mittened thumbs-up.

"How long have you been waiting?" I asked as I held her arm and guided her along the walkway.

"Long enough to advise Jerald on the perfect Valentine gift for his girlfriend."

"Did he ask for your advice?"

Nanny's eyes narrowed. She hated being called out on her nosiness. "Not in so many words, Number One. He told me he was plannin' on askin' the girl to marry him on Valentine's Day. I had to set him straight about why 'twasn't the best day of the year to do so."

I knew I shouldn't ask, but lifelong habits are hard to break. "Why not? It's literally the one day of the year devoted entirely to love. Asking someone to marry you on Valentine's day seems like a good idea to me. It's so romantic."

"Well, since you've only been asked once in your life and if I remember correctly—and I always do—'twas New Year's Eve when you were, you'd be wrong in your thinking."

I'd left my car running to keep the interior warmed for Nanny. As soon as I was settled behind the steering wheel, she started speaking again.

"He didn't think it through when he came up with

his engagement scheme."

Scheme?

"He never considered the lass might say no. Or even if she said yes, an' then somethin' happened to make them break up, Valentine's Day would be ruined for the both of them forever more."

"That's a little dramatic, even for you, Nanny."

She turned in her seat to face me. Well, eyeball me really, because only her eyes and the top bridge of her nose were visible. The rest was lost in the numerous folds of the scarf. "Dramatic am I, now?"

Uh-oh. Whenever that tone was released on me or my sisters—clipped and biting, precise and sharp—we knew it was time to be quiet.

Or run.

Since I was driving, escape wasn't possible. I paid a great deal of attention to navigating the car onto the county road and merging.

Once I was in the appropriate lane, I flicked Nanny a side glance to find she was still laser focused on me and said, "Why don't you explain why you feel the way you do so I can understand your point."

Nanny's sigh was loud and theatrical as it blew through the weave of her scarf. "A great deal like your father, you are," she said, shaking her head.

No argument from me, there.

After a moment she said, "Think about it, Number One. Would ya be wantin' to remember a broken engagement or being told no to a marriage proposal on the one day of the year—to quote you—dedicated to love? Wouldn't it be better to pick an innocuous day, say August third, to make such a monumental request, instead? Then, when the date rolled 'round each year,

35

ya wouldn't be thinkin' and rememberin' a day of love as a day of pain instead."

I had to admit, she made some kind of convoluted sense.

This was life with Nanny Fee, exhibit A.

"I've been asked to marry six times in me life, agreed to four of the proposals, and I couldn't tell you the dates I was asked even if compelled to."

I only remembered two of Nanny's four husbands, numbers three and four. Number one died after a year of wedded bliss from the flu. Number two, my grandfather, died of a heart attack when my dad was ten. Three lasted the longest at twenty years, and number four a short six months.

Nanny had claimed to love each of them completely and was heartbroken with each death. I often wondered if people who knew of her much-wedded reputation thought she might be a black widow.

My mother had a different thought, claiming often and mostly under her breath, Nanny's husbands had taken the easy way out when they couldn't stand living with her anymore. I always thought this was mean and proved how much these two women disliked one another.

When we arrived at the orthopedic office, Nanny was brought right in and examined. I'd been worried she'd have an extensive list of questions to pepper the doctor with, the major one being if she could be discharged back to her home. My sisters and I had been grateful when she'd voluntarily signed herself into the Angelica Arms Nursing Home directly from the hospital. With two functioning arms, she'd been a handful. With one casted, we were concerned no one could be with her during the day to care for her since the three of us had to work. Nanny lived in the house we all grew up in along with Colleen. Recently, Colleen had become engaged, and her fiancé, Slade, was living with her now. While Slade adored Nanny, having her back home might not be the best situation for them.

It was the doctor who broached the subject of Nanny's living arrangements.

"There now, I think I'd like to stay where I am."

I don't know who was more surprised, the doctor or me.

"Nanny? Are you sure?"

"Aye, lass. Being able to see me friends every day without havin' to bother someone to drive me to the home has been wonderful. And Tilly's come to depend on me more each day, ya know."

Tilly Carlisle was a retired Broadway musical comedy headliner, Nanny's best friend, and a fellow resident of Angelica Arms.

"She's a mite more forgetful these days, and I'm afraid what would happen if I weren't there to make sure she takes her meds and eats."

The doctor agreed to her wishes and wrote a medical order for her to continue to stay in the facility.

On the drive back, Nanny was uncharacteristically quiet.

"Are you okay?" I asked when we stopped at a red light.

"Aye, lass. 'Twas the right decision."

"You know you can change your mind anytime, don't you? You don't have to stay there if you don't want to. You can live with any one of us, you know that, right?"

"I do." She reached over and patted my hand. "It's lucky I am to have the three of you in me life. Many at the home never see a family face but for Christmas or a birthday. Ach, it's sad, 'tis, to get to an age where you're forgotten. Where everything you've accomplished in your life is a memory only for you and no one else. Where the people you loved the most barely think about you anymore."

I slid my hand from the wheel, pulled her mittened one into my own, and squeezed. "Well, we'll never forget you or all you've accomplished in your life. Or all you've done for us. You've always been our cheerleader, Nanny, always been there for each of us. We were lucky to have you with us when we were growing up. You were the one who stayed with us after Eileen died, who got us through the terrible time when Mom and Dad…left."

More than two years later and I was still angry about their move to South Carolina, asserting they couldn't live in the house or the town where they'd lost one of their daughters. Apparently, it was easy for them to leave their remaining daughters, though. They hadn't been back once to visit.

"Don't be hard on them, lass. 'Tis a terrible thing to lose a child. A child is your child forever, no matter the age. Some never recover from the loss, the grief."

"I get that, I do. But they forgot they had three other daughters who were grieving, too, and needed their parents to help them through it." I shook my head, still unable to reconcile what they'd done by moving away. "They lost a child, yes, and we lost our sister. Maureen lost her twin, the person she shared exact DNA with, for God's sake."

"Don't be takin' the Lord's name in vain, Cathleen Anne."

Heat washed up my neck from my chest to my cheeks. Thirty-nine years old, a successful lawyer, a grown-ass woman, and my grandmother was still able to make me feel like an errant, naughty toddler with a few words and a forceful tone.

When she called me by my rightful name, I knew she meant business, too. The hated monikers of our childhoods, Number One for me, Number Two for Colleen, then Three and Four for Eileen and Maureen was how Nanny addressed us on any given day. To have our proper names spew from her lips meant she was annoyed, pissed, angry, or disappointed—take your pick. The history behind the nicknames was a long one, involving two alpha females—my mother and grandmother—and their individual quests for dominance in the household.

At ninety-three, Nanny wasn't about to change a decades-old practice, meaning we all sucked it up and accepted it.

Colleen, though, still blanches every time Nanny addresses her.

"Sorry." I put the car into park in front of the nursing home.

I wasn't at all surprised when she told me to include the grievance in my confessions before mass on Sunday morning.

After getting her settled back into her room, I bent and kissed her cheek telling her I'd call her later on.

With an impatient wave of her hand, she said, "Don't be worrying about me, lass. It's fine, I am. Get along to work now. I'm sure you're as busy as your dear father always was."

"More," I said, leaning in for a hug. "But never too busy for you."

A soft and bewitching grin bloomed on her face. It was easy to see the beauty she'd been in her youth when she smiled this way.

"There's a darlin' girl, you are." She lifted up on her toes to kiss my cheek. "Oh, now, before I forget. Olivia Joyner stopped by the other day."

"Olivia? What was she doing here?"

"Her grandmother was admitted after breaking a hip in a fall last week. She's down the hall, and Olivia spotted me name outside the door and came in for a chat. She's always been such a delightful girl."

Olivia was the same age as me, and we'd gone from kindergarten through Heaven High together. I wondered if my grandmother referred to me as a girl when she spoke to others.

"Is her grandmother okay?"

Nanny waved a hand and grinned. "Right as rain, she is, but the doctor wanted her looked after until he's certain she can get up and about by herself again. Olivia wanted to care for her at home, but it was too much with her business and her daughter finishin' graduate school and movin' out, and all."

"I didn't realize Freya was old enough to have finished college, let alone grad school." I should have, because Olivia gave birth to her when we were seniors in high school. Time, as I've often thought, goes by ridiculously fast.

"Aye. She's leaving the nest, but Olivia says she's ready."

The corners of Nanny's eyes slitted a bit as she

regarded me. *Uh-oh.* Whenever Nanny tossed you a slanty-eyed glare, it meant you were gonna have a come-to-Jesus lecture. She opened her purse and pulled something out of it. "Before she left, she asked me to give ya this when I saw ya again."

"What is it?"

"Her business card." She handed it to me. "Said to give her a jingle when ya got the chance."

Olivia's name was written in beautiful calligraphy, her occupation listed below it, and her business phone number in the bottom corner of the card.

I swallowed, my throat suddenly dry as day-old burnt toast. "Why does she want me to call?" I asked, even though I had a sneaking suspicion about the reason.

I hoped I was wrong, and she merely wanted a little legal advice.

"Well, lass, why do you think she wants to speak to ya? Wants to set you up, doesn't she, being a matchmaker and all?"

Nope. It seems I wasn't wrong at all.

Olivia Joyner was a fourth-generation matchmaker, and the fact she wanted me to call her about a possible set up was...uncomfortable to say the least. There were a few other words—like embarrassed and pitiful—I could add.

"It's time, lass," Nanny told me, her eyes softening as she stared up at me. "Time to move on. You're still a young, beautiful, desirable woman. It's time a man came into your life and brought some happiness along with him into it. Gave you babies to love. A fulfilling life. Olivia can help ya with that."

I tucked the card into my coat pocket. "I have a full

life, Nanny. Believe me."

"Aye, lass, it's busy you are with your career. But wouldn't it be nice to come home to someone who loved ya? Who warmed your bed at night? You're a healthy, vibrant woman. Ya've normal needs, you do, I'm sure."

My earlobes burned with heat. There was no way I was having this conversation with my grandmother, a women old enough to have forgotten everything about *needs,* desires, and anything else sex related. Unfortunately, because this was Fiona, the four times married woman who'd been able to fit in love affairs with royalty between her marriages, there was no way she'd forgotten anything need or desire laden.

Looking for a diversion, I checked my watch and said, "Sorry, Nanny. Gotta run. I've got a full schedule this afternoon." I bussed her cheek again and bolted from the room before she could say another word.

Back in my car, I took a deep breath and checked my phone to see if I had any messages, which I didn't, not even from Heaven's current writer in residence.

He was probably still rummaging through the public files. He'd want access to the subbasement at some point, and I hoped it wasn't when I was neck deep in court cases. I could reschedule office hours, not my courtroom dates.

Since I'd finished earlier than I'd planned with Nanny's doctor visit and my stomach was making itself known, I pointed my car in the direction of my sister's inn. Maureen should be about ready to serve lunch to her guests, and if I played my cards right, I could finagle a little of whatever she'd made for myself.

All thoughts about matchmakers and needs were

tucked into the back of my mind.

Chapter 4

"So she's healing? No long-term bone worries or…anything?" Maureen flicked her hand in the air a few times.

"Fit as a fiddle, to quote her."

Maureen nodded, her messy bun bouncing as she flitted around her kitchen. The youngest of my sisters was many things. Caring, smart, business savvy, an incredible baker and cook. One thing she wasn't, though, was ever worried about her appearance. While Colleen wouldn't leave the house unless she was camera ready with makeup, hair, and clothing choice perfect, and I dressed in feminine business attire, knowing clients expected their lawyer to appear professional and polished without being prissy, the baby sister in our family went for comfort over fashion every time.

Standing in her designer kitchen spooning her mouthwatering beef stew into bowls for her dining room filled with guests, Maureen resembled a sixties love child throwback, not the owner of an award-winning New England bed and breakfast.

Over the years, I'd been a witness to more debates than I could count between Colleen and Mo about their footwear choices. Colleen didn't own a shoe without a three-inch heel or higher. Maureen would go perpetually barefoot if health-code violations weren't a worry in a business possessing a commercial kitchen.

As usual, an apron covered her from chest to knees. Today's was black with white lettering and *Get your fat pants ready* splayed across the bodice.

"And she wants to stay at Angelica Arms? Indefinitely?"

"She does." I spooned in some of the delectable, steamy stew, my insides sighing with appreciation. "God, Mo, this is insane."

"Word," Colleen said. "I'm glad I happened to drop by. I didn't even realize it was close to lunchtime."

Maureen slanted our sister a glance, her lips pressed together in a smirk. "Yeah, it's funny how often you lose track of time when it's mealtime."

Colleen stuck out her tongue.

"How old are you?" I asked.

"Younger than you." She slid the spoon into her mouth and shot me a grin.

Maureen shook her head, her lips clamping together, the hint of a dimple appearing on each cheek.

Of the three of us, Maureen was the one who kept her feelings closest to the vest. I knew the tiny smile she tossed me over her shoulder meant she was pleased to have family in her kitchen.

"Hey, who's the new guest with the puppy-dog eyes?" Colleen asked, after finishing her stew. "I spotted him in the dining room when I got here. About six two, needs a haircut? Looks like a runner, and he's got the saddest eyes I've ever seen."

I knew exactly who she was referring to.

"Mac Frayne," Maureen said. "He's writing a book about Josiah."

"Good Lord, who would want to read about him?"

"Apparently, Frayne's publishers," I told her. "He's been given access to the personal archives by the historical society."

"Sucks, for you," she said, her lips dipping into a frown. "Aren't you supposed to babysit him when he's doing his research since Leigh's out on maternity leave? Isn't that one of the dumb society rules you have to follow?"

I told her it was.

"What's up with him?" Colleen asked. "He looks like the weight of the world is on his shoulders."

"He's had a pretty rough couple of years," Maureen, a faithful fan of internet research, said.

"He looks it," Colleen said. Before she could add anything else, her cell phone chirped. "It's tomorrow's groom." She rose from her chair and handed Maureen her bowl. As she left the kitchen for privacy, she connected the call and put on her best wedding-planner-in-crisis-control voice. "Caleb, what can I do for you on this lovely day?"

"It's eerie how fast she can switch to professional mode, isn't it?" Maureen said.

"Scary, too. What did you mean Frayne's had a rough couple of years?"

Maureen was the one of us who resembled Nanny the most and in more than her physical appearance. When she shot me a familiar raised eyebrow and inquisitive glare, I could imagine what Nanny had looked like back in the day when she'd scolded our father for a boyhood malfeasance.

"Don't you ever research anyone?"

"When it's for a court-case background check, yeah, of course I do. Frayne's not a case."

"Still, I'd think since you're gonna be working together you'd like to know a little about him."

"First of all, I'm not working with him. I'm merely, as Colleen so aptly put it, babysitting him. Second, I prefer to find out about people the old-fashioned way, by engaging in conversation face to face, instead of stalking their profiles on social media."

"I don't stalk." She stirred the stew. "I simply like knowing a little something about the people who stay here for more than a night."

"Call it whatever you like. Now, what do you know?"

"I thought you wanted to get to know him yourself."

"That snotty voice didn't work when you were a kid, little sister, and it doesn't now."

She had the grace to pout.

"Frayne's not exactly a talker," I said. "So, spill."

With a sigh deep with resignation, she began adding water to the sink to wash the dishes. "His wife and daughter were killed in a car accident."

"Oh, how horrible. What happened?"

"Distracted driver rear-ended them, sending their car off an elevated road and into a stream."

I shook my head, sickened at the thought.

She turned from the sink, drying her hands on a dishtowel. "Apparently, the teenager who hit them got off. The road was icy and hadn't been sanded. The defense lawyer argued about culpability. You can read about it online. You'll understand it more. The end result was Frayne's family was killed. There was another adult in the car with them, too. A man." Her delicate eyebrows rose.

"Was he identified?"

"Just by name."

"How long ago was this?"

"Three years. Frayne was interviewed after the trial by a local reporter. That's online, too. There's nothing about him anywhere after the interview, though. It's like he disappeared off the planet."

Until he showed up in, of all places, Heaven. We were both silent for a few moments.

"So sad," I said.

"Yeah. It is." She heaved a big sigh and then leaned against the kitchen counter. "I'm sure there's a story there with the other man in the car, though."

"Why?"

Her shrug spoke volumes. "Gut feeling."

I let that thought settle for a moment. Maureen was very intuitive—our grandmother would say *fey*. And she was usually correct when she had a hunch about something.

"So, what's up with you for the rest of the day?" she asked.

"I've got a couple client meets this afternoon." I did a quick sweep of my cell phone, pleased to find no emergency texts or missed calls. "An evening full of prep for tomorrow's wedding, a long hot bath, and then a hot date with George."

"How's he doing?"

"The same. He's stiff when he moves, but once he gets going, he's able to get around okay for a few minutes. I wish I could ease his pain a little."

"Aren't you allowed to give him over-the-counter stuff? When I was trolling around for therapeutic foods, I saw it mentioned once or twice. Some OTC pain relievers are okay in moderation."

I stood with my empty bowl in my hand and walked toward the sink. "Shelby said I could try something, but it might do more harm than good in the long run. His kidneys and liver are failing, which means the meds might get clogged in them and cause him more problems. I don't want that. He's suffering enough as it is." I sighed. "This is way more difficult than I expected."

Maureen wrapped her arms around my waist from behind me and laid her head on my shoulder. "You've been together a long time." Her warm, comforting breath wafted across my neck.

"Most of my adult life. I don't know what I'll do when he dies. The house is going to be so...empty and cold. God, I hate this."

"Excuse me." McLachlan Frayne stood in the doorway, a bowl and a glass in his hands. "I'm sorry to interrupt. I didn't know if I should leave these"—he held up his hands—"on the table or bring them here."

Mo unwove her hands from around me, and, with a smile, moved to him, saying, "You can leave them on the table in the future. No need to bus your own."

Her easy smile drew one from him as his gaze went from her face to mine. His lips took their time going back to their normal, full line. "Mrs. Mulvaney."

"Cathy's fine." I swiped at an errant tear, took a composing breath, and tried to place a smile on my face. "Taking a break from your research?"

I cringed on the inside. Duh! Of course he was. Talk about stating the obvious.

"Just for lunch. I need to get back to the museum in a bit."

Maureen placed a hand at my back and then kissed my cheek. "I've got work to do. I'll see you when I see you," she said.

"Love you." I pursed my lips and blew her a kiss.

"Love you more," she tossed over her shoulder as she made her way to the dining room. She bobbed Frayne a quick nod.

"Are you finding everything you need at the museum?" I asked him when we were alone. "You haven't texted me, so I figured you were occupying your time with the public records."

He slid his hands into his well-worn jeans pockets and rocked back a bit on his sneakered feet. Today's pullover was a deep blue V-neck, a swatch of white peeking up along the collar. He and Maureen could have been cut from the same bolt of comfort-wear fabric. Dark, purple splotches sat under his bottom lashes.

"I have been. There's a great deal of info in those files, some of which I haven't seen published elsewhere. It's been beneficial to help me detail a historical timeline."

"I meant to ask you yesterday—why Josiah Heaven?" I tugged my coat from the back of Maureen's kitchen chair and slipped it on. "Why did you choose him to write about? He's not exactly an important historical figure, or even well known. How did you discover him?"

A tiny lift of his lips, and his entire expression changed. Softened. The clouds in his eyes billowed away, replaced by something an awful lot like subdued animation. "I have my agent to thank for that. She attended a wedding here a few months ago. Stayed here at the inn, in fact. Marci—Marci Edgerton's her name—fell in love with the town and asked about its history. When she heard about the founder, she thought he might be someone I'd like to write about. She knows I tend to gravitate toward historical figures. Plus, I've been searching for a new project. After looking into him, I told her she was right."

"And you got the commission to do so?"

He nodded.

"Well, I know the members of the historical society are giddy you're here. They love talking up old Josiah to anyone, anytime. And those public files are interesting reading, a fact I have personal knowledge of. I had to do enough book reports and papers on our town when I was in school. Lots of small-town snippets about the people who came before us and how they lived and survived day to day. You'll get lots of info from the records. While it all looks mundane, it's actually a fairly accurate portrayal of a small, tightly knit New England community."

Frayne nodded. "I think I'll be bothering you for access to the personal files soon, though."

For the second time in as many minutes, I cringed. With two court dates and a custody trial set to start next week, my available free time was going to be severely limited. For the hundredth time, I cursed my role as keeper of the key. It would be rude to tell Frayne that, though. It wasn't his fault I'd been put in the position.

He cocked his head to one side, those pale, haunted eyes regarding me with a questioning stare. "What?" he asked.

"I'm sorry?"

"What's wrong?"

"What do you mean?"

He took a few steps closer, his gaze trained on my face. The feeling of being a gazelle with a hungry lion stalking me crashed across my brain, which was—of course—a ridiculous analogy.

"You seem a little…troubled, by my saying that."

"Not troubled, no."

"But something?"

He stopped less than a foot in front of me, his entire stance radiating a calm and unthreatening attitude. His breathing was soft and steady and slow. But his eyes, his eyes were another story entirely. Inquisitive. Searching. Perceptive. He'd been able to read my expression perfectly, and I knew I had a great poker face.

The lawyer in my DNA wanted to redirect or deflect the conversation. "It's nothing. I just have a great deal of work-related things in the next few weeks I'm unable to move around. They've been scheduled for some time and can't be changed. It would help if we had an appointed time for me to let you into the personal archives. A time I'm not needed elsewhere."

"Makes sense. I can imagine how busy your days are between your work and your family. What's your schedule look like this weekend? Are you free at all?"

"I've got a wedding on Saturday."

Maureen strode back into the kitchen, a tray laden with empty bowls gripped in her hands.

"Mo, what time's Colleen's wedding tomorrow? I forget."

"Ceremony at one, reception right after." She zoomed back out of the room after placing the tray on a counter.

"I'll be free after two, then," I told Frayne.

"You're not staying for the party?" A tiny groove settled between his eyebrows.

"Sometimes I do, but not tomorrow. Will the time work for you?"

His questioning stare deepened. "Yeah, it's...it's fine."

I got the distinct impression he wanted to press me. For whatever reason, he decided not to. I checked my watch and said, "Okay. I'll see you tomorrow afternoon, then, when I'm done. Now, I'm sorry, but I've gotta run. I have clients this afternoon, and I need a few minutes to prep." I put out my hand to shake his goodbye.

Frayne studied it for a moment, shot his gaze back up to my eyes, and then back down to my hand. With a tiny shake of his head, which made his shaggy hair sway, he took it. Like mine had the day before, his body stilled as soon as we touched.

I was raised to be a practical, commonsense, logical New England woman. I didn't believe in fairies, mesmerism, or magic. I wasn't given to flights of fancy, I didn't read stuff about the paranormal, and I thought scary movies were a silly waste of time, better spent on reading a good book or playing the piano. But I swore on Nanny's 120-year-old Bible, Frayne had somehow cast a spell of immobility on me. I knew—*knew*—I had to move, to get back to work. The message wasn't making its way from my brain to my feet, though, and the only reason I could give was Frayne somehow had entranced me with his warm touch and sad, haunted, questioning eyes.

Maureen's helper, Sarah, burst into the kitchen

laughing at someone she was talking to on her cell phone. The abrupt sound sparked a few of my muscles back to life, and with a little more vigor than I'd intended, I tugged my hand back, blinked a few times to focus, then turned and left him standing there.

I chose to ignore the fact my legs were shaking and my armpits were stress-sweating enough to require a blouse change. What I couldn't disregard was the sight of my hands trembling as I put my car into gear and peeled out of the inn's driveway. Nor could I discount the surge of heat coiled in my belly like a live, splayed wire when Frayne's hand circled mine, or the way his troubled eyes made me want to hug him close and give comfort of some kind. Any kind.

Ridiculous. It was simply ridiculous to feel this emotionally off kilter and discombobulated about a man I'd met barely a day ago.

Why then, I asked myself as I drove to my office, was I?

****

"Cassidy and Caleb, you two have weathered many storms, both legal and emotional, and have managed to survive by the sheer will of your love for one another." I smiled at them. "Lesser individuals would have gone their separate ways long before now. Not you two. To see you both here today, surrounded by the people who love and support you the most, I know your love can withstand anything life throws at you. As your futures unfold and you're tested again and again, as you will be, remember the strength of the love you've pledged to one another here today to help see you through whatever comes at you."

"We will," they vowed.

"I know you will. Well, then, by the legal power vested in me by the wonderful State of New Hampshire, I now pronounce you married for life, partners for eternity. Please seal your vows with your first married kiss. And make it a good one," I added in a very loud stage whisper.

The audience filling the inn's ballroom burst into laughter as the two handholding grooms grinned at one another. In a smooth motion I swear they'd rehearsed, Caleb grabbed his new husband and bent him backward over his arm, kissing him soundly amid the claps, whistles, and cheers of their guests.

Twenty minutes later, Maureen handed me my coat and a heavy shopping bag.

"What's this?"

"Leftover stew for you and ground prime rib with rice, carrots, kale, and spinach for George. I figured he might be getting sick of chicken."

"I don't know what I'd do without you." I pulled her into a hug, disregarding the flour-streaked apron adorning her trim frame. Today's was a pink affair with an embroidered wedding cake on the bottom befitting the celebration going on in her ballroom, and the message *Cake is my happy place* written in Victorian script above it.

"You'd survive." She chuckled as she patted my back. "But you'd be seriously food deprived."

"Truth. I've got to get over to the museum. Frayne wants access to the subbasement, so there goes the rest of my afternoon."

"Can't one of the docents let him in and"—she shrugged—"babysit?"

"Unfortunately, no." I sighed and buttoned up my

coat. "There are times I really wish Daddy hadn't advocated for me to take over his position. Plus, it would have been nice to have been asked if I even wanted it. But, no. He simply made another unilateral decision without telling anyone, like him and Mom moving and not letting us know until the last minute. And *God*, I hate how bitter I sound."

Maureen's gaze dropped to her hands. "I think we all deserve to be a little bitter, maybe you most of all, since you're the one who was left holding all the pieces, and us, together."

"I think Nanny was more responsible for that, than me."

"She's a rock, to be sure. A slightly kooky and theatrical one"—she rolled her eyes and grinned—"but she's rock solid in the family glue department. And we're lucky to have her in our lives, no matter how much trouble she gets into."

"Less now, since she's living at the home. At least I know I won't be getting calls from Lucas informing me he's holding her down at the police station on another civil disobedience charge."

"There's that."

"I'd better get going. Thanks for this." I lifted the bag and gave her cheek a kiss.

Chapter 5

The temperature had dropped a good twenty degrees from the day before. The whipping wind forced me to hold onto my hat while I trekked from the parking lot to the museum entrance.

Once inside, I shucked out of my outerwear as I sprinted down the stairs to the basement.

Frayne was alone at one of the computer workstations, sheets of paper and files scattered about the desk next to him.

I took a moment to observe him before announcing myself. Thick-lensed reading glasses perched on the very tip of his nose, a millimeter from falling from his face. For the life of me, I couldn't understand why that was so endearing, but it was. His hair fell over the collar of his shirt, today covered with a jet-black pullover. A tiny moth hole crossed over his bicep. The notion he needed someone looking out for him, caring for him, making him take care of himself, bounded through me.

The story Maureen related spilled back to me, and my heart sighed. I knew the emotional devastation losing loved ones could wreak, and since I was now aware of what had happened to Frayne's family, I understood the perpetual grief in his eyes.

Another striking thing about Frayne was that for all his awkwardness, some might even say shy demeanor, he was an extremely attractive man, and the very fact I noticed it was astounding. I hadn't looked at nor thought about another man in all the years of my marriage, even while Danny had been away for years on end on active duty.

The only man I'd ever loved, ever considered being with, ever looked at, was Danny Mulvaney. Picturing Mac Frayne as someone I could see myself getting to know on a purely personal and physical level was behavior so far out of my emotional wheelhouse it startled me.

"I'm sorry I kept you waiting." I tossed my coat and bag on a chair "I came as soon as the ceremony ended."

Frayne peered at me over the tops of his glasses through eyes a little unfocused, a little startled, and a whole lot of befuddled cute.

He blinked, and then his gaze swept from my face down to what Maureen calls my *marriage duds*. When I officiate, I pair a plain white silk blouse with a black double-breasted jacket and either a black A-line skirt or trousers, depending on the season. On one lapel of my jacket, I always wear a 14-karat-gold, single rose pin, gifted to me by Colleen, to symbolize the love and affection of the couples I marry.

With a quick flick of his hand, Frayne swiped the glasses from his face, and tucked one of the bows into the vee of his sweater. His gaze made its way up to my face again, and he cocked his head in a move I was coming to recognize signaled he was going to ask a question. "You didn't stay for the reception?"

"Like I told you yesterday, sometimes I do, but most times I simply sign the paperwork, take a few photos with the happy couple, and then let them have their party. If I stayed at every wedding, I'd never get anything done on the weekends."

"I've been to my share of weddings"—he stood and tilted his head to one side—"but I've never had to sign papers at one, other than my own. Are there that many people you know getting married that your weekends are typically so full?"

A grin split my face at his words. "They are when I'm performing the ceremonies."

It took him a second, then the cloud of cute confusion cleared in his eyes. "You're a wedding officiant?"

"Technically, I'm a justice of the peace. But yes, I officiate at weddings. I came here from Inn Heaven after performing a ceremony."

"Well, that certainly explains it." His lips twitched at the corners, and for a brief moment, an image of pressing my own against them burned quick and bright in my head. "I saw them setting up the ballroom for some kind of event before I left this morning. Your sister was everywhere."

"I know that's the truth because I've seen it for myself. Maureen is exceptionally organized, a trait that runs rampant in our family."

His gaze swept down my attire again, the small grin tugging on his mouth, broadening. "I spotted another redhead in commando mode, too. She resembled you and Maureen." His grin grew. "I've never actually seen someone bark orders before."

"The barker was Colleen, my middle sister. She's a wedding planner and was in charge of today's event. I officiate at a lot of her non-religious ceremonies."

Frayne slid his hands back into his pockets. "Cathleen, Colleen, and Maureen?"

"My mother believed in keeping things simple and similar. Maureen had a twin named Eileen."

"Had?"

"She…died. Breast cancer."

His eyes widened. "Maureen doesn't look like she's out of college yet, and this was her twin?"

"Yes. It was a rare form. Less than a year from diagnosis to death."

"My mother is a breast cancer survivor. I know how horrible the fight is. I'm sorry for your loss."

Saying thank you when someone says those words always felt wrong, somehow, given the context, so I simply bobbed my head. "Have you found something you need from the subbasement?"

He blinked a few times at my abrupt subject change. "A bunch of things, actually, but the most important item is a birth certificate."

I jangled the key to the subbasement in my hand. "Do you have the file numbers?"

"Yeah. Hang on a sec. I wrote them down." He shuffled a few books and note pads around on the desk until he found an errant piece of paper. "Here they are."

Before leaving, I pulled my cellphone from my purse and slipped it into my jacket pocket. Life with Nanny has taught me never to be more than an Instagran call away.

I led the way down the cast-iron circular staircase to the subbasement. I hadn't been in the personal archives since taking over my keeper-of-the-keys duties—I was going to call it that forever, now—and I'd forgotten how deathly quiet it could be. And how creepy. What amounted to two stories below ground level, the staircase was lit only by the electric sconces on the wall guiding us downward. The sound of our shoes bounced and echoed off the metal gratings under our feet.

"It's wicked spooky down here," I said when we came to the bottom. "No outside noise. No windows. No people. It's like a perfect tomb. If I ever got stuck down here, the silence alone would scare me into an early grave."

"If I was a suspense or a horror writer, this would be a great setting to kill someone and then stash the body," Frayne said, looking around the space. "With limited, keyed access and no foot traffic, it wouldn't be discovered for a while. You could make as much noise or as much of a mess as you wanted and no one would know. The walls would absorb all the sounds of torture and screaming. We're far enough underground the stench of decomp wouldn't be noticeable. By the time the body was found, you'd be long gone. It's kind of a perfect setup, actually." He perused the area intensely, assessing the possibilities.

A shudder zipped up my spine. Who knew the mild-mannered and reserved writer had such a macabre side?

And why, for the love of God, did I find it so...arousing?

He turned to me, and then cupped the back of his neck with one palm, a half grin lining his mouth. "Sorry. I tend to think out loud without filtering. Side effect of being in a solitary profession. I don't usually have an audience when thoughts are running around in here"—he tapped his temple—"so I tend to say them out loud."

"I think you might have missed your calling in the horror-writing department. The scene you set was a little too realistic and probable for comfort. The next time we come down here, I'm hauling a baseball bat along in case you want to try out any of your ideas."

A heart-stopping grin shot across his face like a bolt of lightning: rapid, blinding, and powerful. "I'm harmless." To underscore his point, he drew an X over his heart.

I didn't know about that. Those dimples were about as harmless as a heart attack.

With a shake of my head and my own grin slipping across my lips, I slid the key into the locked door and opened it. A second door, this one passcode protected, stood a few feet in front of us.

"Double security. Impressive."

"The museum's insurance adjustor insisted on it. Some of the papers and items in here could be considered historically priceless." I typed the seven-digit code I'd had to memorize when I was inducted into the historical society onto the keypad located on the wall abutting the door.

"You know, if I was writing my horror book, I'd make you the sole individual with access to the admittance code," he said, his voice soft and hushed now around us. "I'd worm my way into your trust, then lure you down here to gain access to some treasure sealed behind the door."

He was standing close behind me, so close I could feel his breath trail across the back of my neck. The shiver sliding down my spine this time wasn't from the creep factor associated with the locale. No, this time it was pure excitement fraying my nerve endings. Excitement, want, and...need.

I turned back to face him. A day or two's thatch of black and white stubble grazed his cheeks and jaw, and if I were to scratch my fingers across it, it would be prickly and incredibly alluring. His eyes had gone to half-mast as he regarded me from under thick lashes, and his lips were parted a fraction.

"Worm your way into my trust, how?"

His shrug appeared noncommittal. After a moment, he tugged his bottom lip under his top teeth and slanted me a gauging squint. "Well, since my purpose would be some shade of evil, malicious intent—"

"Good description for a horror story."

He grinned. "I'd have to make sure you trusted me. Maybe I'd write a plot point where you took pity on me for some reason." He stopped, his gaze shooting down to my mouth and then back up again. "Maybe even attempt a simple seduction to ensure my hold over you."

The subbasement was kept at a comfortable, controlled seventy degrees year round. But you would never have known it by me. With each word from Frayne's lips, my inner temperature climbed higher, like a nuclear coil overreacting and heating to dangerous levels.

"A-a simple...seduction?" *Good Lord.* I was relegated to repeating things now because I couldn't form a coherent thought. Not with the heat blazing like a firestorm in his eyes.

"Maybe not so...simple." His voice lowered even more. "The need to be careful with you, with your feelings, would war within me. I'd have to decide what

I wanted more: the hidden treasure…" His gaze flicked to my mouth. "Or you."

I swallowed.

"And after you decide? Then what?" I asked, trying to keep my voice even and not give him a clue what he was doing to my nervous system. "You'd chop me into tiny bits and leave me for the docents to find in six months' time while you escaped scot-free?"

I'd meant it to be a playful rejoinder, following his horror theme, and a ridiculous attempt to lighten the mood. The joke was on me, though.

Frayne took a step closer, stretched out an arm and placed his palm flat against the wall, imprisoning me on one side. I lifted my chin to keep my gaze connected with his.

"No." His voice was as soft as a curl of smoke. "No, I wouldn't hurt you. Never. I couldn't." He shook his head. "I think I'd write it so I stole the treasure…and you along with it. I'd take you both with me." With a tiny crook to his elbow, he leaned in closer and bent his head.

"Where…where would we go?" I asked. While waiting for his reply, I swallowed again—hard—the sound of my throat working loud and rough between us.

With his free hand, Frayne reached up and idly coiled a strand of my hair around his finger. Lovingly, he rubbed it between his thumb and his first two fingers, then lifted it to his mouth. When he dragged it across his lips, I swear on my oath as an officer of the court, I was in danger of losing my ability to stand.

"Someplace no one would ever find us." His voice had gone whisper-soft. "Someplace…far away from"— he sighed—"everything and everyone."

How wonderful that sounded. To go someplace far away from court cases and demanding clients. Loneliness and heartache. Responsibilities and sad memories.

"We'd spend the rest of our lives on a beach somewhere, lying in the warm sun. Drinking champagne, eating lobsters. Sleeping." He let loose my hair. "Making love. No outside concerns. No thoughts about anything except what time the sun set. Sounds pretty perfect, doesn't it?"

That ability to keep standing upright? Yeah, well, I lost it right then and there.

I fell backward against the security door, shoving it open with my body. I stumbled across the threshold and would have fallen flat on my butt if Frayne's reflexes weren't laser swift. His strong hands went around my upper arms and held fast. Even through the layers of my blouse and the warm wool jacket, heat blasted from his fingers, branding my flesh as if he held it, bare, in his hands.

When the door opened, the automatic light shot to the on position and the glare from the overhead fluorescents was blinding.

Frayne held me close in front of him, even after I was sure-footed, his fingers slowly kneading my upper arms as he continued to stare down at me. "Are you okay?"

I swallowed the lump in my throat for the third time—and then tried to take a step back and out of his hold.

His grip tightened. "Cathy? Are you all right?"

"You can let me go," I said, my voice shaking. "I won't fall. Promise."

His gaze shifted to where his hands were clasped around my upper arms. With brows almost meeting in the center of his forehead, he shook his head a few times, as if pulling out of a trance.

Flames shot up my neck and cheeks, and I imagined my face was akin to the color of a vine-ripened tomato by now.

He opened his hands, crossed them behind his back, and then took a step backward. At the same time, I turned and moved into the archives, dragging in a huge gulp of air to calm myself.

It was going to take a whole lot more than a deep breath to quell the tsunami swirling in my belly.

I never entertained the thought Frayne was flirting with me. First, he didn't seem the type. Second, I believed him when he said he was used to working story angles aloud. When I prepared court summations, I routinely read them out loud at home, to hear how they came across, if I was conveying my thoughts coherently, and if everything made sense. I figured he'd been doing the same thing, then got caught up in the moment and let it go a little further than either of us expected. Telling myself this went a long way in soothing my nerves.

The air in the archive rooms, although temperature controlled, had a stale, musty reek to it. It was apparent no one had been down here in quite some time.

"Do you have those location markers?" I asked. Before turning back to him, I sent myself a silent order to keep things professional.

I took the proffered paper and snuck a quick side eye at him. His brows were beetled, and he was staring down at the floor. He'd shoved his hands into his pockets again, and a slight tic in his jawline told me he was chewing on the inside of his cheek. Eileen had done the same as a child and through her teen years whenever she was concentrating.

"Okay." I lowered my voice as it bounced around the metal cabinets and shelves surrounding the room. "What do you want to see first, the birth certificate?"

"Yes."

"According to the numbered indicators, they're in the next room. There's a high-quality copy machine in there to use."

"I can't take it upstairs with me?"

"No, I'm sorry. Nothing can be moved from here because of the controlled environment. Hence, the copy machine."

"Some of the papers will be old and faded," he said, for the first time looking directly at me again. "They might not copy well."

"They will, don't worry. The copy machine is worth every penny the historical society paid for it." I located the archival drawers indicated on his notes and pointed to the box of disposable gloves sitting on top of it. "You'll need to put on a pair of those."

He grabbed two from the box, as did I.

I located the file and gave it to him. "The birth certificate should be in here."

With his glasses perched back on his nose, he opened the file and rifled through the documents housed within it. After a few moments, he stopped.

"Did you find it?"

Whatever he'd been about to say was halted when my cell phone blared, the unexpected shrill making me jump.

"*Jesus.*" I tore off a glove and hit the connect icon. Lucas Alexander, Heaven's police chief and one of my oldest friends said, without preamble, "Cathy, we got a situation."

I closed my eyes and took a cleansing breath. I was doing a lot of deep breathing recently. "Please tell me it doesn't concern Nanny."

His low chuckle calmed me. "Not this time. But I had to haul Seldrine Compton in, and I figured I'd give you a head's up."

"What happened?"

"Neighbors called in a disturbance. When Pete Bergeron got to her house, she was drunk and screaming like a fisher-cat. He had to call me for backup because he couldn't handle her. He's got a nice shiner brewing."

"Oh, good Lord. Is he okay?"

His calm, smooth voice filtered through the phone. "He's fine. Sitting here with a bag of frozen peas over his eye socket. His pride's hurt more than anything, but I've got to add assaulting a law officer onto the drunk and disorderly charge."

"Seldrine's been doing so well lately." I shook my head and closed my eyes. "She's been attending meetings, getting her life back together. She even started classes to earn her GED. I've got her custody case this week."

"I know. Which is the reason I'm calling. Her mom took the kids back to her house with her. She's agreed to keep them until Seldrine's brought before the judge, which isn't going to happen until Monday morning. Asa's skiing with his grandkids in Vermont this weekend."

"This is going to be a black mark on her record for sure." I closed my eyes and shook my head.

"It will. I've got her back at the station, fuming, in a cell, and I'm gonna have to keep her there until her court appearance. I'm hoping once she sleeps it off, she'll be less combative."

"Do you have any idea what sparked this? I know for a fact she hasn't had a drink since before Cam went to prison."

"She wasn't exactly forthcoming with Pete or me. Called us a couple of names I haven't heard since I got back stateside, though. Maybe you'll be able to get more out of her."

"Okay." I thought a moment. "I'll be down there as soon as I can. Tell her I'm coming, would you?"

"Will do. Before I let you go, you're not anywhere near the inn, are you?"

"No. I was there earlier for a wedding. Why?"

I could hear him shrug. "Gonna be a long weekend if I'm stuck here babysitting. I was hoping you could finagle some muffins or something from your sister so I don't starve to death."

I knew Lucas was a frequent visitor to the inn. My sister and her helper, Sarah, each had a soft spot for him and took pity on him more times than not. They never sent him away without a plastic container filled with leftovers from lunch service, or a morning's sample of breakfast items. Lucas was divorced and, in addition to being the town cop, also had his elderly, infirm father living with him. His sporadic hours meant oftentimes he wasn't able to cook a nutritious meal for them and whatever Mo sent him home with was always appreciated.

I told him I'd make a quick stop there before coming to the jail.

"Take your time. Seldrine isn't going anywhere, and neither am I."

I hit the end icon, then called Martha at home. After I explained the situation, she volunteered to come in the next morning and type up a brief I was going to write tonight for the judge so it would be ready to go Monday morning.

One more quick call to Maureen and a promise for a go-bag for Lucas and Seldrine, and I finally shut my phone. When I turned, Frayne's face was a jumble of expressions. His brows were pulled in so tight it looked like he had a unibrow, he was gnawing on the inside corner of his lip, and he was tapping his reading glasses against his thigh. In the other hand, he still held the file I'd given him.

I couldn't determine if he was confused, nervous, or merely antsy from being in the subbasement.

"Sorry," I said. "Client emergency."

"I thought you had weekends free. Except for weddings, I mean."

"My life doesn't run on a normal five-day-a-week schedule." I shook my head. "I have my own practice, and in all honesty, I'm always available for my clients. Any day they may need me and at any time."

"Practice? Wait—you're a doctor?"

I smiled. If he knew how much the sight of blood made me queasy he'd never ask that. "No, I'm not."

He cocked his head again and peered at me, his eyes narrowing.

"Social worker?"

"No, again. I'm a lawyer. That was the chief of

police informing me he arrested one of my clients."

Frayne's entire body went stone still as if he'd been turned into a hardened slab of concrete. His eyes were the only things indicating he was still conscious. A few minutes ago they'd been free of their haunting sadness and replaced with what I thought was something akin to desire. Now they were frozen over like a tundra glacier.

"You're a lawyer." It wasn't a question.

Not understanding the annoyance in his tone, I took a breath then said, "Yes. General law. I deal, for the most part, with child custody, guardianships, wills."

He shook his head and fisted his hands on his trim hips. If I was reading his body language correctly, he wasn't happy about what I'd told him.

"I've gotta say, I don't know what I thought you did for a living, but lawyer was never even a consideration. You seem too nice, too..." He waved his hand in the air. "I don't know. You don't come off like a lawyer."

"How do lawyers come off?"

Fire chased the ice in his eyes away. It was fascinating to see someone's emotions turn on a beat. "Arrogant. Self-aggrandizing. Egotistical. Greedy and self-serving. More descriptions come to mind. None of them are complimentary."

"No, they don't seem to be. I'm sorry you view the profession in such a light."

"That's a laugh. I never met a lawyer who was sorry for anything." His mouth turned down at the corners, scorn screaming through his words. "Lawyers don't care about the lives of the people they deal with. It's all a game. A big chess game with people as the pawns. Who's going to be sacrificed? Who wins? Who makes the best deal? Who comes out on top? Never mind people have suffered, are suffering. Never mind the pain, the physical ache, suffusing them. You all twist things to allow the guilty to go free and the innocent to suffer. *Christ.* I hate lawyers. I hate the entire breed."

When he stopped, he shook his head with such force his hair fell across his forehead. With a furious finger swipe, he shoved it back in place, a deep, dark breath dragging through him.

Frayne's characterization was something I'd heard before. Many people had nothing nice to say about lawyers and had no need of one.

Until they did.

Until a situation arose where having a lawyer meant the difference between getting off with a warning or spending a decade in prison.

I willed myself to keep my tone calm and my voice professional when I said, "Yes. I can see you do."

His gaze met mine. Pain had mixed with anger, both harsh and hot.

"As much as you despise us as a breed, lawyers do have their uses, Mr. Frayne, one being to ensure the safety and welfare of our clients. And I need to go see to mine. I can wait until we find the other items you want, though. You can make copies of the documents in here before we go back upstairs."

Before he could say another word, I turned, the slip of catalogue file numbers he'd written still in my hand and went in search of the records he'd indicated. Frayne said nothing.

It was easy to find the two land deeds he wanted to inspect. What wasn't easy was keeping my hands from shaking when I handed them over. While I'd been searching, he'd taken advantage of the high-tech copy machine in the room. When I gave him the deeds, he returned the file with the birth certificate to me.

Not more than five minutes later we were done. Neither of us had uttered a word as I locked the subbasement door behind me, then made a beeline for my belongings. Frayne walked back to his work station and laid the copies down on top of all the papers and books he'd left there.

I slipped into my coat. After I had it buttoned, I finally looked over at him. He stood next to the desk, his hands in his pockets again, his shoulders drooped. The sad, haunted glaze was back in his eyes as he watched me pull my car keys from my bag.

"I'll make sure one of the docents knows you're in here so you aren't mistakenly locked in at closing time. Goodbye, Mr. Frayne." I turned my back to him and moved to the door.

Frayne's hand shot to the handle the same time mine did. I hadn't even heard him move behind me.

I snatched my hand back as if it had been burned and took a full step backward. His gaze briefly met mine before he twisted the knob and pulled the door open for me.

The gallant gesture after his verbal tirade was confusing, almost as much as why I was drawn to the hurt once again shining in his eyes.

"Thank you." I moved past him.

I managed to get to my car and start the ignition before my nerves finally broke free.

Chapter 6

Sunday morning I escorted Nanny to weekly mass at our family church, Heaven on Earth, and then to a late breakfast at the inn with Maureen, Colleen, and her fiancé, Slade. There was no sign of Frayne, and I didn't ask my sister if she knew where he was.

After dropping Nanny back at the nursing home, I spent the rest of the day preparing legal briefs, writing up a statement to deliver to the judge Monday morning for Seldrine, and snuggling with George. No texts from Frayne blew up my phone, and I was happy I didn't have to deal with him. After his outburst, I wasn't sure I could stand being regarded again with such scorn purely because I'd chosen law as a career. I'll admit I was disappointed he'd been unable to look past my job and see the woman and not merely the lawyer.

For the first time in my adult life, I'd actually considered what being with a man—other than my husband—would be like. There was something intriguing about McLachlan Frayne. Sure, he was handsome in a sexy, scruffy, professorial way, all shoulders and trim waistline. Even though his hair hadn't met a pair of scissors in a season or two, what should have turned me off was, in fact, wildly appealing. When we'd been in the subbasement antechamber, his voice teasing and erotic as he described the scenario he'd pen, my body had responded in a way I hadn't recognized from myself.

I thought it had been desire brimming in his eyes when he'd gazed down at me. If it *was* there, it was surely gone now.

Oh, well.

At least I knew I could feel something for a man other than Danny. All this had me remembering the business card in my coat pocket. I pulled it from its nesting place and ran my finger over Olivia's embossed name.

A matchmaker. Such an old-fashioned way to meet a potential…something. While I wasn't searching for a spouse, it would be nice, as Nanny said, to have someone who wanted to spend time with me.

Before I morphed into lawyer Cathleen and debated sixty reasons why I shouldn't and talked myself out of it, I punched in Olivia's number on my cell.

"This is Olivia."

"Oh, hey. It's Cathy Mulvaney. I figured I'd get your machine since it's Sunday."

Her laugh mimicked the sound of champagne flutes tapping in a toast. "You know what Father Duncan always says about no rest for the wicked, Cathy."

That brought a smile to my face and helped shake away some of my nerves.

"Fiona gave you my card?"

"She did."

"Don't sound like you're walking to the gallows, sweetie. I set people up for a living, not kill them."

This time I laughed. "I'm sorry. I'm a little nervous about this."

"Don't be. When I spotted Fiona at the Arms, I thought, well, why not reach out. Test the waters. See if my old high school chum is interested in meeting someone."

Was I? I still wasn't sure. "This is all new to me, and I'm a little, well…I knew Danny since the dawn of time."

She laughed again. "I get it. I really do. Do you have a few minutes for me to give you my spiel?"

I told her I did and then settled down into my chair.

A half hour later, I was much more educated on the role of a modern day matchmaker and had, astoundingly, promised to attend a speed-dating event she was hosting one town over the next weekend. I wasn't going as a participant—Heaven forbid!—but as an observer to see how meeting people had changed in the twenty-plus years I'd been out of the dating pool. In truth, I'd never swum in it. Danny was my first, last, and only boyfriend. From the moment I'd seen his smiling, front-toothless grin at eight years old, I'd known we were going to be together forever.

Monday dawned cold and windy with the promise of snow in the air. I arrived at the courthouse earlier than I needed to prepare for Seldrine's court appearance. Lucas had already notified me Pete Bergeron wasn't pressing charges for the hit to his eye. In all honesty, the deputy'd said, she probably hadn't meant to hit him, she was simply too drunk to realize what she'd been doing. His resolution to let it slide would go a long way with the judge's decision about whether to keep her locked up for thirty days or release her on her own recognizance. The custody of her children in the interim was another matter I needed to address.

At a few minutes before nine, Seldrine's parents

took their seats behind me. The room was beginning to fill, the judge's Monday docket full, I learned, after conferring with his clerk.

Lucas and Pete walked into the courtroom, Seldrine and two others with them.

At nine a.m. sharp, Judge Asa DuPont arrived, robed and ready.

The judicial system in our little town of Heaven was a bit…different…from other places. Since we were a small, tight-knit community, our civil and legal disputes were oftentimes between people who knew one another. Judge Dupont—or as he was known to me outside the courtroom, Uncle Asa, since he was my godfather—had been a fixture in the community for decades. He and my dad were the very best of friends, and many times had sat on opposite sides of a courtroom dispute, Dad for the defense, Asa for the district attorney's office.

Yeah, it was a little legally incestuous, but Asa was a staunch constitutionalist and the rule of law meant everything to him. I'd appeared before him many times in my career, and while I might have won more cases than I'd lost under his watchful eye, I knew I'd done it based on my abilities and the law's merits and not because he used to toss me up in the air and make me giggle when I was baby.

The courtroom rose as a unit while Asa walked to his chair. One quick gavel *thwack,* and we were in session.

Three cases were heard before it was time for Seldrine's. Piers Grouty, a boy I'd gone all through grade school with and who now worked for the county prosecutor's office, sat across from me as the court clerk read the charges against my client.

"Mr. Grouty?"

"Your Honor, Mrs. Compton is the sole responsible parent for her four children. This act of intoxication with them at home speaks to an issue of the welfare of those children. The defendant has a history of alcohol abuse and was even placed in a treatment facility several years ago. I've been instructed to file charges of child endangerment against Mrs. Compton and to request she be kept incarcerated in the county jail for a minimum of thirty days, while we conduct our inquiry."

A loud gasp blew from Seldrine's mother.

I rose from my seat. "Your Honor, if I may?"

"Mrs. Mulvaney."

I'd known potential incarceration and child endangerment charges would be on the plate. I also knew there was a way around them.

"While Mrs. Compton does have a history of alcohol abuse, she has diligently attended weekly AA meetings for the past three years, and until Saturday, when an inciting incident sparked her to drink, she's been sober. In fact, she received two visits from her AA sponsor and counselor this past weekend. She has been a model parent and has even begun working toward her GED, while simultaneously working fulltime at Angelica Arms. All in addition to caring for her four young children. To file child-endangerment charges against her is not only ludicrous, it's also cruel for the children and disruptive to the strong family unit they've established since my client's husband was sent to prison."

Asa stared down at me from his chair, his wooly eyebrows kissing in the center of his forehead. "What was the inciting incident?"

I reached over to the stack of notes I had on the table. "My client received this letter from her ex-husband, sent from the prison where he's currently incarcerated. May I?"

Asa wagged his fingers at me to approach and sent Grouty a wave, too.

I handed Asa the letter. "Cam Compton sent this to her after he received the papers informing him of Seldrine's petition for the dissolution of his parental rights. I've been working closely with my client for the past six months to legally separate him from those children so he'll have no claim on them when he's released. He's used the children in the past to control my client and threatened them if she didn't comply with whatever he wanted. As you can see"—I pointed to the letter—"he says point blank no legal document will ever keep him from his kids, and he promises to take them away from their mother. Seldrine fell apart when she read it and started drinking. Believe me, she knows she messed up by doing so."

Asa read the letter twice, then handed it to Grouty. "Still want to press charges, son?"

"Your Honor, while I agree this letter is a more than an implicit threat, it didn't make the defendant get drunk while she had children under her care."

"Noted, counselor," Asa said. "Step back, the both of you."

Asa's gaze fell on my client. "Young lady, stand up."

Seldrine's hands visibly trembled even though they were clasped together.

"Explain to me, in your own words, why you're

standing before me today."

In a voice shaking as much as her hands, Seldrine explained about opening the letter from her ex-husband and feeling not only terrified by his intentions, but helpless against preventing them. "Taking a drink was the stupidest, most selfish thing I could ever do, Judge Dupont. I know it. At the time, well"—her emaciated shoulders lifted—"I didn't think of what else to do. I wanted to…make it all go away. I realize now the smart thing, the correct thing, would have been to call Mrs. Mulvaney right away and let her deal with Cam."

Asa nodded. "I'm hopeful in the future you'll remember that before reaching for a bottle."

He sat back in his chair and steepled his fingers. After a few moments, he sat forward again.

"Okay. Mr. Grouty, I've heard what you want. It's Mrs. Mulvaney's turn. And you can sit down, young lady," he told Seldrine. "Let your lawyer do the standing and talking. It's what you're paying her for."

I squeezed Seldrine's shoulder and happened to glance toward the back of the courtroom before speaking. My breath caught when I spotted Frayne in the back row, his arms folded across his chest, his gaze squarely focused on me. His facial expression was unreadable, but his body language was screaming.

"Mrs. Mulvaney? I'm waiting."

"Yes, Your Honor. I apologize." I cleared my throat. "Based on the current circumstances, Mrs. Compton realizes she's made a colossal mistake, especially in front of her children. After being sober for a number of years, she in no way thought she would ever be put in a situation such as this again. Having said that, you can't unring a bell."

Asa tried to hide his grin behind his hand.

"In lieu of being incarcerated, my client is willing to attend daily AA sessions for however long the court determines. She will be attending them even if the court doesn't order them because she realizes she needs the constant positive reinforcement those sessions give her. We believe a period of no less than ninety days is warranted. Afterward, the court can reexamine my client's progress. Mrs. Compton would like to remain at home, keep working, and attend school without any disruption to her future plans to better herself and her family situation. The children are all with my client's parents, which is a much better arrangement than putting them into temporary foster care."

"The parents are willing to assume responsibility for an indefinite time period?" Asa asked.

I turned to Seldrine's parents and nodded. They both stood and said, "We are, Judge." Before they sat down, I caught Frayne's eye on me again.

"My client will do whatever the court instructs her to for the betterment of her family, her future, and herself." I sat back down.

"What happens now?" Seldrine whispered to me.

"He considers both sides and rules on what he thinks is best."

"Do you''—she swallowed, her eyes shining with emotion—"think he'll send me away?"

I clutched her hand and squeezed it again. "Take a breath and have some faith, Seldrine. Asa's a good man and a fair judge. Whatever he rules, you're going to comply with, even if it's going to lockup for a time. Understand?"

"Cathy—"

"Understand?" I gave her my lawyer glare to show I meant business. She swallowed again, jerked her head in a few nods, then lowered her eyes.

My gaze drifted to the back of the courtroom. Frayne was still there, looking down at something in his hand. As if struck with some kind of telepathy, he lifted his head and connected with me in a heartbeat. My mouth fell open in shock at the smoldering *heat* staring straight at me. The hues in his pale eyes deepened to a warm mix of purple and azure, the color of the wild bluebells growing around the lake property my grandmother owned. The haunted sadness had flown, as had the anger I'd seen on Saturday, replaced now with such a well of unfathomable need, I couldn't prevent my breath from quickening, or my heart from racing.

Seldrine touched my hand. "Cathy, what's the matter?"

"What?" I blinked a few times, shook my head and brought her into focus. "What's wrong?"

"You tell me," she said. "You got lost there, for a second."

"No. No. I'm okay. I was just—" Asa's heavy gavel rap pulled me to a stop.

"I've made a decision," he bellowed.

I rose, tugging Seldrine with me.

"Mr. Grouty, I assume your office will begin investigating the home life of Mrs. Compton and her children."

"Yes, Your Honor. It's standard protocol, and I've already notified Social Services and the Department of Child Welfare."

"Of course you have," Asa muttered. "Fine, then, you go ahead with your plans. In the interim"—he turned his attention to our side of the room—"I'm ordering court-mandated substance-abuse meetings for a period of ninety days, every day for the defendant, subject to tagging on more time if I think it's warranted. The clerk will give you the paperwork. In addition, the children can continue residing with their grandparents. I'm a big believer in stability, and shoving them into foster care when they obviously have family who'll take care of them is a waste of taxpayer money. I'm allowing the defendant to interact with her children under court-supervised visits for now, until the prosecutor's investigation is complete."

Seldrine turned to her parents, who nodded at her.

"In addition, since our jail is already crowded enough, I'm releasing the defendant on her own recognizance. Mrs. Mulvaney, you will be responsible for seeing to it your client attends those meetings, and if I hear she missed even a single one, we're gonna be back in here a.s.a.p. Understand me?"

"Yes, sir."

"The defendant will also need to provide the court with copies of her school transcript and her work timetable for the next three months. No sick days and no missed classes will be tolerated. Understood, young lady?"

"Yes, Your Honor."

Asa banged his gavel. "The clerk's gonna set up another hearing in thirty days for all of you. Everybody okay with that?"

"One more thing, if you please, Your Honor?" I said before he could dismiss us.

"Counselor?"

"The issue of Mrs. Compton securing sole parental

custody of the children is scheduled this week. It's been on the docket for over a month."

"Well, obviously it needs to be tabled until this situation is rectified," Asa said. "We'll revisit it when we convene again."

"Yes, Your Honor. Thank you."

Seldrine grabbed my hand. "Does this mean I'm not gonna get custody? Can Cam still be in their lives?"

The fear galloping in her eyes was all the proof I needed of why she'd gotten drunk. Knowing how fragile she still was, and where it could lead again if not checked, I tried my best to calm her anxiety.

"No, it doesn't," I said. "It means it'll take a little longer, is all. Don't let it worry you. Cam has another four years mandatory left on his sentence. He won't be out tomorrow and looking for you and the kids. Put it out of your mind, do you understand me?"

Her eyes spilled over, but she bobbed her head.

The next few minutes were filled with court scheduling business.

"I need to take you to a meeting right now," I told my client, "so say your goodbyes, and then let's get over to the church. Father Duncan has a meeting scheduled in half an hour, and you're going to it."

"Can't I go home first and shower? I've been locked up all weekend, and I reek."

"Nobody will care what you look or smell like. They've all been in the same place you have."

"But—"

"You want your kids back?"

Her eyes glistened, and she swiped a finger under her dripping nose. "You know I do."

"Then no excuses. The judge has made this my

responsibility, and I take it very seriously. You're going to be ready, on time, and compliant for every meeting. Do you understand me?"

She told me she did.

"Okay, let me finish up here, and then we're leaving."

Frayne was no longer in the back of the courtroom.

After a tearful goodbye to her parents, I carted Seldrine over to Heaven on Earth church, parked, and walked her to the basement where the meeting was being held.

"Your parents will be here, waiting for you in an hour," I told her as we stopped outside the rec room door. Since this was a closed meeting, I wasn't going to break anyone's anonymity by entering with her. My responsibility was to escort her to the meeting. It was up to her to do the rest. "Don't screw this up, Seldrine."

"I won't, Cathy. I promise."

"Good. Call me before you go to work later with your schedule for the next two weeks. We need to plan which meetings you go to, and I need to adjust my own days to bring you."

She grabbed my hand and squeezed it with both of hers. "I'm sorry about all this, I really am. I don't know how I'll ever be able to repay all your kindness."

"By getting your life back in order."

She threw her arms around me, and then entered the rec room.

Back at my office, Martha greeted me with a stack of files in one hand and a mug of tea in the other. She handed me both after I'd taken off my coat. "Everything go okay?"

I explained the provisions Asa had handed down,

including my need to escort Seldrine to daily meetings. "She'll call later with her work and school schedules."

"Okay. Hey, did that writer fella find you?"

"Frayne?"

"Yeah. He showed up here at nine. I told him you were in court, and he said he'd drop by there."

"Did he say what he wanted?"

"No. Did he find you?"

"He was in the back of the courtroom while Seldrine's case was being heard, but he left before it ended."

"Couldn't'a been important then, cuz if it was he'd'a waited."

I had to agree.

As I was leaving the office for the day later on, I toyed with the idea of stopping by the inn, seeing if Frayne was there, and asking him why he'd been in court today, observing me.

Observing me? *Ha.* Getting me all hot and bothered was what he'd really been doing. I'd never lost my concentration before like I had when I'd found those pale eyes focused on me.

It was a little discombobulating, to be sure.

I hit the remote starter on my key fob, and my car roared to life, warming the engine before I ever got to it. A quick movement from the parking lot caught my attention.

Frayne alighted from a car and walked toward me.

Since it was almost five on a January day in New Hampshire, dark had descended an hour ago. The lamps along the street were lit, throwing an eerie golden glow of light atop his bare head, haloing it. His face was mostly shadowed, but his lips were pressed tight together, his hands tucked into the pockets of his bomber jacket. He walked as if he were on a mission, with purposeful strides, body erect, eyes fixed in front of him. On me.

I waited, my briefcase in one hand, keys in the other. A flicker of expectation shimmied down my back, the unexpected jolt I kept experiencing whenever we were together making itself known. I should have been on guard against any kind of silly expectation about seeing him, since I knew his opinion of what I did for a living. Unfortunately, this was one of those times when the logical part of my brain warred with the emotional part. It didn't happen often, but when it did, emotion usually won the battle.

"Mr. Frayne," I said when he finally stopped in front of me. I impressed myself with my ability to keep my voice devoid of the sensations clanging around inside me.

His face was partly shadowed under the street light, but I was able to see his mouth clearly. It pulled into a straight line at my greeting. "I know you're done for the day and want to get home to your family, but I need to speak to you about something important. Do you have a few minutes?"

The only family I had to get home to was probably asleep under the kitchen table. A few minutes more wouldn't make much difference. "Of course. What can I do for you?"

He pulled his bare hands from his pockets and blew on them. Apparently, no one had told him how cold it gets in New England in the winter. "Can we go somewhere warmer, like up the street to the diner? They're still open, I think."

"The Last Supper is open until eleven every day of the year." I shut my car off.

He tossed me another one of those confused looks, as if he missed the pun of a joke when everyone around him had gotten it. He tucked his hands back into his jacket pocket and followed me, silently, up the street.

Delicious warmth and the heavenly smell of bacon grease and percolating coffee hit us the moment Frayne held the door open for me.

"Hey, Cath."

"Hey, Ruthie. We're gonna take a booth, okay?"

"Ay-a. Sit wherever ya want. I'll be right over."

We slid into a flaming red vinyl-upholstered booth, which had been new when my parents had gotten married. Old-fashioned jukeboxes were secured to each tabletop, the tunes all from the eighties and nineties.

"I don't think I've seen one of these in years," Frayne said.

Two empty mugs were plopped down in front of us along with two glasses of ice water. "Cost you a quarter if you want to hear somethin'."

Frayne turned his focus to the owner of the Last Supper.

"You the writer feller staying over at the inn?" Ruthie asked, eyeing him from head to chest. "My dad was talking 'bout you at breakfast th'other morning."

"Ruthie, this is McLachlan Frayne," I said. To Frayne, I added, "This is Ruthie Tewksburry. You met her father, Olaf, at the historical society the other day. Ruthie owns the Last Supper."

"Own, operate, cook, and if you get outta line, I'm a second-degree black belt, and I can take you down no matter how big or stupid you are."

Frayne's eyes went wide. Whether it was from her blunt statement or her appearance I had no idea, but once again, he had that paralyzed deer-in-the-headlights stare, exactly as he had the first day at the museum.

Ruthie Tewksburry, all one hundred pounds of her sopping wet, stood a little over five feet, was sixty-two years old, admitted to fifty-one if asked, smoked like she invented the habit, and was universally loved by all of Heaven.

"Good to know," Frayne said.

Ruthie winked. "Coffee for you?" she asked, and then poured him a cup before he could answer. To me she said, "Your tea is coming up, sweetie."

That's the benefit of living somewhere all your life: the townspeople know everything about you. Of course, it can also be a curse because, well, the townspeople know *everything* about you.

Frayne's eyes tracked her as she sashayed to the counter.

"She assumes every male on the planet drinks coffee. If you'd prefer something else, ask."

He looked down at the cup, then shook his head. "No, this is fine. She's…" He let the sentence drag.

"Yeah, she is. Now, what did you need to talk to me about?"

He lifted his cup, took a sip, and his shoulders relaxed when the first taste hit his mouth. Ruthie breezed by and deposited a full pot of hot water and three unopened tea bags in front of me.

"You eating anything, kids?"

My stomach rumbled in answer. With a chuckle as quick and harsh as a car backfiring, Ruthie grinned. "I already know what you want," she said. "How 'bout you, writer-man?"

"Um…"

"Meatloaf's on special tonight. Comes with garlic mashed, green beans, and a slice of pie for dessert."

"What kind of pie?"

A grin split her gaunt face revealing a huge gap in her front teeth. "Apple, blueberry, blackberry, lemon meringue, key lime, chocolate mousse, rhubarb, pecan, pumpkin, tollhouse, chocolate peanut butter, and orange cream."

She rattled of the selections in a swift staccato, and I wondered if he'd actually heard all the choices.

When he ordered the chocolate mousse, I knew he had.

Ruthie's head bobbed a couple of times, and then she left us alone.

The diner wasn't packed as it usually was during leaf-peeping season and on any given weekend day, but it still did a fairly good business, enough so Ruthie was able to stay open seven days a week for the entire year.

While I steeped my tea, Frayne cleared his throat. "Why does she know what you want without asking?"

I took a sip, closed my eyes, and sighed. Nanny Fee had remarked many times that a good cup of tea could solve any problem, soothe any ache, heal any emotional wound. She wasn't wrong.

When I opened my eyes, set on answering him, the words stuck in the back of my throat. As he had in the subbasement, Frayne's stare was penetrating, as if trying to read my mind, even reach down to my soul. I needed a moment to compose the jumble of nerves tumbling through me.

When I was sure I could respond without sounding

like I needed an inhaler, I said, "Because I order the same thing every time I come in here and have since I was a kid, including the three summers I waitressed for Ruthie when I was in high school. Every item on the menu is fabulous, yet I still order the same meal every time."

"It must be good."

I smiled at him and then repeated my earlier question.

He peered down at his coffee mug again. "I know you saw me at the back of the courtroom this morning."

Since it wasn't a question, I didn't answer.

"I asked your sister where your office was, and when I got there your secretary told me you were at the courthouse. I thought I'd be able to catch you when you were done, but I got a phone call I had to take."

"I was surprised to see you in the gallery. After our conversation the other day, I'd think the last place I'd find you was a courtroom."

The tops of his cheeks darkened as he lifted his mug to his mouth. The mist from the hot coffee rose from its center, caressed his face, and for a moment I grew jealous of the steam. I wanted to know what it felt like to run my fingers over the hard, square line of that chiseled jaw, stroke the multicolored stubble crossing it, and drag my fingers into the crevices slipping down the sides of his mouth.

"A courtroom isn't my favorite place on earth," he said, then took a long chug from his mug.

From his silence on the subject, I surmised he wasn't going to tell me why.

I repeated my question.

"I've come across a name in the public files and

then did a search through the personal archives, and I've hit a dead end."

"What do you mean?"

"The last direct surviving member of the Heaven family died about twenty years ago. I found his birth and his death certificates. He was, in all respects, the last of the reverend's line."

"Yes, Robert Heaven. I know. He was Josiah's four, or maybe five times—I forget which—great-grandson. When he died, the line died with him since he never had any kids. What's the problem?"

"He may not have had any children, but he was survived by a wife."

A little bell rang in the back of my mind.

"And I can't find any record of her passing, so I need help locating her. I went down to the county clerk's office, but there's no record of her. I thought you might be able to help me."

He had no idea how helpful I could be.

"Why do you need to talk to her? She's not a descendant. She wouldn't have any information pertinent to the family."

"You can't know that."

Oh yes, I could.

I swear he could read my mind. His eyebrows folded into the middle of his forehead, and he cocked his head in his familiar, pre-questioning way.

Before he could ask it, our food arrived.

"Here you go, kids. Meatloaf special for you, Mr. Writer-man. Heaven in the Morning for you, Cath. I had Alvy put on a few extra pieces of crispy bacon for you. And this"—she placed a wrapped paper bag on the seat next to me—"is a little something for George.

Colleen and her handsome hunk were in here this morning, and she told me your guy isn't doing too good. I know how much he loves Alvy's sausage patties, and I thought this might perk him up a bit."

"Oh, Ruthie, you're the best." I grabbed her hand and squeezed it. "Thank you."

"Give him a kiss from me, and tell him to feel better."

"I will."

"Enjoy your meal, you two."

"I'm sorry," Frayne said when we were alone again.

"For what?"

"I'm keeping you from your family."

I swiped my hand in the air. "Don't worry about it."

He took a bite of his meat while I slathered butter and syrup over the challah bread french toast, sunny-side-up eggs, and bacon Ruthie had placed before me.

"That's what you eat every time you're here? Breakfast?"

"Most important meal of the day. I can always eat breakfast no matter what time of the day it is. In addition to it being divine." I put a huge forkful in my mouth and let the sweet and savory flavors explode over my taste buds. I let out a tiny groan, like I did every single time when the first bite settled in.

Frayne's breath hissed in with the force of a steam valve opening.

"What's the matter?" I asked, fearful he'd burned his mouth on his food.

"*Good Lord.* Do you have any idea, any idea at all what you—" He stopped short, his eyes widening and, as if realizing he'd leaned practically across the table to me, slammed his body against the seat back, the force making the cushion release a *whoosh* of air.

With a violent shake of his head, Frayne dropped his gaze to his plate. "You don't," he mumbled, his head still moving side to side. "Of course you don't. It's obvious you don't have a clue."

"Don't have a clue about what?"

When he wouldn't look at me, I reached across the table and laid a hand over his.

A spark flashed when my fingers came in contact with his skin, powerful enough we both startled. The shock was enough to force Frayne's gaze back to mine.

For the life of me, I had no idea what he was thinking. In the brief moment we sat there staring at one another, he went from annoyed to baffled, and then maybe even little turned on. The man's emotions and reactions were so mercurial I was in the dark about what was going on with him.

"Tell me what I don't have a clue about," I said, in my firm, get-to-the-point lawyer voice, the one Maureen swears is a perfect imitation of our father's.

It was fascinating to see him suck in all those conflicting emotions. He dragged in a cavernous breath, held it for a few beats then slowly let it out, enough so his shoulders pulled down from where they'd settled at the bottoms of his ears.

"I'm sorry. I don't know why I said that." His carefree shrug didn't fool me for a moment. He took a sip of coffee, then picked up his utensils again. "What were we talking about? Oh, right." He speared a slice of meatloaf with his fork. "I meant to say you seem...reluctant, to help me find Robert Heaven's wife.

Why?"

I'd said he was perceptive. Here was more proof I was correct. I *was* reluctant to tell him her identity. Not for any reason he could think of, though.

"I'm wondering what you think she could tell you that's not already mentioned somewhere in the archives."

"Which is my point. There's a big gap in the personal archives. I spent the better part of yesterday backtracking everything through both sets of files listed on the computer. I can't find anything listed from after Robert graduated college until his marriage and then his death. Almost sixty years of data is missing."

"Maybe nothing of significance happened during those years."

His was studying me again with that tilted head, squinty-eyed perusal. "Do you know who his wife was?"

I waited a few beats while I shoved in my eggs. "Yes."

"And is she still alive?"

I nodded.

"Still living in the area?"

"Yes."

"So, you know who she is and you know she still lives around here, you probably even know where."

Once again, because he wasn't asking a direct question, I chose to remain silent and eat my eggs.

"It makes me curious why you won't tell me who she is. All I'm going to do is ask her a few questions, you know."

"Maybe she doesn't want to answer any of your questions."

Okay, as far as a rebuttal went, this one was fairly pathetic. I was a much better debater and rebutter than this.

"How would either of us know if we don't ask her?"

He had me there. His argument was lawyer-worthy, a thought I kept to myself considering his feelings about the profession.

In a soft, dulcet voice made for persuasion, a voice very reminiscent of the one he'd used in the subbasement, he asked, "Who is she, Cathy? Who is Robert Heaven's widow? Tell me."

My tummy muscles jumped when he called me by my given name. It sounded…right, somehow, on his lips. I'd had a hard time resisting him the last time his voice reminded me of a man who'd woken from a night of wild sex and warm bourbon, and this time I couldn't, either.

I waited a breath while I composed my thoughts.

His stare grew more intense. Yup. He'd have made a heck of a lawyer.

"My grandmother."

Chapter 7

Frayne gaped at me, wide-eyed and openmouthed.

"You're a descendent of Josiah Heaven?"

"Not by blood, no. He was married to my widowed grandmother for a time. There's nothing connecting us except for a marriage license."

The moment the words left my mouth, he slid from the booth and called out to Ruthie to box up our meal. Ten minutes later, with him following me in his rental car, we arrived at the nursing home, unannounced.

"Number One, this is a surprise. What brings ya here at this time o' the evenin'?"

Nanny was already dressed for bed even though it was barely six p.m. The white Irish linen nightgown she'd had sent from her homeland several years ago sat under an ankle-length cotton robe Colleen had given her when she'd been admitted to Angelica Arms. At a tiny ninety pounds, Nanny was perpetually cold even though the nursing home blasted the heat year round for the residents. Her waist-length flaming-red hair—a product of two different colors-in-a-box—was coiled into a thick braid slung over one shoulder. A fair face sparsely etched and usually smiling belied her ninety-three years. I didn't have one memory of my grandmother where she looked other than she did right at this moment.

Well, maybe a few where she was actually dressed,

97

not in her jammies, and her hair was coiled around her head instead of over her shoulder.

Eagle-sharp periwinkle-blue eyes zeroed in on the man behind me. "And who might this handsome lad be? You don't usually bring along a beau when you come to visit me, darlin' girl. And especially when I'm not lookin' me finest."

The tops of Frayne's cheeks turned an adorable pink under Nanny's hearty scrutiny. The smile he graced her with, though, was pure male delight.

I made the introductions.

"I have to disagree, Mrs. Heaven," he told her, the skin around his eyes wrinkling and laughter dancing in their depths when he took her withered hand in his. "You look very fetching."

"Ach, now." Nanny waved a dismissive hand at him, her own eyes twinkling at the flirtation in his voice. " 'Tis a good eye physician you need. I've one I can recommend. And it's Scallopini now, darlin' boy. Like the dish, minus the veal. Robert Heaven was me third husband. God rest his soul." She made the sign of the Cross.

"Nanny, Mr. Frayne is writing a book about Josiah Heaven."

"A book about the Reverend? Why, who would want t'be readin' about that old crackpot, I ask ya?"

"You'd be surprised, Mrs. Heaven," Frayne said. "I mean, Scallopini."

"I imagine I would at that, then, since you're here. So. What do ya need with an old woman like me?"

I settled Nanny into the reclining chair she'd been able to bring from home and indicated the other chair in the room for Frayne, while I sat on the edge of her turned-down bed.

I let Frayne take the lead in the questioning.

"I'm doing research on the Reverend at the museum, and I noticed something odd when I began tracing the descendants' files. There's nothing I can find catalogued in the archives about Robert Heaven from after his college graduation until his marriage and then his death," Frayne told her. "I find it odd nothing of note was ever saved by someone about him, when every other family member has literally reams of documents and files associated with them."

"Does seem odd, aye?" Nanny said. "Robert had a very full life before we married. Attended college. Yale. Ran his own company for a number of years. Stayed a bachelor until his late fifties, married to his company, most who knew him said. Then we met, and as the kids say these days, the rest is history."

Frayne's smile was soft and, I had to admit, charming.

"Together almost twenty years before he went to his maker with a smile on his lips and a full stomach, seeing as we'd just dined at the annual Jingle Bell Ball. Good years. Good times."

"You don't happen to still have any of his possessions or personal items, do you? Or anything from his family archives? I realize he's been gone for some time, but if you know of anything, or anywhere I can go to find something, anything, to help in my research, I'd be in your debt."

The twinkle in Nanny's eyes brightened. "Well, now, darlin' boy, it's more careful you should be sayin' those words to the likes of me. We Irish take the grantin' of favors and the payin' up o' debts very seriously, you know."

Frayne must have recognized the devilish gleam in her gaze. My grandmother was many things, with *flirt* holding the number one position, *harmless imp* the second. And as a word of caution—never play poker with her.

His mouth split into a grin rivaling Nanny's. "I'm sure you'll be able to come up with the perfect recompense, Mrs. Scallopini. Like the dish, minus the veal."

Her girlish laughter warmed my heart. "Ach, you're a darlin' man, you are. The charm of the devil himself."

"Oh, Mrs. S. I didn't know you had company."

Seldrine Compton entered, carrying a tray with a pot of Nanny's evening tea and a scone from Maureen. My sister sent a supply every few days to the Arms to be doled out to Nanny and her cronies at their asking.

"It's okay, child."

"I'm sorry, Cathy." Seldrine placed the tray on the table next to Nanny's chair, then rolled it in front of her so my grandmother could reach it. "I don't mean to interrupt." When she stood upright again, her eyes flicked to Frayne, and her cheeks turned the color of ripe strawberries in summer.

I could relate to her response. All that adorable rangy male essence stuffed into a ratty pullover and snug jeans would have the same effect on any girl with a pulse and a functioning pair of eyes.

Frayne's smile left his face, the good humor in his eyes lifting.

Seldrine averted her gaze and settled on me.

"You doing okay?"

Her vigorous head bob told me she understood what I was asking. "I'll come back when your company's gone, Mrs. S, for the tray. Can I get you anything else right now?"

"No, darlin'. I'm good. You run along, and I'll see ya in a bit."

With another head bob for Nanny and me, she ignored Frayne altogether and left.

"That poor child has had more misery in her young life than should be borne in a lifetime. Right when it looks like she's making strides and moving forward, the miserable excuse she has for a husband shoots her back a few paces." Her head shook from side to side as she clucked her tongue. "It's proud of you I am, Number One. You're helping her get her life back together. She deserves it. As do those babies o' hers. It's times like this"—she reached over and grabbed my hand—"I'm happy you followed in your father's footsteps instead of me own."

She turned to Frayne and said, "The lass coulda been more famous than me. Plays the piano like no one's business, she does." She winked and added, "Gets it from her dear ol' gran."

I've got to admit hearing this from a woman I loved without measure went a long way in making my day. From the corner of my eye, I caught the surprised lift of Frayne's eyebrows. It took everything in me not to leap from my position on the bed, grab his shoulders, shake him, and declare, "See? Not all lawyers are horrible, greedy soul-suckers like you think they are."

Of course, I didn't.

But I sure wanted to.

"Now." Nanny turned her attention back to Frayne.

"I don't know anything specific about any documents or whatnot Robert may have had, but the man was a pack rat, a real hoarder if truth be told. And the messiest human being I'd ever met. Never put anything away once he'd taken it from wherever it was stored. A real chairdrobe and floordrobe, was he."

"Excuse me, what?" Frayne's gaze swung from Nanny to me.

Since I have a black belt in Nanny-isms, I translated. "Chairdrobe is what Nanny calls someone who piles their clothes on a chair instead of putting them away in a drawer or hanging them in the closet."

"Me dear departed granddaughter Eileen was a horrible offender as a teenager," Nanny said.

"So, going with the description"—Frayne cocked his head at me—"a floordrobe is…"

"Someone who tosses clothes and belongings on the floor in the same fashion."

Nanny sipped her tea. "Horrible habits, both. 'Twas the cause of many an argument between us. O' course, the makin' up was worth the yelling."

I rolled my eyes, and when I caught Frayne's stare, he was trying to suppress laughter behind his hand.

"When Robert died," Nanny continued, "I packed up a bunch o' boxes he'd had sitting in the basement collectin' dust and mold and put them into storage. They're with the rest of the things I couldn't bring here with me because I've got such limited space."

"They're in a storage unit?" I asked.

"Aye, lass. Do me a favor and reach into me table there. See the little clutch? Give it over."

I handed her the item she asked for.

"This is the key to the locker. Or lockers, I should

be saying, as I've got three."

I tried not to blanch. Nanny was nothing if not eagle eyed.

"I know you're thinking who's the hoarder here, lass, but the truth of the matter is I've lived for ninety-three years, traveled the world, and been married four times. I've got baggage." Her gaze slid to Frayne, and her lips twitched. "In both the figurative and literal senses, to be sure."

Truer words, alas, were never spoken.

"Do you have any idea which unit Robert's boxes are in?" I asked.

Nanny sighed, loud and long. "I'm sorry, lass, I don't. When he died and then I married Vincenzo, Mr. Scallopini"—she clarified for Frayne—"and then he passed—God rest his soul—after a short time together, I simply locked the door of me house and moved in with your parents in me time o' grief. You were married and off on your own by then. 'Twas your father's idea to get rid of everything. He wanted to call in a dumpster company like 1-800-Toss-Me-Crap and chuck it all into the rubbish. We had a big to-do about it. In the end, he saw reason and let me keep me life's possessions."

More likely he simply gave in because arguing with his mother always gave him stomach pains.

"Rented the storage lockers, and in a weekend, we moved everythin' into them. I've been meanin' for years to go and straighten things, look through the piles, and sort it all. Ah, but life has a way of changin' the plans we make, doesn't it?"

She has the gift of stating the obvious, does my grandmother.

"So, I'll give these to you two, and you can rummage 'round and try to find Robert's things. The boxes'll be labeled with his name. Don't be askin' me where to find them, though. You'll have to sift through everything yourselves."

The thought of digging around and hunting through eight decades of my grandmother's life—and no doubt, junk—wasn't exactly appealing. On any level. The excited gleam in Frayne's eyes, though, told me the situation was more than pleasing to him. As a historical writer, he probably lived for the moment he could delve into a person's past, root through their actual belongings, and perhaps unearth heretofore unknown aspects of their lives.

In the purest sense, he was a biographical archeologist.

Nanny handed the keys to me. "You've got me permission to take anything you find pertinent to what you're doing," she told Frayne. "Give it to the historical society for their collection. I've no need of any of it. Anything lookin' like junk, take to the dump. That includes"—she peered at me—"me own things."

"Oh, Nanny, I don't want the responsibility of choosing what to keep of yours and what to throw away. That's not right."

"You hold me power of attorney, don't ya, lass?"

"I do, but—"

"Well, then use the power I gave ya and make some decisions. Anything you feel has sentimental value, go ahead and keep. The rest, well, if I've no use for it now, I'm not gonna. I've a thought there may be some good furniture pieces mixed in with all the other stuff Number Four might find useful for the inn. Other than that, nothing else means much to me. I've got everything I need here, and I'm probably not gonna be movin' again afore I leave this earth."

My heart grew heavy at her words, and a little ping of sorrow riffled through me. "What have you always told me about never saying never?" I reached across the table and took one of her hands in mine.

She laid down her teacup and slid her free hand over mine, cocooning it between them. "You're more than a half century younger than I am, darlin' girl. Those words make sense at your age. I've lived long enough to know it's better to roll with what life tosses at ya instead of trying to dodge and weave."

She squeezed my hand and grinned. "Now, off with the two of ya. I want me evenin' snack, and I've got a new romance book I'm in the middle of on me e-reader I want to get back to. It's just started to get to all the sexy-time parts."

She winked at Frayne. When his cheeks went dark again, I knew in my heart Nanny had meant for them to.

"Give us a goodnight hug and kiss, Number One, and be off home yourself. George'll be waiting."

I did as asked and then kissed her on both cheeks.

"Mrs. Scallopini, it's been a delight," Frayne said, extending his hand to her. "Thank you for your help. I can't tell you how much I appreciate it."

Nanny might look frail, but in truth she was strong as a workhorse, her hands especially. A lifetime of playing piano professionally had made them that way. She tugged Frayne to her and said, "In this family, we hug."

I didn't know who was more shocked, Frayne or me, when his arms circled around her and held on tight for a few seconds.

When he pulled back, both of them had grins on their faces.

"Oh…" Nanny turned her attention back to me. "Before ya leave, tell me. Did ya call Olivia Joyner?"

Heat danced up my neck. "Um, yeah."

"Good." She smiled. "You're in your prime, you are, but getting younger you're not."

That heat turned into a furnace blast. "No worries, Nanny."

Just as we were leaving the room, I spotted Seldrine in the corridor. "Wait up," I called out. To Frayne, I said, "Give me a second."

"You all done with your visit?" she asked, snaking a quick look down the hallway at Frayne.

"Yeah. Look, I know you're working, but I never got the chance to tell you how proud I am of you before I dropped you off this morning."

"Proud? Of what? I made a mess of everything, Cathy. I could lose my kids, my house—"

I took her hand in mine. "You won't, which is why I'm proud of you. You're a strong woman, much stronger than you give yourself credit for. Asa Dupont knows you want what's best for your family, and he's betting on you doing whatever you have to in order to ensure it happens."

"But you heard Grouty. He thinks I'm unfit, and he's gonna try and prove it."

"Then you have to prove him wrong. On all counts. Keep going to school, keep working, abide by the judge's rules, and keep attending those daily meetings. You'll show everyone this was a blip, an aberration, something not to be repeated."

Her gaze flicked down the hallway and then back to me. "He a friend of yours?"

The question took me by surprise as did the distrust I saw flying in her expression when she glared at him.

"Not a friend, no. Not even a client." I explained why Frayne was in town. "What's the matter?" I asked when she stole another worried glance his way.

"Just be careful is all. Look, I gotta get evening care started. I got three baths to do. I'll be ready when you pick me up in the morning, don't worry."

"I'm not. See you at eight."

I walked back toward Frayne who was trying—and failing—to look nonchalant as he leaned against the hallway wall, his hands slung in his pockets.

I didn't say anything about Seldrine, and neither did he.

"I'm sorry for keeping you from your family. I know you want to get home, but can you take a few minutes for us to schedule when to go the storage facility? Obviously, I'm free anytime. You've got work and family responsibilities."

The breath I blew past my lips echoed in the sterile, vacant hallway. "I do." I pulled my phone from my purse and called up the calendar app. "Tomorrow's schedule is light, and I've got no court appearances. When would you like to start?"

"What's the earliest you're available?"

His anticipation was palpable.

"Is ten okay? I've got a client at nine. I should be done by ten, ten fifteen at the latest. Does that work for you?"

He told me it did. I gave him directions from the inn to the storage facility and said he should be able to find it without any problems.

"I can always plug the address into the GPS system in the car if I need to," he said.

I wanted to thank him for being kind to my grandmother and not pushing when she couldn't tell him anything other than she had. I could imagine a less conscientious man would have grilled and prodded her for any memory or bit of information he could elicit.

"You were very patient with my grandmother," I said before we came to the Arms' front doors. "Thank you."

His shrug was careless. "She's a lovely woman, and she's helping me."

I thought it was more and said so. "Were you close to your own grandmothers?"

"Not especially. One was in a nursing home for most of my childhood, and the other died before I was born."

"My grandmother has been a fixture in my life since the day I was born. In all my sisters' lives. It's a blessing we still have her at her age, relatively healthy and still mentally sound." A laugh jumped from me. "Well, the last part is debatable among my sisters and me at times, but you know what I mean."

Frayne peered at me from under the fringe of his eyelashes. It annoyed me I couldn't read what was behind his intense look.

"Family is very important to you, isn't it?"

"It's everything."

I knew now what lay behind the pained, sorrowful expression living in his eyes and the desire to comfort him, console him on his loss was great within me. But I knew he didn't like me, or rather my profession, and I was pretty sure if I offered him any words of solace or support, he'd shoot me down for my efforts and I'd look foolish for the attempt.

"Well," he said, zipping up his jacket, "I won't keep you any longer. I'll see you in the morning."

He held the door open for me, and the slap of frigid, windy air was like a thousand little ice shards stabbing my face. I'd donned my hat and gloves and wound my scarf around my neck and chin when we'd been in the vestibule. Frayne had neither hat nor gloves.

I shot a quick glance at him as he got into his car. He didn't look cold, so maybe he had a body furnace like Maureen. In the dead of winter, she wore flip-flops and was never cold. The passing thought I'd like to snuggle up against someone with heat to spare made me a little uneasy and a tiny bit turned on.

Before driving off, I waved at him. He didn't wave back. That notion about snuggling up against him went the way of the dinosaur as I drove home.

Chapter 8

The sixth sneeze in less than a minute blew from me like a nor'easter roaring along the shoreline.

"God bless you," Frayne said.

Again.

If I had my dates correct, Nanny had filled these storage units more than fifteen years ago and, from the layers of dust covering everything jam-packed into them, hadn't come back one time since the locks were secured.

All three units were side by side, making it easy to go from one to the other. The storage facility was located on the outskirts of town and covered twenty acres of county-owned land. Nanny had the forethought to rent units housed inside the facility and not facing the outside elements. I was thankful we weren't relegated to years of dust *and* frigid temperatures while we dug through them.

I'd run home after meeting with my client and changed from work clothes into sweat pants that had seen me through four years of college, then law school, and one of Danny's old army sweatshirts. If I was going to get dirty, I wanted it to be in comfortable, washable clothes. I checked on George, who was a little doggy-confused about why I was home in the middle of the morning. A few minutes spent loving on him, and then I left.

Frayne was waiting for me at the storage facility when I pulled up.

"We should have brought filtration masks with us," I said. "This dust could be filled with mold spores."

I'd had some foresight on the dirt situation and had packed various rags and multipurpose cleaning solution in addition to Danny's Swiss Army knife to slice open any taped boxes.

We'd unlocked the first two units for convenience. No one was going to be visiting any of the other lockers on a wicked cold January Tuesday, and I was confident we'd have free rein of the hallway to pull items out and strew them along the space for inspection. When I rolled the unlocked door up to the ceiling, I'd sneezed a series of rapid tornado blasts from the cyclone of stale air and dust clouds spiraling up from a decade-plus of confinement. I'd learned my lesson with the first unit, and when I unlocked the second, I covered my mouth and nose with a clean rag.

By mutual agreement, Frayne and I decided to split up and each take a locker to determine if there was any order to their storage.

After two minutes in mine, I knew there wasn't.

"Found anything yet?" Frayne called.

I lifted another huge plastic container filled with Christmas ornaments—the eighth one so far—and yelled back, "Nope. You?"

"No. I've got dozens of bags of what look like formal dresses, like for a wedding, though."

"Those are probably Nanny's concert clothes."

I grabbed another box, this one labeled *Travel.* After slicing the masking tape with Danny's knife, I found it filled with concert programs from all over

Europe. The dates were mixed, but most were from the 1940s and 50s.

"Concert clothes?"

I jumped and dropped the pamphlet I held in my hand. Frayne stood right behind me. He was holding a garment bag, and through the unzipped opening, several beaded gowns in various shades of red, Nanny's signature color, peeped through. Despite being a flaming redhead—or because of it, I never knew which—she wore the vibrant color when she performed, while the rest of the company was garbed in the traditional mix of black and white.

"*Jesus*. You should wear a bell."

One corner of his mouth tilted upward.

"My grandmother was a professional concert pianist and traveled the world with various symphonies. Those"—I nodded to the bag in his hand—"are some of the gowns she wore when she played."

"She must have led some life."

I lifted the box of concert programs. "She did. This is filled with programs from some of the places she performed."

He reached out for it, and I stepped around a pile of plastic containers to hand it to him.

He was dressed, like me, for comfort and cleaning. A pair of ratty, torn-at-the-knees faded jeans cupped his butt and made me want to do the same and covered his long legs. A Dartmouth College sweatshirt with holes in the elbows kept him warm on top. He hadn't shaved today, and the mix of gray, white, and peppery-black stubble over his jaw and cheeks made me want to drag my fingers across it. I don't think he'd showered, either, because his hair was even more of a riot than usual. It needed a good brushing, in addition to a trim. Reading glasses were perched halfway down his nose as he regarded me over the top of the rims. Today, his eyes were clear and focused, the pain haunting them, hidden.

He was such a mix of adorable and sexy, I wanted to fold him into my arms, hold him close, and squeeze his enticing ass.

Because the urge to do it was overpowering, I turned back to work after handing him the box.

"I don't think there's a concert hall in Europe she hasn't played." He rifled through the programs.

"She's been to Asia three times, too." I popped open another plastic container. "*Criminy*. How many Christmas decorations does one person need? This is the ninth box I've opened."

"I've got a few ornament boxes in my unit as well. They look...ancient."

His gaze drifted to the mound of boxes still in the middle and back of the unit and shook his head. I tried to move a large garment container from the top of an old wooden hope chest, but it was awkwardly shaped and heavy, not to mention covered in dust. I started rapid-fire sneezing again and would have dropped the box if Frayne hadn't reached out and grabbed it—and me.

Like an off switch had been flicked, I stopped sneezing. My eyes were watery and my nose was threatening to dribble as I stared up at him. I could imagine how pathetic and unattractive I must have looked.

His clothes and hair were dust-streaked, and tiny particles were stuck to the prickly hairs on his face. A tingle of acute awareness shot through me, and for a moment I simply lost my breath. It had been long, too long, since I'd experienced anything remotely resembling arousal, and I needed a few seconds to make sure I didn't give into my thoughts and jump him.

Why Mac Frayne, a man who I seriously thought only tolerated me because I could help him with something, should be the one my long-dormant and now-screaming hormones were zeroing in on, was baffling.

"You okay?" His voice was low and deep as he peered over his glasses at me. His brows grooved under the wild fringe of hair falling across his forehead, and my hands did that tingly thing again, wanting to reach up and push it back.

"Y-yes. Sorry. The box was heavier than it looked." I took a subtle step backward, and he let go of my arm.

When he appeared convinced I was surefooted, he grabbed the box with both hands and then reached for a rag to wipe the dust.

"There's a label on this. It's pretty faded." He adjusted his glasses and examined it closer. "I think it says *Wedding: # 1*. The word *number* is a hash tag. Is this your grandmother's wedding dress from her first marriage, do you think?"

While he'd been busy with the label, I'd moved back to the hope chest and lifted the top.

"What's wrong?" he asked.

"Nothing. Why?"

"You gasped."

"Oh. I was surprised, that's all. This trunk is filled with stuff from my wedding. I didn't even know Nanny had these things. Let me see that box."

He held it up for me.

"That's not my grandmother's wedding dress; it's mine."

"You've been married more than once?"

"What? Oh, no. No." I lifted out a framed wedding picture of Danny and me. After a quick glance, I put it down on a container. "My grandmother refers to us by numerical order. I'm the oldest grandchild so she calls me Number One, ergo, the label. Colleen, unfortunately is Number Two, a name she still despises to this day but really hated when we were kids. Maureen is four."

"What happened to three?"

"That was Eileen, Mo's twin. The one who died."

While I rummaged through the chest, Frayne went silent. When I turned, he was staring at my wedding photo.

"You look very young in this picture."

"We were both eighteen. Graduated from high school a month before. He left for boot camp a week after the wedding."

Frayne placed the picture back down on the container. His brows were kissing again. "Why does your grandmother call you and your sisters by numbers? It's...odd, to say the least."

"The very least," I quipped. "It's a long-standing feud with my mother. Nanny hated she'd given us all similar names because she wanted to play up our Irish roots. Nanny thought it made us all seem clichéd and sounded kooky."

"Cathleen, Colleen, Eileen, and Maureen."

"Yeah. It's pretty obnoxious sounding when the names are all said in a row. Nanny started calling us by number as a way to annoy my mother. It worked, but it also made our lives miserable when we were kids, especially Colleen. To this day, she's still scarred."

"You're all adults now. Why does she still refer to you that way?"

I shrugged, a tiny dust cloud wafting from my shoulders with the movement. "Habit, more than anything, I think." I opened a scrapbook I found sitting in the chest. It was filled with photographs of my engagement party, my wedding shower, the ceremony. "God, we *were* young," I said as I turned the pages. "I've never even seen some of these."

"I would think this is an example of the items your grandmother didn't want thrown away. Those kinds of memories are precious."

What did old photographs mean to me now? It wasn't like Danny and I were going to be sitting by a fireside one day, regaling our grandchildren about our younger lives. We'd had no children, therefore grandchildren couldn't be considered. End of story. Here I was, thirty-nine years old, no husband, no kids, no prospects of either anywhere in my future. I'd done everything I was supposed to do in life, everything my parents pushed me to do and expected me to. Gotten married, became a lawyer, planned a future. Danny had wanted kids as much as I had. Until he'd decided he didn't.

A ball of anger started to swell within me as the memory of the last time he was home on leave jumped to the front of my mind. The hurtful words, the accusations, the lies, the truth finally rearing its head.

As quick as the anger grew, it died.

"Are you okay?"

I looked up from the scrapbook. He'd slung his

glasses into the neckline of his sweatshirt and moved closer to me, concern filling his eyes.

Was I?

"I'm fine." I snapped the book closed. "Look, this trip down memory lane isn't getting us any closer to finding Robert's things. Help me move this chest out of the way. I want to get to the back wall."

I don't think he believed me, but he didn't argue.

When we'd moved the chest into the hallway, an entire new row of boxes and plastic containers appeared.

"I'm gonna scream if those are filled with more holiday decorations."

A ghost of a grin crossed Frayne's sexy mouth. "I'm going back next door to rummage. Call out if you find anything promising."

"You, too."

An hour later, after opening more boxes and containers, the only thing worthwhile I'd uncovered were some publicity shots of Nanny from her touring days, remarkably preserved, their color still brilliant.

She'd been a looker, for sure. Tumbles of curly, flame-shot hair framed a perfect face of porcelain skin and periwinkle eyes. As an homage to the times, a scarlet slash of red covered her lips, and her cheeks were the color of ripe cherries. It was no wonder she'd taken four trips down the matrimonial aisle. Even at ninety-three, she was still a beautiful woman who looked twenty years younger in any light.

"Found them," Frayne called from the third unit. After moving everything in the second locker out into the hallway with no luck, he'd opened and started on the last one.

"They were right in the front of the pack." He came into the hallway, a box under each arm. "I wish we'd started in this unit. I saw six or seven others along the back wall. There may be even more. This locker is the most jammed of all."

It was impossible not to smile at him. He looked like a kid on Christmas morning who'd found precisely what he'd asked Santa for waiting for him under the tree. He was covered in even more dust, his glasses cloudy with it. I was surprised he could even see through the lenses.

Maureen is the sister with some serious cleaning OCD, but there was no way I could let this go. I reached up and pulled his glasses off his nose. To say the move surprised him was an understatement. Armed with my cleaner, I squirted the lenses and then buffed them dry with a rag. After holding them up to the hallway light to ensure they were now clear, I slid them back on his face, ensuring they were snug around his ears. "Better?"

The lopsided grin he gave me was almost my undoing. "Much. Thanks."

His eyes were huge behind the glasses, and I understood why he wore them the way he did, perched on the tip of his nose. I must have looked distorted and gigantic as he peered at me through the magnification. The brilliant blue of his irises was stark and clear, the sorrowful cast to them, gone.

In truth, I could have stood there for hours staring at them.

"I'll go grab some of the boxes," I said.

Together, we were able to unload fifteen bankers boxes and four huge plastic containers labeled, simply,

Robert.

"There's a lot more here than your grandmother remembered," Frayne said, prying open a container. "This is going to take a while to go through."

"Well, we don't have to do it here." I pinched my upper lip between my fingers and thought for a moment. "This stuff is, for all intents and purposes, property of the historical society now."

"Do you want to move it there?"

"No. Not until I know what we're dealing with. Since I'm the one charged with maintaining the personal archives while Leigh is out, and this stuff definitely falls under that purview, I think we'd be better served carting it all back to my house and then sorting through it."

"I want to help you go through all this," he said, opening another container.

"Don't worry." I tossed him a side eye. "You're elected to help since you're the one who discovered stuff was missing. I don't relish going through all this by myself. And getting some of the other society members involved would be more trouble than I care to deal with."

"Why?"

I rolled my eyes and wiped my hands across my sweat pants. "Most of them have a my-way-or-the-highway mentality. While it isn't necessarily bad, when it comes to organizing and decision-making, they each have a different opinion of how things should be done, and I'd spend 99 percent of my time refereeing arguments rather than getting anything accomplished."

A tiny grin started at the corner of his mouth and then grew like wild fire across dry grass, engulfing his entire face in mere seconds.

"What?" I asked, enchanted.

"I witnessed that for myself after you left the luncheon. A few of the gents got into a shouting match. I don't even know what it was about, but all of a sudden voices were raised and faces turned red. One guy, I think Ollie?"

"Olaf."

"Yeah. Him. He stood up, rammed the table with the flat of his hand, and I thought poor Mrs. Johnson was gonna have a stroke."

"Probably because she thought he might have done some damage to the antique furniture. She's very protective of it. Did that end the argument?"

"Not even close. It was…entertaining, to say the least."

"That's one word for it." I shook my head and looked around. The hallway was stacked with boxes, containers, furniture, two bikes, and at least eight tall garment bags. "Since you've found what we set out to find, we need to put all this stuff back. I'll come out here some other time with my sisters, and we can go through all Nanny's personal stuff."

"You don't want to take any of it now?" He lifted my wedding picture and the scrapbook I'd left on top of the hope chest.

"No. I need a plan, garbage bags, and my sisters to do this any justice. Not to mention face masks to protect us from the dust. Let's get it all back in, and then we can load both our cars with Robert's stuff, okay?"

"If you're sure."

I was.

Getting all the crap back into the storage units was easier than taking it out had been. At least I had an idea of what was in store for me when I could get back here.

After dividing the boxes and containers and cramming them into our two cars, Frayne followed me back to my house.

****

When Danny was home on leave the year after I received my law degree, we decided the time had come to get a house of our own. We'd been renting a tiny one-bedroom apartment in town, and since I was now working for my father, we knew having our own property would be beneficial in more ways than one. We toured a few houses in and outside of town and decided on a one-hundred-and-fifty-year-old farmhouse resembling the home I'd grown up in, something Nanny was quick to point out. When Danny was deployed again, I spent the long lonely months fixing up the house. I became an expert in fuses, electrical wiring, sheetrock, and paint.

Somewhere along the way, the house became more mine than ours; everything in it from the paint colors to the furniture, and even the layouts of the rooms, were all my own choice. When Danny came home on leave, he'd rarely notice any of the cosmetic improvements I'd made, even in the master bedroom, where'd we'd spend the majority of our time when he wasn't hanging out at the Love Shack—our town bar—with his high school friends, drinking and telling war stories.

Now, with my husband gone, the house had turned from my home to my refuge and safety zone. I never had guests over who weren't family, and George was the most stable and committed relationship I'd ever had with a male of the species, including my husband.

Even though I lived alone, I still kept the house tidy and neat, a side effect of growing up with two women who were neatness fanatics—my mother and my grandmother—and a younger sister with cleaning OCD.

"Bring a couple of the boxes inside, and we can start on them," I told Frayne, grabbing two from my car.

George lifted his head, his rheumy, half-closed eyes peering at me in the afternoon light when I came through the doorway. I set the boxes on a counter and dropped to my knees. With his face cradled between my hands, I rubbed his nose with mine. His breathing was faster than when I'd seen him a few hours ago, his tongue swaying back and forth with each rapid pant. He hadn't eaten anything in almost forty-eight hours, not even the delicious food Maureen had sent home for him or the sausage from Ruthie. I'd been able to get him to drink a few ounces of water every few hours, but when I offered him some now, he turned his head.

"Baby, you have to drink something. Just a little. Please."

I sensed Frayne come into the room, then a moment later crouch down next to me.

George's cloudy eyes turned his way, the gray hairs above his eyes lifting, sensing someone new.

"Hey there, old fella." Frayne reached out a hand to let George sniff him. His thick, dry tongue swiped across the tips of Frayne's fingers, something he always did when he recognized a friend.

"How old is he?"

"Almost sixteen."

His gaze swept across George's face and frame.

"Not feeling too good, are ya, boy?" His fingers slid up and around the dog's ear, scratched, and then petted his head.

I don't know whether it was because George was seeing someone new in the house for the first time in a long, long while, but I actually sensed a little sparkle of life come back into his eyes. His shaggy tail wagged and thumped on the floor several times under Frayne's stroking.

"He's not eating?"

I shook my head. "Or drinking. My vet says I should keep trying, though, even if he refuses."

"Do you have a syringe or a turkey baster?"

Talk about a weird request.

"I've got a baster, one I use at Thanksgiving. Why?"

Frayne sat on the floor, his hand still stroking George's head. "My mother had a dog when I was a kid. Old as dirt and as spoiled as any animal I've ever known. She paid more attention to him than she did to me."

The wry grin on his mouth made me sad.

"When it wouldn't eat or drink on its own, she was able to force fluids by using a tiny eye dropper filled with water. It worked, although I think the dog did it because it liked being catered to and not because it physically couldn't drink. Like I said, it was spoiled rotten."

"Do you think that'll work with George?"

Under the shaggy fringe spilled across his forehead, his eyebrows tugged together and the corners of his mouth turned down. His gaze slipped to my dog and then back to me. "This"—he pointed under the table—"is George?"

I nodded.

"This is who you and your sister were speaking about in the kitchen the other day? And the one the diner owner, what's her name, Ruthie, sent home sausage for?"

"Yeah. Who did you think George was?"

"Your husband."

I snorted. Not the most feminine sound to make, to be sure. "Nope. This is George." I rubbed his snout.

"The way people talked about him, I assumed he wasn't, well, a dog. George isn't exactly a canine name."

"True, but it fits him. Doesn't it, baby?" I kissed his snout this time. "Okay." I stood up. "Let me find the baster."

Frayne stayed on the floor and continued rubbing the dog's head and ears. "It kinda does fit you," he told my old friend.

I located the glass cylinder in the bottom of my kitchen junk drawer, rinsed it, then filled it with some of the filtered water from the fridge. "Okay. Let's see if this works."

Carefully, I slid the baster into the side of George's mouth and gave the plunger a little push. George lapped the liquid, then licked the syringe. I squirted in another ounce, then another, until the baster was empty.

"It works." Pleasure floated through me. I turned to Frayne to find him grinning. "I wish I'd known about this a few days ago."

I moved to fill it up again.

"Don't give him too much," Frayne cautioned. "If

he hasn't had anything in his stomach, he might get sick from too much too fast. Dole it out, and see what happens."

"Good idea. Feel better, baby?" As an answer, George dragged his sandpapery tongue across my hand.

I stood, as did Frayne.

"I can't believe you thought George was my husband. That's too funny."

He folded his arms in front of him and leaned back against the kitchen counter. With a shrug, he said, "I don't know if funny is the right word. The way everyone spoke about him, I assumed it was your husband's name."

I shook my head, then took two glasses down from the cabinet, filled them with the filtered water, and handed one to him.

"I don't know if I could ever be married to a George," I said, considering the idea. After a few sips, I shook my head. "Nope. Can't see it."

"What's your husband's name?"

I greased over the present tense. "Danny. Daniel Mulvaney."

Frayne nodded. "Definitely different from George."

I smiled into my glass, then cocked my head like he was prone to do and asked, "Where does McLachlan come from? Are your parents Irish?"

"My father is. Born and bred. Thick brogue and a will of iron."

"Were you named for him?"

"No."

The way his jaw clenched and the finite sound of the word screamed *sore subject*. There was some family drama there, and I was an expert on all things family and drama related. I sensed Frayne didn't want to talk about it so, instead, I said, "Well, we should start on these boxes. See what we've got that's salvageable and usable. Let's bring them into the dining room. There's more room to spread out in there."

I grabbed a few dishtowels to clean off the mountains of dust on each box and lifted the two I'd brought into the kitchen. Frayne followed me.

For two hours, we systematically went through five of the boxes we'd carted from the storage unit. The huge plastic containers were filled with Robert's clothing. They'd make a good addition to the public archives once they were cleaned and ironed. And boy, did they need to be cleaned. Nanny had packed them into airtight containers, but they still smelled stale and musty.

Every half hour, I'd gone back to the kitchen and given George another baster of water, thrilled when he not only drank it, but kept it down as well.

By four thirty, the January afternoon sun was gone and we were almost finished with the first wave of boxes. Frayne had been delighted when he'd found several leather personal diaries dated from the 1940s and '50s belonging to Robert. He placed them in a separate pile and said we should read them together when we were done going through everything else.

Working side by side, we talked little, concentrating instead on the task at hand, but I was acutely aware of him at every turn. Little things filtered through my consciousness as I worked, like how every time he lifted an item from a box he'd readjust his glasses to see it better. Inevitably, the glasses would inch their way down to the tip of his nose. Or how when he went through the clothing containers, he'd methodically search all the pockets in a jacket or a pair of pants, a few times finding small items like an extra button, or in one instance a lighter with a monogramed *H* embossed across its face.

"Was Robert a smoker?"

"I don't remember ever seeing him with a cigar or cigarettes. We can ask Nanny."

He placed the lighter in the pile of personal effects we needed to take pictures of and catalogue.

When my stomach started to growl, Frayne's did as well. It was a contest whose was louder.

Laughing, I went into the kitchen, checked the stores I had in the refrigerator, and then called out, "Slim pickings, I'm afraid. I haven't had a minute to shop this past week. Do you like grilled cheese? I can make us sandwiches."

When I closed the fridge, I jolted. "*Good golly.* I'm buying you a bell."

"Sorry," he said, holding a piece of paper in his hand, the tops of his cheeks going pink.

God, how was it possible for a grown man to be adorable and hot-as-hell sexy at the same time? I had a wild urge to reach up, grab his face, and kiss him silly.

In the same instant, I wondered how he'd respond if I did.

Better not to go there.

"So. Grilled cheese okay?"

With a quick nod he said, "Fine."

"Okay. Give me a few—"

A noise I'd never heard before thundered from under the kitchen table. Both of us turned to see George standing upright on wobbly legs, a thick, white substance covering his mouth. His breaths were harsh, and sounded like a seal barking.

"Oh my God, what was that?" I fell to the floor next to him. His chest retracted with each labored breath, the outline of his entire ribcage visible through his fur. "I don't think he can breathe."

Frayne moved next to me and ran a hand along George's ribs. "I'm no expert, but it feels like he's not moving any air into his lungs."

I wiped the froth from George's mouth only to have it cover him again within seconds. Deep expressive eyes settled on me. Through the clouds of his cataracts, pain engulfed him with each breath he tried to take. His body shook as if he were in the throes of a feverish seizure, his spindly legs quivering, fighting to keep him upright.

"Oh, baby." Tears swelled in my eyes, and I touched my forehead to his.

I knew this day was going to come. The vet had told me I was on borrowed time, but I wasn't prepared to lose George. And because I wasn't, I was still going to fight for him.

I swiped at my tears and chugged in a deep breath. "I'm calling my vet. She'll be able to tell me what to do."

"He's probably dry as a bone, Cathy," the receptionist told me when I connected. "Even though you were able to get him to drink a little, it's not enough. The doc says to wrap him in a blanket and bring him in right now."

"We'll be there in less than five minutes."

"Your car is bigger than mine," Frayne said while I

covered George with an afghan I pulled from the rocking chair in my living room. "He'll be more comfortable in it than he would in my two-door. You sit in the back with him while I drive. I'll need directions."

Together, we carried him out to my vehicle. I slid into the back seat, and Frayne lifted George in as if he weighed no more than a five-pound bag of potatoes. With George's head on my lap and his breathing worse, I sent up a few silent prayers while I directed Frayne to the veterinarian's office.

The waiting room was empty, and we were shown into an exam room the moment we came through the door.

"Put him on the table," Shelby Sinclair, my longtime veterinarian instructed. I'd known Shelby since kindergarten. She'd been interning with Heaven's local vet, Doc Masters, fifteen years ago when I'd brought George in for his first vaccinations. When she'd bought the practice five years later, she'd continued to be the only doctor George ever knew.

"Hey, buddy. Not feeling too good, are ya?" She ruffled his head and slid a stethoscope bell along his ribs. "He's not moving any air, and from the color of the mucous, it looks like he's in congestive heart failure."

"Congestive, like he's clogged with water? Oh, my God, did I cause this? I've been giving him water all afternoon through a turkey baster. Did I do this?"

Shelby fixed her steady gaze on me and, in a stern voice that would have made Nanny proud, said, "You did nothing to cause this, Cathleen. Nothing. This is a progression of his ailments and his age."

"Really? You're not saying that because you want

to spare my feelings?"

"When have I ever said anything to spare your feelings?"

She had me there.

"Okay. Okay." I tried to keep from letting go of my tears. "Can you fix this heart failure?"

"I can try to alleviate some of the symptoms causing it, but we've talked about this." She spoke to me but kept her hand on George. "Combined with all the other conditions he has working against him, I can't fix the underlying cause. George is elderly. A dog's body ages at a much more rapid rate than ours. In people years, he's over one hundred. Old by anyone's standards."

"I know. I know, but I'm not...ready to say... I mean, he's all I have. I can't..." A sob finally tore from me, unchecked, and I shot my fist to my mouth. A strong and steady hand rubbed along my back.

Frayne.

Shelby's dark eyed gaze shot from him, then back to me.

"Please, Shelby. Please. Try something. Anything," I pleaded. "I can't stand to see him this way."

With a quick nod, she called out to her assistant and issued a series of orders. "Okay, let me work. Go outside to the waiting room, and I'll call you back in in a few minutes."

"Can't I stay?" I sounded like a whining child, but I didn't care. My emotions were sliced raw. My life had been filled with too much loss the past few years. I couldn't bear to add George to the list.

"No," Shelby said. "I've known you forever, Cath. You can't stand the sight of needles or blood, and I don't want you getting sick or, God forbid, fainting." Her gaze flicked to Frayne again. She pointed to the door. "Outside, and when I'm set, I'll let you know."

"Come on, Cathy." Frayne's hand circled around my upper arm. "Let's let the doctor do what she needs to."

I pulled against him and grabbed Shelby's hand. "Please. *Please*."

She patted my hand and nodded. "I know, kiddo."

I let Frayne guide me out to the empty waiting room. My bones felt as if they'd turned to unsettled jelly, loose and liquid. I slid into a cushioned chair and folded in on myself, my hands wrapped around my midsection, my body bent at the waist.

I couldn't lose George. I couldn't.

When the army representatives had come to my door to tell me Danny had been killed, I hadn't reacted as everyone assumed I would. Lucas had been with them, and he'd volunteered to be the one to notify me because, as one of my oldest friends, he'd thought to try and temper the emotional blow of the news. With his strong, familiar voice cracking at the loss of his dearest, best friend, he'd told me what had happened.

I kept my cool, didn't shed a tear. I thanked the soldiers and Lucas and then sent them away.

Alone, except for George, I'd sat in my rocking chair for the rest of the day, thinking about how my life and my marriage had turned out so different from what I'd imagined and dreamed it would be. Lucas had been the one to notify my family and as soon as they heard the news, they'd descended on me, seeking comfort, fighting tears, grieving, wanting to be comforted.

I was the one to give it. I was the one who held

Danny's mother up, physically and emotionally, through the endless days of the visitations, the mass, and then the burial.

When my sister Eileen died a year later of breast cancer, history repeated itself. I was the one who notified people, organized the funeral, wrote thank-you responses for the condolence cards, while my sisters and parents fell apart. No one ever knew how weak I was on the inside each time I was called upon to be strong.

Those same emotions whirled inside me now while one of my oldest friends worked on a dog I loved beyond all end.

Frayne's hand squeezed my shoulder. "Can I call anyone for you? Your sisters? Your husband?"

His face was a mask of concern. Seated next to me, he leaned in close, his gaze fixed on my face. His fingers were doing a little kneading thing on my shoulder, and a soothing calm, like the sensation you get right before falling asleep, flowed through me from his touch.

I was used to being the one doing the comforting; the one who stayed strong and focused. Through the haze of my amazement to actually be the one receiving comfort, Frayne's words seeped through.

I squinted at him. "My husband?"

"Do you want me to call him to come and be with you? I would think you'd both want to be together in case…" He didn't need to finish his thought.

I sat up so abruptly, his hand slipped from my shoulder. Heat shot up from my neck, and my face burned as if I'd been caught out in the bright sunshine all day without sunblock.

"What? Cathy, what? Did I say something wrong?" His concern morphed into confusion.

I shook my head. "No. No, you didn't. I just realized you don't know a thing about me."

"What does that mean?"

I sighed and stood, prepared to pace. "My husband is dead. He was killed in combat three years ago. And you don't need to call my sisters. I'll handle this like I do everything else."

Frayne's hands shot out and halted me, his fingers now flexing and extending their grip on my upper arms. The movements were careful and controlled. The emotion swimming in his eyes was anything but.

"Your husband is dead?"

I nodded.

"You're a widow?"

"Yes."

"Why didn't you tell me?"

"Why would I?"

Frayne shook his head, the disheveled hair I'd fantasized about clutching on to, swishing side to side. His eyes bore into mine. No longer kind and caring, they were now hard and questioning. "All the times we've been together, at the museum, the storage locker, *Christ,* even your own house, you never once mentioned your husband was dead."

"Again, why would I? It's not like we talked about anything other than your research. What does his being gone have anything to do with, well, anything?"

It was as if he hadn't heard me. Or if he had, chose to ignore my words. "The other day in the basement, you knew, you had to know, how much I wanted to kiss you. Take you in my arms and slake this hunger, this need to feel you, hold you against me. You had to know what I was thinking. It took everything in me to rein in the need running through me."

"*What?*"

If he'd told me we were twins separated at birth, I couldn't have been more stunned.

"But I didn't give in to the craving," he continued, "because I thought you were married and there are rules about that. Everything I'd heard, every indication said you were. If I'd known then"—his fingers pressed a little harder into my arms—"I would have—"

Shelby's tech interrupted whatever he'd been about to say. "You can come back in, Cathy. Doc's all done."

I wanted to move, but it was like a magnetic force field held my feet rooted to the floor.

He'd wanted to kiss me. *Me.* Good God, the notion alone was equal parts terrifying and arousing. The truth was written in his eyes, though. He wasn't playing with me.

"Cathy?"

The tech's voice penetrated through my paralysis, and I tore out of Frayne's death grip and bolted back into the exam room.

Shelby stood, observing George from next to the metal exam table, her gaze moving from the intravenous bag connected to a rod above the table down to my dog. A tiny green face mask was secured over his snout, plastic tubing connecting it to an oxygen tank on the wall. His labored breaths echoed and wheezed through the mask.

"How is he?" I laid my hands on his back and head. His eyes were closed, and he gave no indication he knew I was there.

Shelby glanced at Frayne as he came into the room, and then to me. "Not good. I gave him a bunch of meds to try and help his breathing, get some of the fluid out of his lungs. It'll take some time to see if they work, but I have to be truthful with you; I'm not hopeful he's gonna come out of this."

I choked back a sob and bit down on my bottom lip to stop it from quivering. My entire body went numb at her words.

This was it. This was the day I'd prayed would never come.

"Is—is he suffering?"

When she didn't answer me right away, I knew the truth.

"If the meds are going to work, it should be in a few minutes," she said. "I'll know better, then. Stay here with him. I've got to go check on a dog I did surgery on a few hours ago. I'll be back." She pulled a stool out from under a desk and shoved it over to me.

When she left, I plopped down on it and leaned in close. "I'm here, baby. I'm here. You rest. Let the medicine work."

I don't know how many minutes I sat there, stroking the fur on his head, his back. Time stopped moving.

Memories are funny things, and they pop up at the craziest times. While I sat there, listening to my best friend's jagged breathing, watching the fluid drip down the IV tube, I remembered the day I'd brought George home from a local breeder. I was lonely with Danny gone for months on end and wanted a dog for company during the long days and nights alone. He'd been the runt, surprising the owners when he'd survived, the twelfth of the litter and the tiniest. I'd come into the room where mama was nursing her pups. All but George. He was splayed on his belly, his four legs spread out at all corners. He spotted me and then on those tiny, weak legs, pushed up and tried to walk to me. I lifted him, and I swear he looked right in my eyes and smiled. From that moment, he held my heart, and each year his grip grew more snug around it.

Shelby returned, listened to George's heart and lungs, and then sighed. "He's not any better, Cath."

"Can't you give him more medicine?"

"I already gave him the maximum doses—"

"Well, maybe he needs more than the maximum." I knew I was shouting, but I couldn't help myself. "You're the one who told me his organs are failing. Maybe he needs more to be able to, I don't know"—I flapped my hands in the air—"*metabolize* what he needs."

"It doesn't work like that, Cath." Unlike me, she kept her voice low, her tone controlled. "Look. I know this is hard. You need to come to grips that this is it for George. He's lived a long life, longer than a lot of Labs I've taken care of. He's been loved by you and spoiled and given a great existence. But his poor body is tired. You need to face it, understand it."

"*I can't.*"

George startled at the pitch of my wail, shocking me into silence. In the next moment, he took a huge, deep, tortured breath, and then his entire body went still. His legs stretched out and relaxed, and his chest stopped moving. The panting echo of his breathing against the mask grew silent.

"*Shelby.*"

She was moving before I screamed. Stethoscope out, she called to her tech and then moved to George. She listened to his heart, her eyes trained on me. I held my breath, fearful to move or make a sound. My heart was hammering like a pile driver against my ribcage. Frayne pushed off the wall and came to stand next to me, took my hand in his and then slung his other hand around my shoulder, tucking me close to his side. I clung to him like a lifeline.

Shelby dragged her hands all over George's chest, his back, his abdomen, examining every bit of him. After an eternity, she stood tall and removed the stethoscope.

I knew what her words were going to be before she opened her mouth.

I shook my head. "No."

"I'm sorry, Cath. I'm so sorry."

"*No.*" I pulled against Frayne's grip, but he held on to me. "Do something," I pleaded with her. "Please. There has to be something, anything—"

She reached out her arms, and when Frayne let go of me, she pulled me into a fierce hug. With her hands rubbing down my back and holding me tight against her, she said nothing more, simply held me while I cried.

Shock was such a weird sensation. You could either become lost in a fugue state when it occurred, unable to understand anything going on around you, your mind shutting down and your body going numb; or you could become hyperaware of every movement, every sound, every *thing* around you.

I fell into the latter category.

The feel of Shelby's fingers sliding up and down

my back sparked my nerve endings, the sensation jolting all the way to my feet. The sound of the oxygen whooshing through the mask still attached to George, blared. When Shelby's tech turned it off, the silence was deafening.

Like being underwater, background sounds grew muffled. My head suddenly felt as if I'd taken one too many sleep aids and was fighting the effects to stay awake.

After a while, I became aware Shelby was speaking. I pulled back from her embrace and pressed my fingers against my eyes. When I swallowed, my ears popped.

"Sorry. I'm okay." I took a deep, rough breath and cleared my throat. "What do I need to do? Sign something? What? Tell me."

Shelby wound her hands around my arms again. "Cathleen. Stop. You just lost your best friend. Your baby. Take a few minutes with him. We don't need to discuss what comes next right this second."

"No, I know. But I want to." I squared my shoulders. "Tell me what I need to do."

The tech brought in some papers for me, and then Shelby and I decided what to do with George's body. I almost lost control when I made the decision to cremate him, but I was able to keep myself in check long enough to get everything secured.

When she left the room, Frayne asked, "Do you want a few minutes alone with him before I take you home?"

I nodded. With one last swipe down my back, he left me with my best friend.

"I'll be right outside," he said.

The tech had pulled the IV from George's leg and removed the oxygen mask. His body was still and peaceful, and it was only if you noticed his chest wasn't rising and falling you'd ever think anything was amiss.

I leaned down and hugged him before kissing his snout. When his whiskers tickled my cheek, I bit back another sob.

"I love you, old friend. More than anything. Be at peace now," I whispered. "I love you."

Chapter 9

It was deep dark by the time Frayne pulled away from the clinic. We'd run out of my house with just the clothes on our backs, and now the brutal January cold impaled us with its harsh and ruthless bite. Neither of us said a word on the ride home. In truth, I was exhausted. Emotionally, physically, *hell*, even spiritually. I don't know if I could have answered anything he asked me with more than a yes or no reply, if that.

Shelby's tech had given me back the afghan I'd wrapped George in. I held it in my arms as we drove, its warmth doing nothing to soothe my soul or the chill seeping through my bones.

Frayne pulled into my garage and parked. We'd left in such a hurry we hadn't closed the door. I hadn't taken my purse, or my phone, or anything, in my haste to get George attended to.

The warmth of the kitchen enveloped me as soon as I came through the door.

George's doggie bed sat under the table, the cushion rumpled, the empty turkey baster lying next to it. I bit back a sob right as Frayne started talking to someone.

"Cathy." Maureen flew into the kitchen, dropped a shopping bag on the floor, and then pulled me into her arms. My head fell against her shoulder as she squeezed me in a full body hug.

"What—what are you doing here?"

"Mac called us," Colleen said as she slipped her arms around me from behind. "We came as soon as we heard."

I lifted my gaze and found him. He looked…unsure. Maybe even a little embarrassed. I'd told him I didn't need anyone, but he'd called my sisters regardless.

"We didn't want you to be alone," Maureen said. "We know how much you love George. We do, too."

That was Maureen, the perceptive one.

"Yeah," Colleen, added. "He's the only nephew we have."

And that was Colleen, the say-it-plain-and-simple one.

I glanced at her over my shoulder. "Nephew?"

She shrugged. "You know what I mean. George is family."

Tears threatened. I willed them back.

"Don't do that," Maureen said.

"Do what?"

"Suck it up."

Perceptive, remember? I stared at her, trying to keep my face expressionless.

"You don't have to," she added. "We know how hard losing George is for you. That's why we came." She swiped her hands down my arms, her eyes soft and caring as she regarded me. "You're always the one who stays strong, who comforts the rest of us when we're upset."

"You're always the rock," Colleen added.

I lifted my shoulder in a "so what?" gesture.

"It's your turn for us to be that for you. You don't need to hold it together. Not for us."

"Yeah." Colleen nodded. "Let us, for once, take care of you. Maureen brought food, 'cause it's what she does. I brought wine and chocolate."

I turned around to her again. " 'Cause it's what you do?"

A perfect smile filled her face.

"Don't you have guests to tend to?" I asked Mo.

"Sarah's looking after everything, no worries. We're here, and we're staying."

She might be quiet and keep her thoughts hidden more times than not, but I've always thought Maureen was the most determined and resolute of us.

"I love you guys, I do, but I'm fine."

"Cath—"

"Really." I squeezed Maureen's hands to underscore the point. "I'm sad, of course. Heartbroken, to be truthful. But Shelby was right. I didn't want to lose George, and I kept him alive longer than either of us expected because I didn't want to let him go. What I did was selfish."

"I don't think it was," Maureen said. "I think it showed how much he meant to you. And you know he loved you."

"Boy, did he ever." Colleen shook her head and rolled her eyes. "Loyal. Sweet. He followed you everywhere, and every time he looked at you, it was as if you hung the moon for him. If he'd been a guy, he'd have been perfect."

I shook my head again. She was right.

I pulled both of them in for side-hugs. "I'm glad you guys are here. Thanks for coming."

"Of course we came," Maureen said. "You're our big sister, and we adore you. Now, when was the last time you ate?"

My gaze drifted over her shoulder to Frayne. He was propped against the kitchen counter, much the way he'd been in Shelby's office, with his arms crossed over his chest, his glasses slung from the collar of his sweatshirt.

"Actually, I was starting to make supper when George…well. We'd been working all afternoon."

Both my sisters turned their attention to Frayne at the same time. The tops of his cheeks darkened under their intense scrutiny.

Maureen cocked her head at an angle. She could be my grandmother's clone when she did this. When all of us were younger and Nanny Fee put her all-knowing, penetrating, you-can't-lie-to-me expression on her face, we'd confess to anything and everything whether we'd done something naughty or not. It seemed Nanny's powers had passed down to Mo.

"Well, good thing I brought enough food to feed us all."

"Slade's gonna be here in a few," Colleen said. "I texted him when we were on the way, and he said he'd meet us here when he was done with a conference call."

The back doorbell chimed, and without anyone answering it, Lucas Alexander walked into the kitchen.

"Hey," he said, by way of greeting, to the room. His eyes grazed over Maureen, settled for a moment, then moved to me. Mo moved out of the way so he could hug me.

"Sorry about George, Cathy. The old guy had a good life."

"How do you even know?" I asked, my voice muffled against his massive chest.

"Shelby's tech, Marnie. She's seeing Pete and called the station to tell him she'd be a little late for their date. Since it was you, Pete told me."

"The curse and blessing of living in a small town," I said, with a shake of my head. Lucas let me go, and I stood back from him a bit.

"Including all your dirty little secrets," Colleen said. She was opening the wine bottle she'd brought. "Not that you have any. Or any of us do. But still."

"Knock, knock."

The kitchen door opened again, and Colleen's face broke into a cheek-wide grin filled with adoration as her fiancé walked in.

He graced her with a loving look, then grabbed me in a hug. "Counselor. My condolences."

God, I loved these people, this family.

"Well, since everyone's here," Maureen said, "let's eat. Who's starving?"

"I am," Lucas said, as he removed his coat.

"You're always starving," Mo shot back with an eye roll mimicking Colleen's to perfection.

"What's all this crap?" my middle sister called from the dining room. "There's a ton of junk on the table." She walked back into the kitchen, the open wine bottle in one hand, napkins in the other, a look of bemusement on her face.

My gaze shot to Frayne.

"It's stuff we found in Nanny's storage locker. All that *crap*"—I shot my younger sister a speaking glance—"is Robert Heaven's personal effects. Nanny gave Mr. Frayne permission to go through it all to see if any of it was appropriate for the museum."

"Oh, good Lord," Colleen said. "I'd forgotten all about poor Robert."

"Who's Robert?" Slade asked.

My two sisters clued him in while Frayne caught my eye and gave me *follow me* head bob.

We walked out of the kitchen and in to the hallway.

"I'm gonna head back to the inn," he told me, his hands shoved in his pockets again. He cocked his chin toward the dining room. "Your family is here now, and I'm intruding."

"No, you're not."

The look he shot me was doubtful.

I reached out and wrapped one of my hands around his forearm. He jumped.

"I don't know how I would have gotten through the past few hours without your help. I really don't." I shook my head and dropped my chin to my chest. The sight of Frayne's old, worn, and battered sneakers shot straight to my heart. I looked back into his eyes.

"Please stay. If for no other reason than I promised you a meal after all the work we did today, and Maureen's cooking is way better than my grilled cheese would have been."

Indecision ran across his face. He tucked his chin as he regarded me from under brows that had lowered to half conceal his eyes. "You don't need to do that, Cathy. I can grab something to eat on my way back at the inn."

Before I could respond, Maureen popped into the hallway.

"Hey, we need guidance about where to put all Robert's stuff. Colleen's about to shove everything back into boxes to make room for the food. She hasn't eaten anything today, and you know how she gets when she's food deprived."

She ducked back into the kitchen.

"Well, now you have to stay," I said, nodding. "Or all the work we did this afternoon will be ruined. Colleen takes no prisoners when she's *hangry*."

One corner of his mouth lifted up, and those tiny lines in the corners of his eyes deepened.

I squeezed his arm, and when I turned to go, he stopped me.

I glanced down at the hand circling my arm and then up to his face. He'd gone back to being serious.

"I want to say…to tell you…" He swallowed and, like a magnet shunting to true north, my body moved in closer to him.

His gaze darted across my face, searching, seeking. For what, I haven't a clue.

"I'm…I'm sorry…about George."

I wasn't convinced it was what he'd meant to say, but I didn't push. "Thank you. Again, I don't know what I would have done if you hadn't been here to help."

"Hey, let's go." Colleen's voice rang out clear as a crystal bell with none of the musical beauty from the dining room. "I want to eat."

I couldn't help but laugh because, this was after all, typical Colleen. "Come on." I grabbed Frayne's hand and tugged.

When he shook his head and grinned, a warm, liquid pleasure shot straight through me.

****

In the end, he didn't stay. Nothing Maureen, me, or

anyone else said could convince him to. With a final word of condolence, and a request to text when I was up to going through all the locker boxes again, he left.

After being fed and petted and cared for by my family, I'd gone to bed for the very first time in this house, alone. No husband. No dog. When I was huddled down under the covers, I let my grief loose and cried until I had no tears left to shed.

My life was nothing like I'd envisioned it would be at this age. Widowed, childless, lonely for the comfort and love of a man by my side. No happily ever after, no lifetime companion. I had myself a real pity-party for one while I lay there, staring up at the ceiling and letting my tears flow without issue. In the span of three short years, I'd lost my husband, a sister, a dog who meant more to me than most people did, and—by virtue of their decampment south—my parents. How do people soldier on when they're faced with such insurmountable loss?

With exhaustion gripping me, I finally fell asleep.

When I lifted my head from the pillow and shielded my eyes from the harsh, stark light shining through my bedroom window curtain, I groaned. In a heartbeat came the realization George was gone. Determined not to let my sadness overtake me again, I did something Nanny Fee has instructed often when we've had to deal with issues we'd rather not: I girded my loins. As a kid, I hadn't a clue what she'd meant.

As a grown-ass woman, I had a fairly good idea.

Okay, in reality? I closed my eyes again, took a whopping deep breath, and then let it out, super slow. There. Emotions in check, thoughts calmed. Almost ready to start the day.

An hour later, showered, two mugs of caffeine on board, and with half a scone Maureen left in my fridge devoured, I drove to Seldrine's house to pick her up for her meeting.

She'd heard about George from Nanny after Colleen had called our grandmother to tell her.

Remember the curse and the blessing of living in a small town?

"I'm really sorry, Cathy. I feel bad you have to drive me every day. I wish Judge Dupont hadn't made you do it."

"No worries," I said. "This way we get a chance to chat about how things are going. How are your kids? They all settled in at your folks'?"

A deep breath huffed from her. "The kids are confused. They keep asking why can't they come home, sleep in their own beds. I tell them this is like sleep-away camp only with Grandma and Grandpa instead of counselors. It's a special treat, but I don't think they're buying it. Especially Cullen."

Seldrine's four children ranged in age from four years to nine, Cullen the oldest.

"He's a smart kid, Sel. And he remembers what life was like with Cam."

"Too much so. In the beginning, after Cam got locked up, Cullen wouldn't go to sleep. He'd be exhausted and cranky but pushed to stay awake as long as he could."

"Why?"

"He told me he was worried Daddy was gonna come home and start hitting me again. He wanted to protect me."

"Oh, sweetie." I reached across the cab of my car

148

and squeezed her hand.

Seldrine's free hand slammed down on mine. "I'm wicked pissed at myself for allowing Cam's letter to get to me. For ever taking a drink. I just wanted to…run away. Someplace he wouldn't be able to find me, torture me. I was only thinking about myself, about *my* pain, *my* fears. I never considered what it'd do to the kids and their lives. And look where being selfish got me. I might lose my kids. *Christ*. I'm such a loser."

"Stop saying things like that." I channeled Nanny's stern, catechism-instructor voice. It worked. Seldrine stopped castigating herself and gaped at me. "You did what you did. You can't change what happened. You can only get over it and work to make it better. Understand?"

Speechless, she nodded.

I pulled the car into the front U-shaped driveway of the church, put it in park, and left the engine running. "By going to these meetings every day, by keeping your job and continuing with your education, you're negating the one momentary lapse you had. You *will* get your kids back. I believe it. I know it in my heart." And I meant it. "You will get through this. Focus on one day at a time. Nothing else. Okay?"

It was advice I'd given myself more than once in the past three years.

Seldrine squeezed my hand and sniffed. "Thanks, Cathy. For everything."

I pulled her in for a hug. When I let her go, a familiar figure bounded up the front church steps to greet my parish priest, Father Duncan, at the main door.

Seldrine must have noticed me stiffen, because she pulled back and turned to look out the window. "*Him*," she said. The word was filled with rancor.

"What do mean?"

"Mac." She crossed her arms over her chest.

"How do you know his first name?"

"Simple. I don't know his last. *Anonymous*, remember?"

It took me a moment.

"Wait. You mean…?" My gaze shot to the front steps again. Frayne stepped into the church with my priest.

"Yeah. He's a *Friend of Bill*, like me. What? You didn't know?"

"I had no idea."

"Huh. I figured you'd sent him to, you know, keep an eye on me. Make sure I actually went into the meetings and not cut out after you dropped me off."

I stared at her. Hard. "I would never do that, Seldrine. I trust you."

An embarrassed rose colored her cheeks.

"So he's been at the same meetings as you?"

"Yup. Doesn't talk much. Share, you know? Father Duncan tries to get him to testify, but—" She shrugged. "He listens mostly. Stuck in his head. You know?"

Frayne to a T.

"You'd better get inside," I said. "You can't be late."

The frigid air blasting through the open door when she got out of my car shot right to my bone marrow.

After she entered the church, I drove to my office.

Martha greeted me with hugs and condolences (Maureen had called to tell her about George) and a notice that one of the guardianship cases I'd been working on had developed a snag. I made a quick call to Lucas and then the courthouse.

The rest of the day was filled with client appointments and writing briefs for upcoming cases. I made it through most of it on a fairly even keel, not letting my thoughts drift to George. The moment I walked back into my house, though, it all came back.

There was such a huge difference between being alone and being lonely. While I was used to being alone with just my dog for company, I was never lonely. Even after Danny died, I could truthfully say I was content by myself. George was a companion—a silent one to be sure—but always there in the background with me. I wasn't alone.

And now I was.

The tears I'd been able to keep contained all day broke free. In the shower, I let them fall without constraint. After climbing into bed without dinner, my head hurt too much with emotions barreling through it, so I simply closed my eyes and drifted off to sleep.

Three days after George died, I was better able to deal with my loss and didn't feel like crying every other second. My sisters had both texted me daily, and Maureen had dropped off a week's worth of food while I'd been at the office.

Friday morning dawned, and I replayed the busy day's schedule in my head. Within an hour after I was showered and dressed, I was standing back in Asa Dupont's courtroom. As I was mentally preparing how I wanted to argue the case, I received a text.

—*Are you free to go over the Heaven artifacts?*— Frayne wrote. It was the first time I'd heard from him since he'd left my house the day George died.

—*In court. Don't know how long I'll be.*—

After I hit send, Asa walked into the courtroom, and I shut my phone to silent mode.

When we were done, I left the courtroom to find Frayne out in the hallway.

"I didn't expect to see you here," I said. "I figured you'd be working at the museum."

"I was hoping to spend some time today going through Robert's things, and I was wondering if you'd allow me to do it at your house while you're working."

"My house?"

"Yeah. I've exhausted everything in the public files, but I haven't wanted to bother you. I wanted to give you some space, but I can't go any further with the archival stuff. I realize you're supposed to be present at all times when I go through any personal property, but I thought since the stuff isn't officially logged in yet, maybe you'd make an exception. I realize it's asking a lot, but…"

I knew I shouldn't. If Clara Johnson ever found out I'd let someone go through items unsupervised, I'd never hear the end of it. But I was tied up all day and this unexpected court visit had put me back several hours.

"Sure," I told him.

Surprise kicked the shadows out of his eyes.

"There's a spare key under the sconce on the outside garage wall. It lets you in through the kitchen door. Everything is still in the dining room."

He stuffed his hands into his coat pocket. "You don't mind? Me being in your house without you?"

I shook my head.

"You won't get…in trouble with the historical society if you're not with me, overseeing my work?"

I wanted to say what they didn't know wouldn't hurt them (or me) but thought better of it and simply said, "It's fine. Do me a favor and don't remove anything from the house, okay? We still need to get it all catalogued."

"I promise I won't."

An awkward silence blossomed between us.

"Okay," he finally said. "I'll let you get back to work. Thank you."

He gave me a tense head bob and then walked away. After a few steps, he stopped, turned and, over his shoulder said, "Thank you," again.

Chapter 10

There was a note on the kitchen table when I got home.

Thank you for letting me do this. I started putting Robert's journals in date order. Left everything on the dining room table. I think we need to go through this all together, though. Let me know when you're free. Mac.

He'd brought in the remainder of the boxes and containers we'd unloaded in the garage and had started going through them. Sticky notes with the contents of each box were adhered to the tops. Everything was orderly and neat.

I thought about the shaggy hair many weeks beyond a trim, the battered sneakers with the tattered laces that had seen better days, even the pullover with the moth holes. Frayne took care with the things he thought were important, like these artifacts, but neglected himself. Why that facet of his personality was endearing, I couldn't fathom, but it was. He reminded me of a wounded little boy who needed looking after, warm hugs, and lots of attention.

In my home office, I booted up my laptop and finally typed in a search of his name. Dozens of articles were listed, most centering on his writing work. I hadn't known in addition to the biography of Emily Dickinson, he'd also penned three bios on eighteenth- and nineteenth-century American writers and poets plus one president. I narrowed my field of inquiry down to the deaths of his wife and daughter and started reading.

An hour later, I forced myself to stop.

I was no longer surprised about the loathing he exhibited for the judicial system. If what I'd read had happened to me, I would have been a nonbeliever in justice as well.

In my bathroom, I splashed cold water on my face and then slipped back into my coat. Ten minutes later, I was at Inn Heaven. My youngest sister was in her kitchen putting the final touches on an elaborate wedding cake for the weekend wedding Colleen was in charge of and at which I was officiating.

"Hey. This is a surprise," Maureen said when I kissed her cheek. "How are you doing? Have you eaten yet?"

"I'm good. Listen," I said. "Is Frayne in?"

"Yeah. He was in the gym for a while. Sarah said she saw him go back up to his room a few minutes ago. Why?"

"I need to talk to him about something. What room is he in?"

"Blue-one."

"Thanks. That, by the way"—I pointed to the four-tiered cake as I left the kitchen—"looks fabulous."

I sprinted up the main staircase, which was reminiscent of Scarlet and Rhett's red-carpeted one in the movie version of *Gone with the Wind*. Nanny referred to the color as *harlot scarlet*, and she wasn't wrong.

I knocked on Frayne's door, running over in my head what I wanted to say, and then lost the capacity to think at all when the door opened.

All thoughts of him resembling an emotionally damaged little boy dashed out the window when he stood before me with a towel secured around his trim waist, another in his hand, mopping the water drenching his hair and sluicing down his body.

And, *Holy Mother of God*, what a body.

Broad and thick shoulders connected to arms with biceps as wide as my thighs. His chest was a solid mass of muscle, scattered with thick, damp, curly black hair dropping all the way down to below his belly button and disappearing under the towel. Where in all creation had he gotten those abs? Perfect grooved trenches lined both sides of his torso and waist, and for a moment I had the ridiculous notion they were fake.

But they weren't.

Who knew those baggy, worn pullovers and tattered jeans covered a body carved from marble and perfect in every way? The idea blew through my mind that this was how Lois felt the first time she got a gander at what was under Clark's suits.

"Cathy?"

I had to drag my eyes back up to his face.

A look of befuddlement crossed his features as he rubbed the extra towel over his hair. "What are you doing here?"

"I—" Words wouldn't form. By an unseen force, my gaze was dragged back down to his mind-boggling chest.

Frayne repeated my name.

"I wanted…"

His eyes widened, and he dropped his chin as he regarded me. "Yes?"

"Um."

Okay, this had to stop. I was a lawyer, for pity's sake. I made my living with my ability to form complete and convincing sentences.

I cleared my throat and then my mind. "I wanted to take you to dinner. I-I never got the chance to thank you for being so kind the other day. And you didn't stay afterward, so I want to buy you a meal. Dinner. To thank you."

Good gravy. One minute I couldn't string words into a coherent sentence, and now I was talking like my mouth was having difficulty keeping up with my brain.

He slung the extra towel across his shoulders and neck and casually grabbed onto the ends. "You don't have to. It's not necessary."

"No, it's not," I countered. "But I'd like to."

A silent debate played over his face. His teeth clamped down on a corner of his mouth, and he'd cocked his head like he was going to ask me a question. Before he could refuse me again, because it sure looked like he was going to, I added, "Please."

Something flashed in his eyes, and after a moment, he nodded. "Okay. Give me a few minutes to get dressed. I just got out of the shower."

Yeah, that was obvious.

I told him I'd meet him downstairs whenever he was ready.

When the door closed behind him, I fanned myself to cool the raging heat of the desert storm cycloning through my system.

Mac Frayne might look like an absent-minded, desk-bound writer, but those shabby clothes hid the truth: the man possessed the hard, sculpted body of a god.

Who knew?

"Back already?" Maureen asked when I came into the kitchen again.

"I'm waiting for Frayne."

She piped a row of creamy white seashell scallops along the bottom tier of the cake.

"You do that so fast," I said.

Her shrug was careless. "Practice."

I sat at the kitchen table and watched her work.

"Nanny called me a little while ago," she said when she switched decorating tips. "Her scone supply has dwindled. Can you drop off a box from me? I'm swamped from now until Sunday with Colleen's wedding party, plus my regular guests."

"Do you have them ready? I'll drop them off tonight before I head home."

She pointed with her chin to a large bakery box sitting atop the counter. When I lifted the top, the delicious aroma of a dozen scones of varying flavors hit me and made my empty stomach growl with need.

"I heard that," Maureen said, never lifting her head from her work. "I thought you ate."

"I'm planning to in a few minutes. I'm taking Frayne with me."

For the first time, she stopped working on the cake. Turning, the piping bag suspended in her hands, my youngest sister's eyes widened as she stared across at me.

"What?"

"Since when do you take a man out to dinner?"

I rolled my eyes. "It's not like *that*. He helped me a great deal with George. I simply want to thank him, and since he's here all alone and you don't cook dinner for your guests as a rule, I figured buying him a meal would be a nice gesture."

She didn't reply.

"Why are you looking at me like I have three heads?"

"A nice gesture?"

"Yeah. A way of saying thanks for the help."

"Hmmm."

Remember I said my little sister was the one who routinely kept her thoughts and emotions close? Who never let anyone see what she was thinking or going through? Well, right now, standing in her kitchen with a pastry bag gripped in her hand, the look on her face was as clear and transparent as fresh seawater pooling around a Caribbean island.

"Stop," I commanded. "Just…stop."

With a tiny tilt of her head, she asked, "Stop what?"

"The whole plot scenario I know is raging through your brain right now."

One corner of her mouth tipped upward, and a tiny, knowing smile tugged at her lips.

"This is a simple thank you-for-helping-me-through-something-horrible meal. That's all."

"So the fact you've never invited a man out to dinner before—let me finish." She aimed the pastry bag at me—tip first—when I opened my mouth to argue.

I clamped it shut.

"Or shown any interest, professional or personal, in any guy other than your husband, whom you'd known since the dawn of time, and I'm not supposed to think you're feeling a little something other than gratitude for him? Especially a guy who looks like he does?"

"What do you mean, looks like he does?"

She waved the pastry bag in the air. "All haunted and Byronesque and…buff."

"How do you know he's buff?"

"*Duh*. He uses my gym every day. Pounds miles on the treadmill and lifts weights like nobody's business. I've seen him in nothing but running shorts." She fanned herself with her free hand and smiled. "Toned abs, hard thighs, and a tight ass. The very definition of buff."

"Who's buff?"

The smile on my sister's face disappeared at the sound of Lucas Alexander's voice as he walked into the kitchen.

"Why are you here?" she asked him over her shoulder.

"I was driving by and saw Cathy's car." He turned his attention to me. "Saved me a call. A buddy of mine up at the prison notified me that Cameron Compton was shanked in the dining hall this afternoon. It hasn't been made public yet. Injuries are life threatening. He's not expected to live through the night."

"Oh, sweet Jesus. Seldrine—"

"I was on my way over to Angelica Arms to notify her, and when I saw your car, I figured you might want to come with me, maybe ease the blow a bit."

"Yes, definitely." I stood and grabbed my bag at the same moment Frayne walked into the kitchen.

He was dressed now, the ends of his hair still a bit damp. His tattered bomber jacket covered another pullover, and he'd forgone his jeans for a pair of black trousers fitting what Mo had described as *hard thighs* well. His glasses were tucked in the V of the pullover.

"Cathy? Is everything okay?"

I quickly explained about Cameron.

"We don't have to go," he said.

"Yes, we do," I said. A quick look at Lucas, then my sister, and I added, "One stop at the nursing home for the notification. You can visit with Nanny while Lucas and I deal with this. I'm sure she'd love the company."

"Especially if it's male company," Maureen told him with a smile. "Bring her these." She handed him the bakery box. "She'll be your best friend for life."

With bemusement crossing his face, he accepted it.

"You can ride with me," I told him. "Lucas, we'll follow you."

"Here." Maureen handed Lucas a paper bag she'd pulled from the refrigerator. "I'm assuming you haven't had dinner yet. This is some leftover soup from lunch, and herb bread for you and your dad."

"You make the bread?" he asked.

She answered him by merely lifting an eyebrow.

I kissed her cheek. "Bye."

"Hey," she whispered before I could pull away. "A little buffness in your life wouldn't hurt."

"I'm pretending I didn't hear that," I whispered back. "Love you," I said in a normal voice.

"Love you more."

In the car, I jacked the heat up to high while I pulled out behind Lucas's truck. "I'm sorry we have to make this stop."

"You don't need to apologize."

"Still."

"What's in here? The aroma is making my mouth water," he said, holding up the box.

"A supply of Maureen's breakfast scones. Nanny is addicted to them. As are her nursing home cohorts. Maureen bakes her a bunch once a week to share with her cronies."

"I thought that's what it was. I think I'm getting addicted to them, too. I've been eating more than I should every morning. Way more."

"Good thing you've got Maureen's gym to work off all those carbs."

The minute the words came out of my mouth I wanted nothing more than to pull them back in. Just mentioning the gym had me thinking about Mo's description of him in running shorts—*toned abs, hard thighs, and a tight ass*. I'd seen the proof of his abdominal muscles for myself. The thought of what it would feel like to be squeezed between those thighs made me press my own together to stop me from squirming in my seat. It did nothing to counteract my desire.

"She's got a great facility," he said. "I usually run outside, but with all the snow here and the frigid temps, I'd rather not."

I said a silent prayer of thanks he hadn't known what I'd been thinking.

Lucas turned into the nursing home entrance, parked his car directly outside, and I pulled up behind him. I figured I wouldn't be ticketed because I was with him, and since he was the one who would ticket me—well, I wasn't worried.

The three of us went straight to the dining hall, where I knew dinner was being served.

"It's never good news when people show up at suppertime," Nanny announced when she spotted us, "especially when one of them's a law man. Number One, what in blazes are ya doing here?"

Lucas answered for me.

"Seldrine's tidyin' up me room," Nanny told us, eyeing the box in Frayne's hand.

I tilted my head to him, and he got the hint. We left him with Nanny and her friends while we went in search of Seldrine.

"I have to admit," Lucas said as we walked up the stairs to the second story, "I won't shed a tear if Cam dies."

"I don't think his wife will either."

Twenty minutes later, after leaving a shocked Seldrine with Lucas, I made my way back down to the dining hall. Nanny and Frayne were nowhere to be found.

"That lovely man took Fiona to the solarium," one of the residents told me.

I found them huddled together on a sofa in the sunroom. They were both laughing, and Nanny had a hand flirtatiously placed over Frayne's forearm. His laughter, rich, deep, and husky, was a sound I could have listened to all day long. *Hell,* all year long. A tingling sensation tripped up my spine when his eyes narrowed, practically disappearing from his face as he smiled. He threw back his head and howled at whatever my grandmother was saying.

It was delightful to see him relaxed and happy, and I have to admit, my heart stuttered a bit when he brought Nanny's gnarled hand to his lips and pressed a sweet kiss against her knuckles.

"Number One, all done, are ya?" Nanny asked.

I came into the room, a grin tugging on my lips.

"Nanny, what tall tales have you been telling Mr. Frayne? I could hear the both of you laughing from the hallway."

"Ah, lass, nothing bad, to be sure. Merely sharin' a few simple stories about me time touring."

"Oh, good Lord." I knew exactly what she'd told him. Nanny's days as a concert pianist were legendary in our family. Legendary and naughty. She'd had affairs with at least two dukes, one baron, and a smattering of lesser-titled men throughout the royal houses of Europe before coming back to Heaven and marrying her second husband. And then her third. And fourth, who was, thankfully, the last.

"Your grandmother has led an extraordinary life," Frayne said, the light in his eyes bright and clear. "Tales of her touring life would make for a terrific book."

"Salacious, more than anything," I said.

"Don't be gettin' any notions to write about me escapades, young man." She swatted his arm with a grandmotherly thwack. "If I ever decide to write about me life, I'll be doing the tellin', not someone else."

"I'd be thrilled and honored to be your scribe," Frayne said. "Anytime. Simply say the word."

"Ah, go on with ya." She swatted his arm again. "I expect the two of ya will be off to dinner now. Seldrine okay?" she asked me.

"She's fine. Lucas is with her, taking her through everything she needs to be prepared for."

"She's a strong lass. Well…" She sighed deep and, because this was Nanny, theatrically. "Off with ya both now. Go enjoy a good meal and you"—she pointed at Frayne—"don't be forgetting I want a full report on

Robert when you're all done with your research."

"That's a promise," he told her.

"Good. Now, give us a kiss and run along."

I wasn't surprised when Frayne bent and bussed her cheek.

"And you," she said when I bent to do the same. "I want to hear all about this event Olivia told me you're signed up for. I want all the deets, as the kids say."

I nodded, my cheeks scorching.

"Your grandmother is a remarkable woman," Frayne said once we were back in my car.

"That's one word for her," I said, slanting him a side eye. The grin on his face was equal parts heart stopping, sexy, and adorable. "Pathetic." I shook my head.

"What is?"

"You and your whole gender."

He turned in his seat to look at me. "What have I and my entire gender done to be labeled pathetic?"

I cocked my head his way, then turned my attention back to the road. "A little wink, a few arm taps, and a girlish giggle and you fall like a ton of bricks."

"What?"

The sigh I exhaled was almost Nanny-worthy in its theatricality. "You have a crush on my ninety-three-year-old grandmother."

Complete bafflement filled his face. A half second later, his eyes widened, and he tossed out another of those deep, throaty laughs. The lower half of my body turned molten-lava hot.

"Tell me I'm wrong." I turned the car onto Glory Road and spotted a parking spot on the street right outside the place where I wanted to eat. This was another one of those reasons I loved living in a small town: you never had to search for parking.

"You're not. *God.* You're not." His head shook back and forth while his smile turned into a wicked grin.

I put the car in park and got out. Over the hood, I said, "See? Pathetic. Every man I've ever known falls for her the moment she shines those twinkling blue eyes at him. I swear she casts a spell with a glance." I shook my head. "I hope you like pizza because I've been craving it for days."

I walked toward the front door of Paradise Pizza, but Frayne stopped me in my tracks. With his hand circling my arm, he turned me around to face him. Gone was the playful expression, the laugh a mere memory. "Cathy."

Talk about casting a spell. I'd never really liked my name, thinking my parents had chosen one plain and common and not exotic or fancy because they wanted it to be easy to remember. It was way better than being called Number One any day of the week, though.

But still.

"Y-yes?"

He moved in closer, his hand still gripping my arm. Through my coat, and even the suit jacket underneath it, the heat from his hand singed my flesh. The back of my throat suddenly clogged and my tongue turned the consistency of sandpaper when I rubbed it against the roof of my mouth.

"What…what were you going to say?"

His pale eyes did that little tilting thing down to my lips again before coming back up to settle on my own.

The hint of a grin kicked up one side of his gorgeous mouth. "I love…pizza."

"Oh. Okay. Well, good." I reached to push the door open, but he beat me to it. "Then you're gonna love this place. Best pizza in the state."

The pungent aromas of fresh garlic, basil, oregano, and a dozen other mouthwatering spices filled our senses when we walked into the establishment.

"Hey, Counselor," Sal, the owner of Paradise Pizza called out from behind the counter. "How you doin'?"

"Good, Sal."

"Grab a seat. Gina'll be right with ya."

We shucked off our outerwear and slid into a booth, facing one another as we had at the diner.

Frayne opened the menu on the table and slid his glasses on.

Was there ever going to be a time I didn't get a little hot and bothered when he wore them?

"Anything you order is going to be delicious. Don't feel you need to get pizza simply because I am."

He peered at me over the top of the menu. His eyes were huge from the magnification.

My toes started to tingle.

"I told you I love pizza. Why don't we split one? As long as you don't like crazy toppings."

"What do you consider crazy?"

His tugged the glasses down a bit so he didn't have to look at me through the lenses.

I had to press my knees together to keep my feet from tapping up and down.

"Vegetables," he said. "Vegetables on pizza are crazy. And just plain wrong."

"Agreed."

"Meat is good," he said, considering. "Pepperoni or ham. Sausage. Extra cheese is even better."

"But no vegetables."

That corner of his mouth ticked upward again. "No vegetables."

"Got something against them in general, or just not feeling them as a pizza topping?"

"In general."

I couldn't stop the smile from blooming across my face. "Good to know I'm not the only adult who doesn't like them. Despite the persistent efforts of my mother and grandmother when I was kid, I'm still not a fan."

"Hey, Counselor. Good to see you." Gina, Sal's wife, set two tall glasses of water down in front us, along with cutlery. She pulled her order pad from her apron pocket and asked, "Know what you want? Sal's got his veal parmigiana on special tonight."

"As mouthwatering as I know that is," I told her, "I think we're going to split a pie." I looked across the table at Frayne. "Extra cheese over meatballs sound okay?"

He nodded.

"You want salads or something other than water to drink?"

"No on the salad, and I'll take a large ginger ale."

"What about you, hon?" she asked Frayne. "You want a beer? A glass o' wine maybe?"

The tops of his cheeks turned pink, probably because she'd called him hon. Aww. Really, this guy was a walking advertisement for endearing and sexy. If he'd been a dog, he'd be a sexydoodle.

I mentally blanched. Okay, I really needed some food in my system if I was starting to concoct new dog breeds.

"Water's fine, thanks," he told her.

"Okay. Be about ten, twelve minutes."

When she left us, Frayne tucked his glasses back into the collar of his sweater.

"Can I—"

"Listen, Cathy—"

We both stopped.

"Sorry," Frayne said. "You first."

In the car, I'd debated how I could ask him what I wanted to know without making him defensive or angry. What I'd discovered about his family was horrible and went a long way in explaining why he wore his emotional pain like a full body jacket. The few minutes he'd spent with Nanny had erased those mournful shadows, and I was reluctant to ask something that could bring them back. In a perfect world, he would be the one to open up and tell me about their deaths without prompting. The likelihood of it happening, though, was dim.

I tried a different tack. "I want to thank you for allowing me to buy you dinner. I felt bad you didn't stay the other night after…well, after everything with George."

He folded his hands together and leaned his elbows on the table. "I didn't stay because I thought it would be better if you were with your family. I didn't feel right about horning in."

"You wouldn't have. Goodness, you helped me through one of the worst days of my life. George was the child I've never had, and even though I knew I was going to lose him, I still wasn't prepared."

Frayne gazed dropped down to his hands. "I don't

think we're ever prepared to lose the ones we love."

As an opening toward asking him about his family, this was a pretty good one. Still, I didn't know how'd he react if I pressed.

The decision was torn from me when he added, "I know I wasn't."

Lawyers employed many varied skills when eliciting information from witnesses, clients, whomever. One of those skills was the open-ended response. "Oh?"

He lifted his gaze back to me and cocked his head. The shadows were back. "I…lost…my wife and daughter a few years ago."

I reached across the table and placed my hands over his folded ones. "I know it sounds trite to say it and offers no comfort at all, but I truly am sorry."

"Thank you. "

Gina returned then with our drinks and a plate of cheese sticks.

"Sal says these are on the house, Cath. He appreciates everything you've done for Seldrine, says he's happy she's got you in her corner for the legal stuff."

Frayne pulled his hands back and rested them under the table in his lap at her words.

"Thanks, Gina. Tell him I've got his niece's back."

"He knows that. Hell, everyone in this town knows that. You're the best lawyer we know, better than your old man even, which is saying a whole lot."

Frayne's breath hitched as he crossed his arms over his chest.

Gina squeezed my shoulder and left to check on her other customers.

When I turned my attention back to him, those painful shadows were gone and a muscle in his jaw twitched.

Nanny's voice filled my head with *gird your loins, lass*. I took a mental breath before I said, "Can I ask you a question?"

His nod was curt.

"The reason you dislike lawyers and the legal system is because of what happened to your family, isn't it?" I held my breath as I waited for his answer.

"You know what happened?"

"Yes." Before he could ask me how, I offered the truth. "I did a Google search."

"On me?"

"Yes."

"Why?"

It took everything in me not to confess the agony in his eyes touched my heart and I wanted to eradicate the pain. "It's been my experience when someone has such an intense response to something, there's usually a real, legitimate, and unsettling reason for it."

He stayed silent.

"You were denied justice for what happened to your family. In your shoes, I'd feel the same way."

"I find that hard to believe since you work for the judicial system. Justice means nothing to lawyers. It's all about winning at any cost. No matter who gets hurt or left in the wake."

The lawyer in me wanted to set him straight. The woman in me, though, could appreciate his anger. "While I understand why you feel the way you do— because believe me, I've heard stories about lawyers who take advantage of loopholes in the law to benefit themselves and their clients—I can only defend myself. I work for my clients, yes, to guide them through government red tape, even defend them when I need to. But I value the letter of the law above all else, and I believe with all my heart and soul in the legal system."

His hot gaze raked across my face.

"It's not a perfect system," I said. "Not by any standards. And, yes, mistakes get made every day. Mistakes, like the one in your wife and daughter's case, which have far reaching and injurious consequences."

"And yet you still work for the system."

I shook my head. "I work for my clients and their rights."

"What about my wife's rights? My daughter's?" His voice hadn't risen, but the controlled fury spitting through his lips made it seem as if he'd bellowed in an empty room. "Their rights to be protected against the person who killed them? Their right for justice? What about that?"

"I agree, they were denied those rights—"

"You can agree all you want; it doesn't change anything. My wife and daughter are six feet under, and the teenager who killed them because she thought texting her friends while driving was more important than keeping an eye on the road is out free and clear. And alive. She has her family intact. I've got nothing." The fury in his voice finally vaulted, and he must have realized it, because, abruptly, he stopped.

He lifted the water glass in front of him, his hand shaking, and chugged half of it down in one draft. I wanted to reach across and cover his hands again, but they'd drifted back to his lap after he put the glass down on the table.

The justice system had failed Frayne, and nothing I could do or say would change that, make him feel better, or despise the system less.

"Again, telling you I'm sorry does nothing to eradicate your pain or change the outcome of what happened. Nothing will ever bring back your family, and nothing I say will ever make the loss less devastating." I stopped and considered how to erase the fury in his eyes.

His gaze connected with mine again. All the fight suddenly went out of him. His shoulders relaxed, his back slumped a bit, and a huge sigh blew from deep within him. "I'm sorry," he said, softly.

"For what?"

"Getting angry."

"You have a right to your anger," I told him. "Every right."

He leaned his elbows on the table and folded his hands together again, while he stared down at them. "I shouldn't displace it on you, though. Or anyone else not directly related to what happened. It's that girl's fault and her lawyer's. Maybe even the judge who presided over the case. No one else's."

"Again, you have every right to feel the way you do. I know what it means to be filled, even consumed, with rage after someone you love is taken from you during a senseless act."

He lifted his gaze to mine, a question burning in his eyes.

"My husband, Danny, was a career soldier. He was killed while on a tour of duty a little over three years ago." I shook my head. "Almost twenty years without a mishap and then one day he couldn't outrun a sniper's bullet."

The line popped up between his brows again. "That's…horrible."

I nodded. "At the time, I was filled with immeasurable rage. But I couldn't give in to it. I had to get his mother through her own grief and fury, had to bury Danny, and then deal with all the stuff that came afterward."

The line thickened, and he cocked his head in his familiar way. "Your sisters said you're the one who takes care of everyone in a crisis."

I nodded again.

"Why?"

A good question and one I'd debated with myself for most of my life. "The easiest answer is I'm the oldest and have always been what my parents termed the 'responsible one.' "

"That doesn't seem…fair."

"Fair?" I shrugged. "Maybe not. As the oldest, I assumed responsibility more times than not, as a kid. It stuck through to adulthood."

"Why?"

I was charmed when the tips of his ears went florid.

"I ask because family dynamics are intriguing and alien to me. As an only child, I don't have any kind of firsthand knowledge about"—he flipped his hand in the air—"sibling pecking order and such."

It was another good question and the answer one I'd never discussed with anyone. Why I was compelled to with him, though, seemed right.

After a moment to collect my thoughts, I leaned back in the booth and stretched my hands out on either side of my plate. "When the twins were four, my mother decided to go back to work a few days a week. Nanny was touring again, and my parents figured it would be fine if I was left in charge of watching my sisters for an hour or two after school. Mom didn't need to work. My father made more than an adequate income but"—I shrugged—"I guess she needed some time away from kids, crying, and sister drama. Be with adults, you know?"

He nodded.

"Anyway. I hated being in charge of them. Colleen was okay because she was only a few years younger than I was and she never caused any trouble, but the twins were rambunctious. And wicked spoiled. They never listened to anything I told them, and I finally started ignoring them, left them to watch television or play by themselves. One afternoon, I was doing homework when I should have been minding them. They were screaming they wanted to go to the park, but I was tired and I had a test to study for, so I banished them to their room and forgot about them. Eileen, somehow, managed to get outside. She was always a little Houdini when it came to crawling out of her crib or high chair, but I never for a moment thought she'd be able to unlock the door and leave the house."

The terror I remembered feeling when Colleen ran into my bedroom to tell me Eileen was missing wormed its way up from my memory and made my body start to shiver.

"Good Lord. What happened? Did she get far, or get hurt?"

I shook my head. "Luckily, a neighbor boy out walking his dog spotted her, right as Colleen and I sprinted down the road to search for her. The minute I saw her, I started screaming, which made her cry. Even Colleen was bawling. Maureen, who Colleen was holding, started up then. Mitchel Kineer, the poor kid who found her, was so uncomfortable with all of us standing in the road sobbing our eyes out, he beat a hasty retreat. When we got back to the house, I sat them down in the living room and read them the riot act. In truth, I think I was more frightened than they were. Colleen recovered quickly since she wasn't in trouble and told me I was lucky Eileen hadn't been hit by a car, or worse, and that our parents were going to be angry when they came home and found out what happened."

"As a parent, I can understand that feeling."

"It was the 'or worse' that got to me. My baby sister could have been taken by some psycho, or even wandered off into the woods and been lost forever. She was only four. She had no survival skills, no sense of right or wrong. Right then and there, I vowed never to complain about being left in charge or being the responsible one again."

"You were a kid, Cathy."

Was I ever just a kid?

"When my parents came home, I confessed what happened. Of course, Colleen added her own sense of drama to the situation. If I wasn't distraught enough about the whole incident to begin with, the looks of disappointment my parents gave me solidified the fact I was a horrible and irresponsible child. My mother quit her job soon after that. Like I said, she didn't need to work. It took a long time before they trusted me again."

I didn't add I'd gone out of my way for years to prove I was a good, trustworthy, worthwhile daughter. I did chores before I was ever asked to, got straight A's in school, helped my sisters in whatever way they asked or needed, all without being told or asked to by my parents.

"Didn't you ever feel…I don't know? Resentful, maybe?"

I was sure he wasn't only talking about my status as the oldest sister. "Honestly, no."

His brows were almost touching now, the skin around his eyes tight. "You're a much better person than I am."

"Better? I don't think so," I said. A smile bloomed quickly before I told him, "Nanny claims it's because I'm a control freak like my father. Falling apples and trees, you know?"

My heart did a little stutter dance when the corners of his lips twitched.

"The same has been claimed about me a time or two."

We ate our cheese sticks in silence for a few moments. I'd have given anything to know what he was thinking. The fact I couldn't read him, read his mood and his thoughts, was frustrating. And I'd be lying if I didn't say it was also wildly appealing.

"How did you get through it all?" he asked. "How did you get past it? The anger? The all-consuming fury after your husband was killed?"

"Day by day. I know it sounds clichéd, but it was really the only way I could. When it looked as if everything was going to settle down and I could give myself permission to vent my anger, Eileen got sick."

"Cancer."

"Yes. Before I knew it, we were all wrapped up in her care. Taking her to chemo treatments, staying with her when she was ill so Maureen could run the inn. Then at the end, sitting vigil. The year after Danny's death flew by, and by the time I could actually let myself feel anything again, I realized I couldn't change what had happened. Danny was dead. I was a widow, and nothing was going to alter that reality. Acknowledging it, knowing it, I finally laid it all to rest."

"I wish I could do that. There are times I can forget what happened." He blew out a breath thick with pain. "I'll get involved in a project or with writing, or even go for a long run and not think about it at all. But the anger is always there, waiting to creep back in."

"Have you talked to anyone about it? Anyone who can help you through it?"

"Like a therapist?"

I shrugged. "Or a friend? Family? Talking with my sisters and Nanny made everything…easier, somehow, on me."

He lifted his glass and took another sip of his water. "You're lucky. My relationship with my family isn't like yours. My parents are…older. Both of them are in their eighties now, and they have their own problems to deal with. We're not…close. Never have been."

That sounded so sad to me.

"After the case was dismissed, I went…well, I went a little off the rails. Started doing things I shouldn't and lost myself for a year or so."

I reached across the table again and slid my hand over his. I had a pretty good idea of how he'd gone off the rails after my conversation with Seldrine, but I wasn't about to reveal that. When my hand came in contact with his, he startled again, glanced down at it, and then back up at me when I gave it a gentle squeeze.

"I started drinking," he said. "A lot. A whole lot, to be honest. I wanted to forget everything, block it all out, forget it ever happened. Being drunk helped. Stupid, I know." He shrugged. "I missed a few deadlines for a project I'd been commissioned to do but didn't care. My agent, Marci, was the one who realized what was going on. She got me checked into rehab, and after a three-month stay, I was better, physically. I still go to AA meetings. They...help. Some." He took another big breath, and I let go of his hand. "Nothing helps with the pain though."

"It doesn't. It's always there, right under the surface." I leaned back against the booth back. "I know that's true for Maureen. While she'd never admit it because she wants everyone to think she's fine, I know she's still processing everything. Losing a sister is tough. Losing a twin...well, it has to feel like a part of yourself is gone. They were the best of friends, did everything together, even attended the same college so they wouldn't be separated."

Frayne's eyebrows rose.

"The one area they differed on was cooking. Eileen hated it. To Maureen, cooking is an extension of her heart, you know what I mean?"

He nodded. "I've seen it firsthand at the inn. She's always willing to make anyone something to eat, no matter what time of the day or how busy she is."

I nodded. "I've always thought feeding people is her way of coping with what happened to Eileen. If she feeds us all, we'll stay healthy. We won't get sick because we're well nourished."

This time, Frayne nodded.

Finally, because my curiosity got the better of me, I said, "I read there was a third person killed in the car."

He stared across the table at me. A streak of anger slashed in his eyes, hot and swift. Just as quick as it came, his gaze shut down, his expression blanking like a clean slate. When he stayed silent, the notion he'd make a good lawyer blossomed in my mind again. The ability to wait the other person out before giving a knee-jerk response was one most people didn't possess. Frayne did.

But so did I. He stared at me, and I stared right back, hoping against hope the expression on my face was one of open acceptance.

It must have been, because Frayne's shoulders relaxed again. "Thomas Roadman. He was a family…friend."

I thought he might be a little more than that.

"Well, more Cheyanne's friend than mine. He and I had a professional relationship since he was my editor."

"Were they…close?"

A harsh cry shot from between his lips as he threaded his hands through his hair. "If that's a polite way of asking if they were lovers, the answer is yes."

Saying I was sorry sounded ridiculous. Once again I kept my mouth shut.

"Apparently, they had been for some time," he continued. "I found out the night of the crash when I got to the emergency room. His wife told me. They'd been separated for a few months, and Tracy explained Cheyanne was the cause."

I shook my head.

"I was clueless. Had no idea at all. There was a bit of a rough patch after our daughter was born. Cheyanne was resentful because she didn't want to put her career on the back burner, but I thought we'd worked through it." He dragged in a deep, heavy breath. "Obviously, I was wrong."

He lifted his gaze back to mine. The hollows and shadows were back, full force. "I'm not like you," he said. "I can't let the anger go completely. I'm mad at Cheyanne, at Tom, at the teenager who was driving. I'm angry at the entire judicial system. There are still days I can't contain it, and all I want to do is have a drink and forget everything that's happened."

"Do you?" I asked, even though I pretty sure I knew the answer.

"No. No, I do what was suggested at rehab and find a meeting. That...helps get past the anger for a time."

"That's a good thing."

He dragged in a big breath, and when his gaze settled on me again, some of the shadows had lifted. "That girl who works at the nursing home with your grandmother? The one you represent? Seldrine?"

"What about her?"

"I spotted you dropping her off at the church a few mornings ago. I've...we've both been attending the same meetings. She recognized me the other night when we were with your grandmother but pretended she didn't. Anonymity, and all."

I stayed silent.

He continued to stare at me, his head tilted. Finally, he shook it, a ghost of a grin pulling at his lips. "I get the feeling you're an exceptional lawyer."

Surprise warred with elation. I wasn't exactly sure

it was a compliment, though. "Why?"

"Aside from the fact you have a great poker face?"

Still not sure I was being complimented here, but...

"Without divulging too much of what's been said, your client thinks the world of you. She's lucky to have you in her corner."

It broke my heart he had no one in his.

"I've said some horrible things to you about lawyers. Hearing how you've helped her has made me rethink a few things, so I want to apologize again for what I've said. I know you're not anything like the lawyers I've had to deal with."

Elation turned to a warm, all-consuming joy at his words. "For the record, most lawyers are more like me than not."

He took another breath and nodded.

For a few moments, we ate in silence.

"Did you ever consider filing a civil suit against the girl?" I asked. "Was the option presented to you by your lawyer?"

His brows pulled together again as he regarded me.

"Justice comes in many forms," I added. "It would be a way to make the girl—and her family—assume responsibility for what happened. I've found when a monetary punishment is sought, if the offending party complies, then some sense of justice is afforded to the complainant."

"Isn't that a little like putting a price on the lives of my wife and daughter? Reducing them to dollar signs?"

"No, not the way you're thinking," I said quickly, fearful he wasn't understanding my point. "It's not the money you're seeking. It's righting what you feel is an injustice by making the driver take responsibility for her actions in the eyes of society. Whether it's one dollar or ten million, she would have to face—legally, ethically, and financially—what she'd done, in a court of law and in the court of public opinion."

I went on to tell him about a case I'd studied in law school about a father who'd lost his daughter in a car crash where his son-in-law had been driving. The man had fallen asleep at the wheel on the way home from dinner and lost control of the car. A subsequent investigation had proven he'd had a drink at the restaurant. While not legally drunk, his action combined with fatigue had caused him to grow groggy on the drive home. The court had ordered the husband to send the father one penny every day for twenty-five years.

"That's an unusual…sentence."

"It was a way to make the husband remember the consequences of his actions every single day for the foreseeable future. His wife's father wanted him to know, although his behavior hadn't been deemed criminal, a life had been lost." I shrugged and added, "It's something to consider."

He went silent again. In all truth, I was happy he wasn't railing at me for suggesting another legal maneuver.

I tried to figure out a way to get him to open up a little more, share more of himself, and decided on a topic that might get him to do so.

"In case you haven't noticed, my grandmother is a talker," I said. "She can drone on for hours on end, barely drawing breath, and she's a big believer in talking about people we've lost. Sharing happy memories, she feels, can lessen the pain of their absence by keeping them fresh in our minds. I know she's right because when my sister died, talking about her helped us all get through the grieving period. So…" I took a breath, reached over for another cheese stick, and said, "Why don't you tell me about your daughter?"

Surprise drifted across his face. "Mabel?"

I grinned and nodded. "Can I just tell you how much I love that name? It's so old-fashioned and…girly."

My smile pulled a small one from him.

"That describes her perfectly." He mimicked my actions and pulled a cheese stick onto his own plate. "Mabel was an old soul wrapped in a five-year-old's body. Wise beyond her years. And"—he shifted his gaze to me—"extremely girly."

His whole expression changed while he talked of his daughter. I got him to tell me of her love of reading, and her desire to be a writer like her father while we finished off the appetizer. The shadows in his eyes flew while he spoke, the hard lines from the corners of his mouth to his jaw softening as he remembered her. He'd loved his daughter deeply.

"Was your wife a writer, too?" I asked as Gina brought our pizza to the table. With a quick nod and a query if she could get us anything else, she left us to eat.

"No." Frayne shook his head and laid his fork down next his plate. He took a deep breath and said, "Cheyanne was a graphic designer. We actually met when she was in charge of my first book cover."

"So a writer and an artist. Was Mabel talented as well?"

He nodded. "Our apartment walls are filled with

pictures she drew. I can't—won't—take them down."

"That's just lovely." My voice went a little wistful. Frayne must have heard the change.

"You and your husband never had any children, did you?"

"Just George. And he was more mine than Danny's."

"Did you want kids?"

"Always. We talked about it all the time when we were first married. We'd planned on it as soon as I was all done with school."

"You said he was career army?"

I nodded.

"But you live here, in your home town. I always thought families of career soldiers lived on a base or in a military community. Am I wrong?"

"No. The answer is simple. I never wanted to leave Heaven. I love it here and couldn't envision living anywhere else. In my opinion, this is the perfect place to raise a family. Danny accepted that."

"And yet you never had kids."

"Unfortunately, we didn't."

I didn't bother revealing the reason we hadn't. Especially since I hadn't known the real one until the day Danny walked out for his last tour. Up until then, I'd thought he wanted them as much as I did. I was wrong. More wrong than I've ever been before about something.

"If you like pizza, you're gonna love this," I said, tugging a slice from the platter and quickly changing the subject. "Sal does something ridiculous to the dough. It makes all the taste buds in your mouth stand up at attention and beg. It's a top-secret recipe, and no one, not even Nanny, who's an excellent interrogator, has been able to wrangle it from him. Gina claims even she doesn't know what he does to it."

I practically inhaled my first bite, not caring a whit when the roof of my mouth protested against the piping hot sauce. My eyes automatically closed, and all my other senses went dormant, shutting off everything but my taste awareness.

I moaned the moment the sweet sauce and tangy cheese dissolved in my mouth. When Frayne's quick hiss split the air around me, I figured he'd burned the roof of his mouth as well. When I opened my eyes, the thought proved true. He was burning all right, but he hadn't taken a bite of the hot pizza.

My brain shut down and left me paralyzed, unable to do anything but stare at him. Those pale eyes were almost obliterated by his dilated pupils and were laser focused on my mouth. One hand rose in slow motion and inched toward my face.

That paralysis? Yeah, it was a real thing. I couldn't have moved if someone had screamed "Fire!"

He dragged his index finger across my bottom lip in a slow, torpid slide from one corner to the other.

Then he slid it back again.

The burning sensation on the roof of my mouth was nothing compared to the cauldron of heat in his eyes.

His finger was still on my bottom lip and with a tiny bit of pressure he pushed my lips apart. For a hot second, I almost sucked his finger into my mouth to…feast on him.

Good Lord.

Where the thought came from, I don't have the

foggiest, but the only reason I didn't pull Mac's finger into my mouth and give in to the erotic fantasy spinning in my mind was because the front door opened, setting the bells above it off, the noise jarring me back to reality.

My immobility flew, and I pulled back until I was plastered against the booth cushion. I shook my head like a dog shucking water from its fur. Frayne's hand stayed outstretched for a second, then, he too, pulled back and slammed into the seatback. With his eyes scrunching in the corners, he looked first at his index finger and then lifted it for me to see.

"Sorry." He shook his head as I had. "You had...sauce...on your mouth."

"You kids doing okay?" Gina's sudden appearance startled me. "Want anything more to drink? More water? Another soda, Cath?"

I mumbled a yes. Frayne shook his head.

He cleared his throat as if he were going to say something, and my phone pinged at the same time. Olivia Joyner's name crossed my screen.

"I'm sorry. I've got to take this."

While the matchmaker reminded me of tomorrow's event, I snuck a peek at my dinner companion. He lifted his shoulders and bobbed his head right and left as if working out a kink in his neck.

"You have an appointment tomorrow?" he asked after I ended the call.

I cleared my throat, as he was wont to do, and said a silent prayer my voice would sound controlled and mature. "A morning wedding at the inn and then tomorrow evening I have an...event, I promised I'd go to."

No way was I sharing what the event was. Forget awkward. I would have felt sixteen levels of mortified saying it aloud.

"Will you have any free time for me to come over and go through some of Robert's things? There are still three boxes I haven't gotten to."

I nodded. "The wedding starts at ten. I should be home by eleven thirty. I can text you when I'm free."

"Since you'll be at the inn, I'll know when you're done."

"You're not going to the museum tomorrow, then?"

"No. I've gotten as much as I can from the public files. But I'd really like to delve back into the stuff at your house."

Talking about his project and the reason he was in Heaven went a long way in dissipating the tension that had blossomed between us. His face was calm again, his features relaxed, his voice animated as he began telling me about the entries he'd already read in Robert's journals.

We finished our pizza without any further interruptions or uncomfortable moments.

Back in my car with the heat jacked up to ward off the arctic chill in the air, Frayne said, "You were right about the pizza. It was amazing."

Since it was, I smiled.

We were silent on the ride back to the inn, but it wasn't a strained silence like it could have been.

"I'm not going in because I've got to get home and prepare for tomorrow's vows," I told him when I pulled up to the front on the inn. "If you see Maureen, could you tell her Nanny says thanks for the scones?"

The quickness and power of his grin made me gasp. In the darkened cab of my car, the brightness of it lit the entire space up as if he'd turned on a spotlight.

"I will," he said, adding, "and I'm requesting a batch to keep in my room for when I'm working. Think she'll let me keep some there?"

"All you have to do is ask. It's a guarantee."

The grooves at the corners of his mouth deepened as his grin widened. I couldn't help but smile back at him. It was the little things in life, Nanny commented often, like the taste of Maureen's scones, that gave us all the most pleasure. She wasn't wrong. I was going to add Mac Frayne's smile to my list of simple pleasures.

For a moment we sat there, silently grinning. The thought he might kiss me bloomed when his gaze slid down to my mouth and lingered for a moment. It wasn't my imagination or wishful thinking either when he moved a little closer to me from his seat. His gaze came back up to my eyes and dawdled for a few seconds before a sigh pushed from him and he said, "I'd better let you get home. You've got things to do."

What would he have done if I'd admitted I wanted *to do* him?

He alighted from the car, then dipped his head to look at me again. "Thanks for dinner. I'll see you tomorrow."

Because I didn't trust my voice right then to scream for him to stop, get back in the car and kiss me, I took the safe way out and gave him a quick head bob.

After he'd closed the front door of the inn behind him, I let out the breath I'd been keeping prisoner and shook my head a few times before driving home to my cold, empty house.

Chapter 11

"These are the three you haven't gone through?" I asked Frayne, pointing.

"Yeah. I've got detailed notes about the items in the others, including the clothing boxes. It should be easy to start cataloging them for the historical society." One corner of his mouth lifted a bit in a charming smirk. "I'm assuming you want everything out of here as soon as possible. It can't be pleasant to have your house so…invaded."

I waved my hand as I slid open one of the boxes.

"It's fine. It's not like I have company coming or people trampling through this place every day and I'm embarrassed about the clutter. I'll take this box."

I ripped off the tape, pulled back one of the corners, and was overcome in a sneezing fit.

Frayne watched me as I sneezed five times in rapid succession before I came to shattering stop.

"God bless you."

"I hate torpedo sneezes. And I could shoot Nanny for being such a hoarder." I swiped my sleeve under my nose. "But if she weren't, I guess we'd never have these items for the museum."

I'd started my morning by officiating at a wedding Colleen was in charge of at Inn Heaven. Since it was a second marriage for both parties, they'd opted for a small ceremony and brunch overseen by Maureen.

During my reading of the vows, I happened to look up and I spotted Frayne leaning against the doorjamb of the Morning Room. For a moment, I lost track of what I was saying. He looked so damn hot and manly, all I could think about was crossing the room, clamping my lips onto his, and finally getting to know what he tasted like.

After dropping him off the night before, I'd climbed into bed with the memory of his confession in Shelby's office. He'd wanted to kiss me in the historical society basement but hadn't because he'd thought I was married. Well, now he knew I wasn't, and yet he still hadn't put action behind that desire.

When my part of the ceremony was done, I made a quick stop by the kitchen where Maureen handed me a shopping bag filled with food for the weekend. Thank God for my baby sister, because I still hadn't had a moment to get any groceries in the house, and now with Frayne coming over, I at least had something I could offer him if he got hungry.

The fleeting thought I could offer myself up to be devoured flitted through my brain. Despite sensing that he was attracted to me, I didn't know if I should make the first move. And let's be real here: I didn't even know how to begin. This was an issue of marrying the first boy I'd ever kissed and loved forever. Because Danny'd been my everything for most of my life I didn't know how to flirt, date, or let a man know I was attracted to him without coming across as aggressive.

Or…pathetic.

The box I'd chosen was easy to go through because it held nothing more interesting than Robert's yearbooks from grammar school up to college.

"You'll probably have more fun going through these than I will," I told Frayne, shoving the box across the table to him. "Historically speaking."

He glanced up from the leather-bound journal in his hands to peer at me over the tops of his glasses, which were covered with dust. I reached out my hand and said, "Give me those."

Without questioning why, he did.

In the kitchen, I doused them in glass cleaner and then rubbed them spotless with a paper towel.

"I'm beginning to think we really should be wearing masks while we go through all this," I said when I returned them to him. "We could be exposing ourselves to mold spores. Or worse."

"What do you think is worse?" he asked, holding the glasses in one hand.

I shrugged. "Some dormant bacteria, maybe? Plague? *Aspergillis niger*? Isn't that what killed the King Tut archeologist who opened his tomb?" I rubbed my nose again because it had started twitching.

"That's actually a myth," he told me. "And it wasn't Howard Carter, the archeologist, who died. It was George Herbert, the Earl of Carnarvon and the one paying for the dig, who did."

I pointed my finger at him. "See? He probably caught some airborne killer fungus unleashed when the tomb was opened."

"I think it was from an infected mosquito bite." He glanced down at the journal. From the way he'd dipped his chin almost to his chest, I got the impression he was trying to hide the fact he was stifling a laugh.

"Why am I not surprised you know that," I mumbled and lifted the remaining box onto the table.

This time when I pulled back one of the flaps I turned my head and held my breath.

"More journals." I pulled one out. "These look old. Like, *old* old."

The pages were held together between two pieces of thin, shaved wood with a string knotted across the middle.

He stuck his glasses back on and reached a hand out. I gave him the book. "There are five more in this box," I told him.

"I can't undo this knot."

"Here." I handed him a box cutter.

Gingerly, he tugged on the cord and cut it with one swift slice. Holding the paper securely between the two pieces of shaved wood, Frayne put the book down on the table and folded back the front cover. I moved next to him to see what, if anything, was legible.

"The handwriting's pretty faded," he said. "The paper's fragile, too. I don't want to rip it if I lift it up."

"Can you make out the date?" I asked, peering over his shoulder.

He leaned in closer and adjusted his glasses. "I can't make it out for sure; the ink is so faded."

"Hold on a sec."

I ran into my office and grabbed a magnifying glass.

"Here."

Frayne held it over the page while I shone the flashlight from my cell phone across the page.

"Seventeen eighty-nine," he said, his eyes huge as he peered at me through his glasses. It was impossible to miss the excitement in his voice.

"Try to turn the page."

Again, with infinite care, he fingered a corner of the page and ran it under the paper, lifting it from the one underneath it. The paper was dry and brittle, and a crackling sound, like when you crumble paper to use for kindling, pushed through the air around us.

"I don't want to damage it," he mumbled.

Slowly, he flattened his palm, face down, under the page and with his other hand, lifted it back.

"*Good Lord,*" he whispered when the underneath page was revealed.

I echoed his sentiments, but I said, "*Holy crap!*"

Written and clearly legible on the second page were the words *Josiah Heaven, the year of our Lord 1789. The town begins.*

"Is this what I think it is?" I asked.

Frayne's attention stayed glued to the page in his hand. He didn't speak, but his breathing got a little faster, and I swear the air around us turned electric.

He folded the page in his hand on top of the cover and slipped under the next one. The paper was unlined, but the author had written in a clear, fastidious way across the page so the lines themselves were even and straight.

"Can you move the light closer?" he asked me.

I did, and we were able to read the first line of text clearly.

The fifth day of April in the year of our Lord 1789. The first structure began today, the Moody brothers, along with the Johannsen men, in charge.

"*Holy Christmas.*" I turned my gaze to Frayne.

A shiver slipped down my spine when his gaze shot down to my lips, lingered, and then took its time coming back to my eyes.

"Cathy." His voice was a whisper, filled with reverence and awe. "These are Josiah Heaven's journals. Do you know what a find this is?"

I had a pretty good idea.

"There are five more in the box," I repeated.

With extreme care, he closed the journal we'd opened and then peeked into the box.

"Josiah supposedly showed up around 1787. That's two years before that"—I nodded to the now-closed journal—"was written. Maybe the others are from before then. That one was on the top."

"The only way to find out is to look."

I stepped back, letting him take the lead. Since this was his project, it felt like the right thing to do.

Frayne reached into the box and pulled out five more identically wrapped journals. "He must have handmade each of these." He laid them out on the table, one next to the other.

"Well, it wasn't like he could drive to the local convenience store to get a new one when he needed it," I said, eyeing each of the journals.

My toes curled at Frayne's deep chuckle.

With care, he first tried to untie the journals but, when they proved as resilient as the original, gave up and sliced each one open. He lifted the top covers and bent to see the dates written on the first page.

"These pages are even more faded." He cocked his head to the original. "Can you shine your phone on them again?"

I did, while he held the magnifier over each page.

"You're right," he said. "These are older. Let's put them in order."

When we were done, the journals ranged from

1786 with one volume, two for 1787, 1788 with two, and the last one with the 1789 date.

"There aren't any more after this." Frayne examined the boxes we'd opened. When he turned his attention back to me, I almost lost the ability to stand upright. "Cathy." His voice was hushed and filled with awe, his eyes fully dilated now. "This is...unbelievable."

"If you hadn't asked Nanny about Robert, these wouldn't have been discovered until after she died." I shook my head. "Maybe not even then, because I can see me and my sisters tossing out all this stuff, never going through it, thinking it was just part of Nanny's hoard."

His expression changed from wide-eyed with excitement to something entirely different. Something deep and dark and—*gulp*—wild.

He repeated my name, and before I could blink, a pair of strong arms wrapped around my waist and a torso I knew was as solid and defined as a redwood tree flattened against the front of me.

He dipped his head, those dreamy eyes dark now with desire, and zeroed in on my own like a laser pointer. Hypnotized by the naked need facing me, I took a breath—a physical and a mental one—and pushed up on my unshod toes until my lips pressed against his.

For a nanosecond, Frayne stilled. The notion that he didn't want this blew across my mind. A beat later and the thought died as his arms tightened and he pulled me fully against his body.

And then kissed me back.

I'd already seen the fabulous body he kept hidden

under his clothes. When his mouth claimed mine and took it prisoner, I discovered another secret about him: the man knew how to kiss.

My head dropped back when one of his hands rose from my waist to cup the back of my neck. I might have initiated the kiss, but Frayne assumed complete control of it. And I gladly, willingly, *thankfully* surrendered. My arms wound around his neck and held on for purchase, and a quick thought filled me that I never wanted to let go.

A groan, deep and savage, heaved up from his chest. He changed the angle of my head with one swift move and bent me even farther back. The forearm, solid and steady across my lower back, was the only thing keeping me upright.

Well, that and the death grip my arms had around his neck.

The edge of the dining room table hit the back of my thighs, hard. A heartbeat later, I was sitting on top of it, those same thighs now spread wide apart with Frayne nestled between them.

His torso wasn't the only thing rock-hard.

He cupped my jaw. In a rhythm that stoked the fire blazing inside me even hotter, he drew lazy lines back and forth across my cheeks with his thumbs. As tender as his touch was, the action made me squirm on top of the table as each little drag of his fingers ricocheted straight down to my core.

My thighs tightened in response and served to pull him in even closer.

His hands dropped down to my waist and slipped under my sweatshirt, then skimmed up my sides to the bottom of my bra. One finger from each hand slipped under the lower edge. My nipples bulleted to two, aching points as the pads of his fingers, coarse and rough, caressed them.

Frayne kissed my temple and murmured my name right before his lips sucked my earlobe between them.

When I gasped, he lifted me from the table, my legs anchored around his waist. His mouth, drawn like a magnet, found its way back to mine.

In the next moment, my back thumped flat up against the dining room wall. Braced against it, held in place by Frayne's hands harboring my backside and the exquisite pressure of his body fully pressing into mine, I increased the hold I had in his hair.

"Cathy," he mumbled against my mouth. "I can't tell you how much I've wanted to kiss you." His lips slid across my cheek, licked the tiny mole at the corner of my mouth, and then found his way home again.

Oh, I had a pretty good idea since I'd been feeling the same way for days.

When his shoulders lifted and his mouth pulled up into a smile, I knew I'd given voice to the words.

"Good to know I'm not the only one." He nuzzled my nose, his heart-stopping grin playing across his face. The dimples I'd only had fleeting glimpses of were deep and darling. The urge to slide my tongue into them was almost unbearable.

Just like the day in the museum basement, I lost all capacity for rational thought when he smiled at me. My heart stuttered, and a tiny tug reverberated through my chest. With his eyes cleared of the haunting shadows and filled now with such intense craving, I knew I was seeing the real Mac Frayne. To know I'd been the one to clear away those sad thoughts he wore like a shield, was empowering.

Then he put his mouth on mine again, and I stopped thinking. I might have even stopped breathing. The only sensation I could experience right then was touch. His. On my skin; across my mouth.

His heart pounded through his shirt, thumping against me. Mine matched his, beat for blessed beat. The only thing separating me from finding the release my body sought was the inconvenience of our clothing. In my head, I did a quick calculation on how fast we could lose what we were wearing.

It wasn't nearly fast enough.

Off in a quiet corner of my mind, a familiar noise rumbled from the next room. When the realization hit that it was the door to the garage opening, my body went stone still. Frayne lifted his head and peered down at me, his forehead trenched with concern.

"Cathy—?"

"Hey sis, where are you?" Colleen called out.

Wordlessly, I uncrossed my legs from around his waist, slammed them to the floor, and pulled my hands from his hair. I was more than a little wobbly when my feet hit the ground.

Confusion mixed with naked lust danced on Frayne's face. When I stumbled, his hands wound around my upper arms to support me.

I shoved against him, but it was like trying to move a brick wall. He didn't budge. When Colleen's voice rang out again, he blinked, pulled back, and dropped his hands, understanding in his gaze.

I bolted around him and tried to put as much distance as I could between us before Colleen waltzed into the room.

"Oh, here you are." Her gaze ran from me to Frayne, her left eyebrow riding up to her hairline in a slow glide of suspicion. I could only imagine what we looked like. My cheeks were screaming with heat and probably resembled two ripe apples in the middle of my face. Frayne slid his hands into his jeans pockets, but his careless slouch couldn't quite pull off the nonchalance I figured he was aiming for.

Before Colleen could pepper me with a thousand questions, I drew first blood.

"Why are you here? Don't you have the afternoon off?"

"I did. Nanny had other plans."

"What?"

With her trademark eye roll, my sister said, "She called me at the crack-ass of creation this morning and asked me to make sure you looked—her words—approachable tonight."

Oh, sweet baby Jesus. Tell me she didn't."

Colleen lifted her hands. In one she held her makeup kit, a see-through bag filled with hair products and equipment in the other. "No can do, sister mine, because she did. And you know when Nanny asks you to do something—"

"It's not a request, it's an order." I slid a side eye at Frayne.

"You're going out," he said, with a nod.

If I weren't so embarrassed about what had just happened, the tightness in his voice would have done wonders for my ego. Before I could respond, Colleen, in typical middle child fashion, butted in.

"She's going to a speed-dating mixer organized by the local matchmaker."

If the floor had opened up right then and there and swallowed me whole, I wouldn't have minded a whit.

Silence bounded around the room. The tiny hairs on the back of my neck shot straight up when Frayne inhaled deeply. I couldn't tell if he was trying to suppress a laugh or if he was surprised by Colleen's words. I lifted my head and turned to him.

It wasn't amusement on his face.

"There really are such things?"

"Speed dates?" Colleen asked.

He tossed her a puzzled squint. "Matchmakers."

"In this neck of the woods there are." My sister has no verbal filters and because she doesn't, tends to talk more than she should.

Frayne shook his head. "Amazing." He turned his attention back to me. His head was tilted in his I'm-going-to-ask-you-a-question posture and there was no way I wanted to get into a discussion about Olivia Joyner, so before he could ask, I said, "You know, we should notify Leigh James about those." I pointed to the journals. "They're the very definition of historical artifacts. They're priceless and should be placed in the subbasement where the temperature and atmosphere are controlled. Plus, as curator, Leigh really needs to know about them."

"I thought you didn't want to tell anyone until we'd gone through everything."

"When it was clothes and yearbooks, I didn't think it would matter. But these"—I indicated the journals again—"are fragile, and I'm afraid they're going to deteriorate in this climate. I'd hate if anything happened to them. Besides, in addition to being temperature controlled, the museum has a powerful magnifier that'll make it easier for you to read them."

Frayne stared at me a moment, and I could tell he was weighing what I'd said.

On one hand, having the documents here at my house where he had total and unobstructed access to them without any time constrictions, such as the museum's closing hours, was one thing. But along with that, I was bending several rules by keeping everything here. Even though no one at the society knew of their existence, it didn't make keeping them a secret the right thing to do.

With a nod, Frayne said, "You're right, of course."

The lack of enthusiasm in his words told me everything I needed to know about how he felt.

"What are you guys talking about?"

I explained about the journals.

"Isn't Leigh still home on bed rest?" Colleen asked.

"Yes."

"Then she's not gonna come running over here to scoop everything up and take it over to the museum tonight. Why don't you keep it all here for now and let him"—she pointed to Frayne with her makeup bag— "go through it while I get you ready. Call Leigh tomorrow. One night won't make any difference. I mean, it's not like the paper's gonna fall into a pile of ash. If it could survive years in Nanny's icky storage locker, another day won't hurt it."

Sometimes it was scary how much sense she could make, considering most of the time she spoke before a thought ever bloomed to fruition in her head.

"Cathy?"

I looked at Frayne. Quiet expectation oozed from

202

him.

With a shrug, I said, "I guess one more night won't hurt. I'll call Leigh myself tomorrow. But," I added as I walked back toward the kitchen, "I don't want to take any chances." I pulled an unopened pair of dishwashing gloves from under my sink. "I remember reading somewhere the oils found on skin can cause damage to antique paper. Wear these."

His lips pulled into a tiny smirk that made my fingers tremble when I handed them over.

"Great minds," he said. "I was about to ask if you had any for the very same reason."

I wanted to ask when the thought had bloomed—when he first kissed me or when he had me against the wall. I kept the question to myself.

"So now that's all settled," Colleen said, "can we get started?"

An hour later, I took one last look at myself in my cheval mirror and nodded.

This was about as good as it was gonna get.

Colleen had brushed, straightened, styled, and then sprayed my hair into a look I was never able to achieve on my own no matter how hard I tried. My curly, kinky, mostly frizzy hair looked nothing like it usually did, but was jet straight, not a curl, a kink, or a frizz in sight. She'd rubbed a balm oozing of tropical coconuts through it and then with a flat iron I swore was heated to a volcanic ash-producing temperature, pulled sections through it until steam floated around my head and my hair was tamed.

"Your hair has never been this long," she said, brushing the ends that now drifted above my waist. "When it's curly, it's so much shorter. And since you wear it pulled back or up most of the time, no one ever sees how long it really is."

"I smell like a pina colada," I said, sniffing the ends.

Colleen laughed. "Not exactly a bad thing."

She'd then proceeded to do all sorts of amazing things to my face.

I was thankful each day all three of us had been blessed with my grandmother's genes and skin. It made keeping my makeup profile low since I didn't need much to cover up any imperfections or wrinkles. Under Colleen's expert hand though, my eyes now popped, my lips were so luscious even I wanted to kiss them, and my skin glowed with dewy freshness.

"If you ever decide to give up wedding planning," I told her while I tugged the one and only little black dress I owned over my hips, "you could make a killing in cosmetology."

While she rubbed her makeup brushes with a clean cloth, she chuckled. "I've had to repair too many faces—brides, mothers, and attendants—over the years when emotions got the better of them and tears were wreaking havoc. No bride wants to look like a raccoon in her pictures. Learning how to do all this"—she swiped her hand across my bathroom counter where she'd set up the tools of her trade—"was a necessity of the job."

"Well, for whatever reason, even I can admit I look good."

"You always look good, Cath. But tonight," she said, stepping behind me to zip up my dress, "you want to look alluring and approachable. That's the reason you're going to this thing, isn't it?" She swiped her hands across my shoulders and then squeezed them.

"In all honesty, I don't know why I'm going. I'm terrified."

"Of what?"

I shrugged and stared at her reflection in the mirror.

Good question.

"I don't know what to expect or what's expected of me, and that's got me a little anxious. I hate walking into something without knowing what's going to happen."

She squeezed my shoulders again and grinned. "You not being in total control of a situation is something I'd pay cash money to see."

I tossed her a stink eye in the mirror.

Her grin grew. "What's going to happen is that, hopefully, you'll have some fun, flirt a little, and unwind for once. Maybe even meet a guy you could see yourself spending some time with. There are worse things, you know, than all that."

What would she have said if I'd admitted I'd already found a guy I wanted to spend some time with, but he came with so much emotional baggage I needed a luggage carrier to cart it all?

Knowing my sister and the fact she could talk about a subject for hours, it seemed wise to keep the thought to myself.

"Well…" She started packing up all her beauty products. "My work here is done. I got you camera ready. What happens next is on you. And BTW, Nanny says to tell you she wants a full rundown tomorrow morning when you pick her up for Mass. 'Tell Number one I want all the deets, as the kids say these days,' she told me before she hung up this morning. So, prepare to be grilled like a raw steak."

On that pleasant note, she kissed my cheek and waved.

I stood, rooted, as I heard her say something to Frayne and then laugh before the kitchen door closed.

"What have you gotten yourself into?" I murmured, shaking my head. After a quick check of my watch, I pulled a small clutch from my bedroom closet and went back downstairs, carrying my kitten heels in one hand.

Frayne was at the dining room table, his glasses one deep breath away from falling off the tip of his nose and the ridiculous yellow gloves on his hands. A wave of such intense desire washed over me, I must have inhaled audibly from its power, because he lifted his head, his gaze connecting with mine over the rim of his glasses.

Surprise turned to confusion and then morphed into a hooded, wicked, smoldering stare. Unshod, my toes curled into the carpet for support. Frayne's gaze never left mine as he rose in one fluid motion, tugged the gloves off, then tossed them on his now-empty chair. He shoved his glasses up on his head, pushing the moppy fringe back from his face, letting me see the full force of the desire drenching his eyes.

Holy Mother.

I stood rooted, *paralyzed*, as he moved toward me. My clutch in one shaking hand, my shoes in the other, I couldn't have moved if Lucas Alexander had barreled into the room, gun drawn as he chased a criminal, and ordered, "Get down!"

Frayne reached out and caressed a stand of my hair

between his thumb and index fingers.

"Your hair is so long when it's straight." His voice was a whisper.

"I-I've been meaning to get it cut. Shorter, you know? But"—I lifted a shoulder—"no time."

Nanny's disapproving voice shouted in my head, *For pity's sake, Number One. Get a grip.*

"Don't," Frayne commanded, his brow grooving. "Don't ever cut it. It's beautiful." He dropped the tendril, took a tiny step closer. "You're beautiful, Cathy."

My heart pounded against my ribs. There was no way on earth he couldn't hear it. His gaze held so much intent as his finger came up to stroke my jaw, move up my cheek, and then slide around my neck.

That small space separating our bodies? Yeah, it was pretty much obliterated as we each inched in closer.

Frayne dipped his head while I lifted up on my still curling toes, our mouths a fraction from coming together. My brain was silently high-fiving what was about to happen, when the spell was broken by the scream of my front door bell.

Frayne startled, frowned, and murmured, "Not again," while I dropped back down, flatfooted.

"That's my ride," I said, regret drenching me.

He dropped his hand and then folded both of them into his pants pockets, a look of annoyance mixed with disappointment scowling his face.

"Hey, you look nice." Olivia smiled when I opened the door. She gave me a complete head-to-toe eye rake. "You all ready for this?"

She'd offered to drive me to the event when she'd

convinced me to attend, to free me up to have a glass of wine or a cocktail if I wanted one.

After a quick hug, her gaze drifted past my shoulder to spy Frayne. I couldn't quite tell if her concentrated wide-eyed perusal was professional interest or feminine intrigue.

I made the introductions, annoyed when Olivia's hand stayed in his a beat more than I thought it should have. I explained, briefly, why Frayne was in town.

When I excused myself to get my coat from the hall closet, I heard her ask, "Is your wife with you while you're conducting your research?"

"No," he answered. I waited a heartbeat to see if he'd elaborate.

He didn't.

Olivia's face was calm, her professional smile in place when I returned.

"I don't know how long this will be," I told Frayne while I shrugged into my warm coat. Before I could get one arm into a sleeve, he was behind me, assisting me. A noise remarkably like a purr whirred from Olivia.

My cheeks burned. "But you can stay and continue working if you want. Lock up when you leave, though, okay? Since I don't have George anymore, I'm a little more diligent about not leaving the house open than I used to be."

He nodded, flicked a glance at Olivia, and then back at me. I got the distinct impression he wanted to say something, but didn't, because of her presence.

"I'll remember."

"It was lovely meeting you," Olivia told him as she slipped her leather gloves back on. "Enjoy your…research."

Just as I belted myself into her warm car, she said, "Well, I never expected to find a man at your place. And such an adorable one, at that."

"His research is intense."

Honestly, could I sound any more lame?

"Intense, is it?" She cocked her head in my direction, a knowing smile on her perfectly plump lips.

I hummed a response, praying she'd let it go. I was in no mood to be interrogated. I was due to be cross-examined enough in the morning by Nanny. From a family member, I would accept it. Not so much from a fringe friend like Olivia.

A seductive chuckle filled the front of the car. "Okay. I can see why you're such a good lawyer. Since you're not gonna indulge my curiosity, let me give you a little rundown on what you can expect tonight."

Chapter 12

The lights were still on inside the house when Olivia dropped me back home three hours later.

"I don't want you to be discouraged, Cathy," Olivia said as I unbuckled my seatbelt. "This was just your first event."

And if I had anything to say about it, it was my last.

"Tonight was a mish-mash of personality types and age groups. I invited you so you could get a feel for what's involved in the process. I didn't expect you to meet or connect with anyone. We need to get together privately so I can figure out the type of man you're interested in. Then, I can set up something in the future more to your taste level."

My *taste* level? Good Lord. If tonight was any indication, there were no men out there who even came close to an appetizer much less a main course.

"Liv, I don't know if I'm ready for this. I'm busy with the practice, handling Nanny's affairs." I swiped my gloved hand in the air. "I'm not sure I have the energy to be involved at the moment."

She smiled and nodded. "Going out to dinner or a movie with a nice guy doesn't mean you have to sign a marriage contract, Cath. According to Fiona, all you do is work."

"Well, yeah. Because I'm busy."

Duh.

"I get that. But you can take a break every now and again, you know. Just think about it," she added when I opened my mouth again, ready to protest.

Resigned, I nodded.

"I'll call you in a few days, and we can grab some lunch, okay?"

"Sure," I said.

The house was lit and warm when I walked through the front door. I thought Frayne had left the lights on so I wouldn't come home to a dark, empty house. The moment I closed the door behind me, I realized I was wrong, because the house wasn't empty at all.

Mac Frayne was seated at my dining room table, a laptop opened in front of him.

"You're still here."

Why that blue-eyed and befuddled stare meeting me through those thick lenses was such a turn on was a mystery I didn't think I'd ever solve, but the moment his dazed gaze zeroed in on me and then cleared, his eyes widening, then narrowing, my legs got a little wobbly and my pulse jumped.

He tugged the glasses off and tossed them onto the table, his gaze never wavering from my face.

"And you're back early," he said, rising.

I draped my coat over my forearm, kicked off my shoes, and shrugged. "It wasn't supposed to be a long, drawn-out evening."

Frayne took a few steps toward me, the lines in his forehead grooving deeper. "How was it?"

"Horrible," I said, before I could stop myself. I shook my head as I moved toward the hall closet.

"That's unfair," I added, as I hung up my coat. "It wasn't horrible, as much as something not for me."

I turned and barreled into him. His hands shot out and braced my upper arms.

"*Jesus.* You don't make a sound when you move."

"A lifetime of apartment living," he said. Once I was sure-footed and guaranteed not to fall into him again, he lowered his hands.

If I'd had any nerve, I would have asked him to put them back. Instead, I swallowed, turned, and walked toward the kitchen, as he asked, "Why wasn't it something for you?"

I ignored the question. "I'm starving. Have you had anything to eat?"

I wasn't surprised when he followed me.

"Not since lunch at the inn. Maureen had soup and sandwiches today, which, like everything else she's served since I've been here, were delicious."

"Mo only knows how to do delicious." I peeked inside my fridge. "And speaking of..." I pulled out a glass container. "This is fried chicken she gave me this morning. Want some?"

He leaned a hip against the counter and cocked his head. "You don't mind sharing?"

"We both have to eat." I put the mashed sweet potatoes she'd sent along in a microwave bowl, then set the timer. "I hope you like your chicken cold because I'm in no mood to wait for the oven to heat."

That darling little curl popped up in the corner of his mouth. "Cold is fine."

"Did you read any more of Josiah's diaries?" I asked while I pulled plates from the cabinet.

When he didn't answer, I looked over at him. His

quizzical head cock was in place again.

"What?"

"I'm curious why you won't answer my question."

I stared at the microwave, taking a moment to formulate my answer.

"The whole concept of dating is alien to me. I knew Danny since the second grade, and we got married when we were eighteen. He was the only guy I ever went out with, and it wasn't even what anyone would consider dating, since we'd been together forever. Having to start all over at this age is"—I lifted one shoulder—"mentally exhausting."

"Why did you agree to go, then?"

"Because, as my grandmother succinctly put it, it's time to move on."

"And you thought hiring a matchmaker was the way to meet someone?"

"I didn't seek Olivia out. I kind of got railroaded into it."

I explained how the situation came about while I put the food on the kitchen table. Once seated, I continued. "Before I knew it, I'd agreed to go to tonight's"—I waved my hand in the air—"thing."

"So, again, why wasn't it for you? I don't know a lot about speed dating, but from what I've heard, it's popular among millennials. Along with right-swipe hookups." The jagged shake of his head told me all I needed to know how he felt about the way people met these days.

"And that's the problem." I pointed my sweet-potato-laden fork at him. "I'm in the wrong age bracket. Call me old-fashioned, but I prefer to meet someone and get to know them organically and over time, not try and stuff the story of my life into three minutes before an egg timer beeps. Even though I didn't participate, I was tense and stressed watching the others who were. It all seemed…desperate to me."

I stopped, mortified I'd admitted it, because in truth, that's what I'd been feeling watching the group tonight.

From the moment we'd arrived at the restaurant, I could tell I'd made a big mistake. The women present were all older than me, had hungry, hopeful gleams in their eyes, and when they caught sight of me, a few of their stares turned hostile. I was all set to beat a hasty retreat when Olivia's hand at the small of my back propelled me forward.

Part of the restaurant had been cordoned off, a half-dozen tables for two set up in a semicircle. Six women, six men, I assumed.

What was that saying about what happened when you assumed something?

A quick glance back at the hostility bowling my way and I realized it wasn't because of my outfit or my age, but the fact I had the wrong chromosomes.

With me included, there were eight women. I was better at words than math, but even a five-year-old knew that left a smaller number of men.

With a gentle prod, Olivia shoved me toward the gaggle of women. For the first time in my life, I understood and sympathized with how Daniel must have felt walking into the lion's den.

"Ladies," I said, with a head bob and a forced smile.

Silence came back at me. I could stare down the most antagonistic of witnesses in a courtroom without flinching, but for some reason, all my courage flew south as these women glared at me through overly made-up, amateurly applied smoky eyes.

I swallowed the golf ball of fear in my throat.

"How's everyone doing tonight?" I asked.

Lame, I know, but I was truly out of my element.

"You're new," a voice said. "Haven't seen you before."

"Y-yes. I'm a...friend...of Olivia's." If they thought I posed no dating threat, I figured they wouldn't disembowel me.

"You joining in tonight, then?"

"Just an observer," I assured her.

"Hey, aren't you Fintan O'Dowd's oldest?"

Another quirk of small town living, especially with a well-known parent: everyone knew who you were and who you were related to whether you knew them or not. Since I didn't recognize the woman asking, I nodded.

"Thought you was married." Yup, accused was the correct word.

"I was. I'm a widow. My husband died...was killed. In Afghanistan."

Immediately, their collective animosity flew right out the restaurant's front door. They approached me in a cluster, cooing and clicking their tongues in sad support of my plight.

If I'd known that was all it took to get them to put away their invisible pitchforks and blunderbusses, I'd have led with it.

And yes, I know that's dramatic, but their facial expressions up until then were fifty shades of scary.

A few moments later, Olivia clapped her hands and called us to order.

I stood with her off at the side while she read the rules and held a stopwatch. A small bell sat on the table in front of her. At the first ding, the room went into motion.

The seven women all took their seats while the five men inspected them like hunters evaluating prey, and then made their way to the tables of their choice. I felt bad for the two women who sat solo.

"Don't worry about them," Olivia said, when I voiced my concern. "Everyone will have a chance to meet. You want to sit down at one of the tables and give this a go?"

Having a root canal without anesthesia while simultaneously getting my fingernails removed had more appeal. I declined, nicely, and said I just wanted to watch.

"I imagine living in a smaller community, it's difficult to meet people you don't already know in some capacity," Frayne said after I told him what had happened.

I could add wise and sage to the words I used to describe him.

I nodded.

"So." He took a long pull of water. "You haven't been involved with anyone since your husband was killed?"

"No. I've been busy with my practice, with settling Eileen's estate, with Nanny." To my ears, the excuses sounded lame, much as I feared they had when I'd voiced them to Olivia. "Have you, since your wife died?"

He looked down at his plate, then back up at me. "No."

The haunted shadows were back in his eyes.

"Unlike you, I didn't get married young. I wasn't even considering marriage before Cheyanne came into my life. She was a...force."

There's a description you don't hear every day.

"She was the cover designer for one of your books?"

He nodded. "We met at the publisher's office, discussed the book and her ideas for it. Then she asked me to join her for coffee. Coffee turned to dinner, and within a week she moved into my apartment. Three months later, we were married."

"Wow. Talk about whirlwind romance."

His lips pulled in at the corners. "I don't know if that's how I'd describe it."

"Three months from meet to marriage? Colleen would label that whirlwind, and be thankful she didn't need to plan the details of the ceremony. Nanny Fee would probably sigh—theatrically, because it's Nanny, after all—and say it was a romance novel come to life."

"More responsibility than romance, I'm afraid."

This time I was the one who pulled the head-cock move.

"Cheyanne was pregnant."

"Oh."

"Yes. *Oh*. I did what my parents called the honorable thing and asked her to marry me. In truth, I was surprised when she said yes. Neither one of us was in love with the other."

He took a long pull of his water while I digested that little piece of info.

"I told her I fully supported whatever she wanted to do with the baby, but I was delighted when she told me she was having it. After we got married and Mabel came along, our lives were, I thought, content."

Until she died in a car crash with her lover in the front seat, her daughter in the back.

"Anyway." He shook his head as if clearing it. "Since I've gotten out of rehab, I've been putting one foot in front of the other every day. Doing everything I can *not* to fall apart and start drinking again. Having this commission is helpful in keeping my mind occupied with something other than the accident and the aftermath. Plus it's gotten me out of New York and my apartment."

In a weird kind of way, our lives were very similar. He'd lost his family, discovering a devastating secret with their deaths, and I'd lost my husband to enemy fire. The difference was I'd already known the secret Danny had kept from me before he died.

"Memories don't have to be sad," I said, rising, my empty plate in my hand, and walked to the sink. "My grandmother taught us remembering the good stuff from the past is helpful in moving us all forward."

This time when I turned around, I wasn't startled when he was right behind me.

After placing his plate and utensils alongside mine in the sink, he leaned back against the counter, dropped his hands into his pants pockets, and shot me that adorable head tilt, his gaze piercing. "Your grandmother is a wise woman."

"About most things." I shook my head. "Some would call her overly involved in her granddaughter's lives."

"I envy you that."

My heart broke a little for him. From what he'd

said, and what I'd surmised, his wife and daughter had been his world, his parents uninvolved. He'd mentioned no friends other than his agent. What a sad existence, to be so alone.

Maybe it was the wistful pitch in his voice or the feeling of loneliness lacing it that I understood so well. Maybe it was what Colleen had called the saddest eyes she'd ever seen. Or maybe it was the way he took care with, and cared about, everything except himself. Whatever emotion sparked it, I gave voice to the question plaguing me all evening.

"I need to ask you something."

"Okay."

I licked my lips and, as a shout-out to Nanny, girded my loins. "At Shelby's office, you told me you'd wanted to kiss me that day in the museum but hadn't because I was married."

His brows tugged together as he nodded. "At the time I thought you were. And like I said, there are rules about things like that."

I returned his nod.

He tilted his head a bit.

I swallowed and took a chance. "Do you still want to?"

"Kiss you?"

"Yes."

He huffed out a breath, ran his hands through the hair at his temples, and then folded his arms across his chest. "More than I want to take my next breath." With a swift headshake and mirthless laugh he added, "I think I proved it before your sister arrived."

The answer I'd hoped for. "Okay, then."

Before I lost all my nerve, I closed the distance

between us, unfurled his arms, and hooked them around my waist like I'd dreamed of doing earlier.

His eyes narrowed. "Cathy?"

With my own hands flattened on top of his chest, his heart banging against them, I told him, "I'm no good at games, Mac. I never learned how to play them. I'm a simple girl, so I'll say this plainly."

I took a breath, my gaze locked on his. Neither of us blinked. Or moved.

"I want to kiss you, too. For the record, I want to do a whole lot more than kiss you. But I'd like to start there and see where we go."

"You—what?"

Actions, I've always felt, speak volumes. Instead of clarifying with words, I showed him what I meant.

And what I wanted.

The moment my lips pressed against his, my feet left the floor as Mac lifted me up fully against him. One firm tug and I wound my legs around his waist as I'd done the last time I was in his arms, the hem of my cocktail dress riding high up on my thighs to my hips.

With my butt supported and cradled in his warm palms, Mac turned and sat me down on the counter, stepping into the space between my thighs. He never broke contact with my lips.

Now that I'd had a sampling of how delicious he tasted and what an accomplished master he was at the art of kissing, I wanted to learn more. My head fell back as he changed the angle of the kiss and delved deeper, his tongue taking possession of mine, our breaths blending.

Pulling back from the mind-blowing kiss, his forehead grooved, his eyes squinted in the corners as he peered so intently at me he had to be able to glimpse my soul.

"Cathy." His hands cupped my jaw.

Every nerve in my body was spliced raw from his touch. I squirmed on the cold countertop and lifted my thighs higher around his waist, tugging him in closer.

"Are you sure this is what you want?"

"What? You?"

When he shrugged, I swear his muscles snapped.

"By your own admission, you haven't been with anyone since your husband died," he said. "Saying I don't want to take advantage of it sounds a little ridiculous and archaic, but I mean it. I want you to be sure this is what you want. That I'm…what you want."

It was my turn to take his face with my hands. When I settled them across his cheeks, he snuggled into them and placed a sweet kiss across one palm. My heart simply sighed.

"I could ask the same thing of you," I said. "Are you sure you want to do this? With me? Do you want…me?"

"I can't find the words to tell you how much." One corner of his delicious mouth lifted as the skin around his eyes pulled in at the corners. "Which is asinine, considering what I do for a living. But yes. I do. I want you. So much."

He touched his forehead to mine and released a sigh filled with such longing, it literally sang through the air between us.

Or maybe that was me.

"Well, then…" I trailed my hand across his jaw, little pleasure pulses tripping across my fingers from the scruff there, and quipped, "It seems both sides are in agreement. I don't see the problem with proceeding."

His face went blank for a moment, and then a quick, free, and utterly charming smile bolted across it. "That sounds an awful lot like lawyer-speak."

"Obviously, because I'm a lawyer. And I'm done talking."

With that, I lifted my chin back up and reclaimed his lips. If I thought about it, I could probably trace this uncharacteristic boldness straight back to Nanny's influence. The woman was nothing if not audacious and daring in her romantic life, two things I've never been nor even considered before meeting this man.

In the time it takes for a finger snap to echo, Frayne skillfully seduced my lips apart and then, with a slow, steady, and determined exploration that left me panting and aching, proceeded to make me forget I was anything other than a woman. Lawyer, daughter, widow, *be damned*.

I was a woman who wanted…craved….*hungered* for the man my legs were wound around. And from the feel of the material straining below his waist against me, he was ravenous as well. I squeezed my thighs tighter.

He dropped his hands to my thighs—my naked thighs—the roughened pads of his fingers pressing into them. Behind his back, my toes flexed.

I slid my hands up and around his shoulders, cupping his neck all the while nipping and sipping at his delicious lips. The thought sailed through me that I could get used to a daily diet of the taste of this man.

Frayne slid his mouth across my jaw, trailing tiny, wet kisses down the column of my throat. When he took my ear lobe between his teeth and bit down, my butt vaulted up from the counter.

"Your skin is like velvet," he whispered as he cuddled my ass in his hands. "I've never felt anything as soft in my life."

"Good genes," I managed to say, while he nuzzled the hollow behind my ear. How I was even able to form a sentence was mind-boggling.

His shoulders shook, and when I pulled back to see his face, my heart stuttered. The dark and sad shadows in his eyes were a memory, replaced now with a glow that turned the pale blue to a brilliant crystal. His mouth was plump and wet—*Holy Mother!*—and the corners were lifted, two deep and adorable dimples crevassing his cheeks. The thatch of hair had fallen across his brow, delicately shading one eye. I reached up and feathered it back with my fingers. My hand settled across his cheek and temple as I did, and once again Frayne nuzzled against it, as if seeking warmth and solace. The gesture was so tender, so damn endearing, I sighed before I could stop myself.

This man, this damaged, mercurial, heartbroken man, stirred a myriad of emotions within me I was powerless to fight against. His abhorrence of my profession provoked anger and outrage. The tenderhearted manner he exhibited toward my grandmother filled me with a sense of intense joy. The single-minded and focused way he went about his research awed and impressed me. And the attention he gave to everything but himself made me want to pull him into my arms, hold on tight, and do everything I could to care for him and show him how special he was.

Frayne touched my heart in ways no man ever had. The realization was both profound and terrifying.

If I'd learned anything in life, though, fear could either paralyze you or propel you into actions you never knew you were capable of.

The kiss he gave me now was gentle and soft, his eyes open and focused on me. A question flashed in them, and I answered it the only way I could.

The only way I wanted to.

I gave him a gentle shove. When he moved, I slid out of his hold and stood, barefoot, on my kitchen floor.

"Come on." I grabbed his hand and tugged him out of the kitchen.

Chapter 13

Without a word, I walked him up the hall stairs to the second floor.

To my bedroom.

The risers sagged and creaked from our ascent. I'd been up and down these stairs thousands of times over the years, and the sounds were white noise to me.

At the landing, I turned left, pulling him along.

Frayne's gaze ran along the wallpapered walls, taking in the dozens of photographs grouped along the hallway. Most were of my sisters, Nanny, and George.

I wondered if he realized there were none of Danny.

Freeing his hand, I entered my bedroom and switched on the bedside light. Frayne stayed at the doorway, his gaze still on me, his head ticked to the side.

"Second thoughts?" The wisecrack was meant to hide the jumble of nerves coursing through me.

"None," he said with a definitive headshake.

There was something in his eyes, though. "What?"

He took a step closer to me. "This is the bedroom you shared with your husband, Cathy. Are you sure you want me—us—to—" He lifted a shoulder.

Add thoughtful and respectful to every other description I'd already assigned to him.

I closed the distance between us and kissed his

cheek.

"After Danny died, I redid this room," I said. "All the furniture, the bed itself, the linens, even the drapes are new. This my room, Mac. Mine alone. George was the only one who ever slept in here with me."

Before I could blink, his heart-stopping grin was back. "Good to know."

I slipped my arms around his waist, kept my gaze connected with his. "You're the only man I've ever invited into this room. The only man I've ever wanted to invite."

He pulled me flat against his body. Right before he took my lips with his again, he whispered, "Also, good to know."

My smile was absorbed by his kiss.

While his lips did wild and wicked things to mine, he shifted and tucked one arm behind my knees, the other across my back and lifted me as easily as he had George when he'd placed him in my car. I've never been what anyone would call a waif, but the effortless way he carried me made me feel as light as a wisp of air.

With one knee bent on the bed, he placed me down in the center of it.

Hovered over me, his weight suspended on his elbows, he said, "I'm gonna ask one more time, because I need to hear you're absolutely sure about this."

I answered him the same way I had before. I pulled his head down and took his mouth with mine.

Every doubt he had must have evaporated, because he kissed me back without any hesitation or worry.

Soon, kissing him wasn't enough. I needed to feel his skin next to mine.

That boldness gene took over again as I slipped my hands under the hem of his pullover and cotton tee and discovered another thing about Mac Frayne: he was a furnace.

My hands slid up and down his back, kneading the tight muscles, reveling in the heat pouring from him. For all the rangy, trim physique his clothes covered, the actual man was a mass of concrete, hard and carved to sculpted perfection. Feeling all that defined brawn against my hands was one thing, but now I needed to see it.

I gripped the bottom of both garments and tugged them upward. Mac got the idea of where I was leading pretty quickly. He pulled up from kissing me, a cheeky smirk across his face, grabbed the sweater and tee, and in a move so smooth I gasped, yanked both over his head with one hand, then tossed them over his shoulder.

"You've done that before," I said. I smoothed my hands up from his trenched abdomen to trail across the perfection of his pecs. His nipples were two flat chocolate disks, until I pinched them between my fingers. They pebbled into solid points under my touch.

Settled on his knees, his hands fisted on top of them, he stared down at me through the wild thatch of hair flopping across his brow.

"Your turn," he said. Before I could form a response, he slid his hands around my back and dragged down my zipper. I shot my arms up, and he yanked my cocktail dress up over my head, then casually tossed it to join his clothes on the floor behind us.

I'd partnered a strapless black push-up bra and matching thong to wear under the dress. The bra dipped low on my breasts, but provided adequate coverage and the support needed.

When Frayne's gaze dragged down to my torso, I swear his eyes started to glow. The blue in his irises changed from crystal, to azure, to the color of ripened blueberries in the rain as his heavy-lidded gaze trailed across the swell of my breasts. Against the satin cups of the bra, my nipples throbbed, tender and taut, from the heat in his glare. He softly trailed the roughened pads of his fingertips across the flesh peeking up from the bra's top edge. My eyes closed and my head fell back as he dipped one finger below the edge to graze across a swollen nipple.

I think I gasped. Or maybe it was a moan. I couldn't be sure because I was having an out-of-body experience from how amazing his touch felt against my skin.

The bra had a front clasp, and with the next breath I took, he had it unhooked, my breasts now displayed bare before him. With a hand plumping each, he kissed one, then gave equal time to the other.

By now, I'd lost the ability to support myself on my elbows, so I'd flattened down on the bed, Frayne straddling me.

I arched up when he sucked one of my nipples into his mouth, simultaneously rolling the other between his fingers.

"You taste like vanilla drenched in sweet cream," he whispered. "Delectable and delicious."

His tongue lapped back and forth across the hollow separating my breasts, then, with clear intention, began trailing downward. He stopped at the edge of one hip, his hot breath warming my skin when he said, "This needs to go." I wasn't given the time to ask what he meant before he pulled the band of the thong between his lips and drew it downward, over my thighs and calves. The subtle plop of it hitting the rest of my clothes rang out, clear as a bell.

A nervous laugh started in my throat and then died quickly when his mouth came back up and swept across my mound, nuzzling my thighs apart in a silent entreaty.

Happily, I complied.

"Gorgeous," he murmured while he skimmed one finger down the long, wet length of me. Fireworks of light exploded behind my closed eyes in the next moment as his tongue mimicked the move and then slid into me.

Then pulled out.

And slid back in again.

With my hands fisted in the sheets so I wouldn't fly off the bed, it took all the control I could summon not to scream. Somewhere between the time he sucked my clitoris into his mouth and slipped two fingers inside me, my control snapped, wrested from me to escape in one long, uncontrollable cry of release.

In all my memories of having sex, I couldn't remember one time an orgasm had occurred so fast and thunderously, nor made my entire body shake with such pleasure. When I was able to take a full breath again, I opened my eyes, the vision hazy around the edges but clear enough to witness the delighted smile covering Frayne's face.

"Do you have any idea how beautiful you are right now?" he asked.

My entire body flushed from the compliment.

Frayne stretched and pressed his lips against mine.

The salt and musk taste of myself on him ignited those tiny pulses again. With each pull and tug of my tongue, I writhed and fidgeted beneath him, the new throbbing in my pelvis combined with the aftershocks of my orgasm growing almost unbearable, seeking relief, begging for release.

"Take these off," I commanded between kisses, slapping at his jeans.

He rose in a fluid line and stood next to the bed, his gaze locked with mine, a mind-bending grin traipsing across his lips. The jagged, metallic rattle of the zipper slowly being dragged down over the sizable bulge in his jeans was loud in the silent room. My toes flexed into the sheets at the erotic sound it made. Frayne hooked his thumbs inside the waistband and in one swift jerk, hauled both the jeans and his underwear down. He kicked them off and then stood before me, naked and free.

I wasn't some simpering, fearful virgin, unschooled in the male anatomy. I'd been married, seen a man naked and fully erect with arousal many times.

Many times.

But gazing at the perfection that was McLachlan Frayne was a unique experience. A slim waist slid into narrow hips, the head of his pelvic bones visible on both sides. Two thick, corded, and powerful thighs showed proof he was a runner. Swirls of inky black hair circled his navel and spread downward in a happy trail toward the part making him a man.

I imagine my eyes dilated as I got my first full glimpse of him, because my vision went all kinds of blurry around the edges.

He was magnificent.

Fully erect, his thick penis jutted out and upward, proud and wanting.

The fact it was me he wanted filled me with indescribable joy.

I stretched out my hand to his, and with a gentle tug, he was back down on the bed, propped up on an elbow next to me. My newly discovered boldness gene took over. I pushed him down to lie flat on his back, straddled him, and held him in place with my hands on his shoulders.

"Cathy?"

"Shhh." I bent forward and nipped at his chin, then licked the column of his throat down to the notch on his neck.

He swallowed—hard.

"Your turn," I whispered against his skin.

I trailed a long, slow line of butterfly kisses down his neck, across those powerful pecs, and then skimmed my tongue over and through the sculpted trenches in his abdomen. Frayne's washboard abs contracted at my touch, and heat flooded my body when he fisted the sheets underneath him the same way I had.

Who knew dominance could be such an aphrodisiac? I certainly hadn't, but with each ragged breath Frayne dragged in, the knowledge I could make this man tremble was awe inspiring.

I dawdled over one hip, nibbling at the prominent bone with my lips, while my hand drifted down and skated across his straining shaft. Encircling it, I tightened my fist and gave him a none-too-subtle squeeze, while sliding my hand up and over the moistened tip. This time, I drew a moan along with the deep inhale from him. His thighs contracted, lifting his butt from the bed. His response pushed me to do it again.

And again.

Many times, in fact.

"Stop." His hand covered mine.

I glanced up at his face and almost came again on the spot. There was no doubt about it now—his eyes *were* glowing.

"Why?"

Frayne shifted as I let go my grip. "Because I want to make you come again, and I want to be inside you when you do."

There was no way I could hide the full-on body blush his words elicited. Even in the subdued light shining from my bedside lamp, it had to be visible.

Frayne grabbed my hand, and with one swift shift, I was on my back again. He covered my body with the length of his while his knees nuzzled between my legs, shifting them apart.

In a move one of Nanny's romance novels would have described as wanton, I spread my legs.

Frayne groaned again. "Cathy, wait."

Balanced on his elbows, he pressed his forehead against mine, closed his eyes, and took a breath. Something about that breath gave me a moment of pause.

Oh, *good Lord.* He'd decided he didn't want to do this with me after all.

"What's…what's wrong?"

His eyes took their time opening. A small grin tugged on one corner of his mouth. "I hadn't planned on this happening between us tonight," he said. "Thrilled though I am that it is," he added, the other corner of his mouth lifting, too. "I'm not…prepared."

I squinted up at him.

He must have read my befuddlement because he clarified, "I don't have a condom." His eyes drifted closed again for a moment, then opened. With a tiny shake of his head, he told me, "I don't routinely carry them in my wallet or my back pocket like other guys do. I never have."

That little confession sang right to my heart and went a long way in showing me the type of man Frayne truly was.

"I have nothing to protect you with," he said, on a sigh.

"Move," I ordered, shoving at his shoulders. When he gave me another of those head tilts, I repeated the word.

He sat back on his haunches, and I scooted toward the edge of the bed.

For Christmas last year, Colleen had informed me it was time to leave—in her words—the land of the solitary widow and start dating. She was the one who'd gifted me the strapless bra and thong set I'd worn to tonight's shindig and, along with it, a jumbo box of condoms. I'd never used them during my marriage since I'd always been in baby-hopeful mode whenever Danny was stateside. Colleen, knowing I'd never venture to buy them on my own, thought it was always better to be prepared should a *situation* (her word) arise.

If she'd been born a boy, she would have made an excellent scout leader.

Well, this appeared to be the very definition of a *situation*. She'd been the one to put the box in my bedside drawer in the event I should need it.

I slipped my hand into the drawer and slid out a strip of condoms from the box. Since I'd never used them before, I'd assumed—incorrectly—they were all individual packages. Nope. Five condom packets made up a strip.

Frayne laughed when he looked down at my hand. "Should I say thank you for the vote of confidence or be terrified I won't live up to your expectations?"

That full body blush made itself known again. I closed my eyes and sighed. "Sorry. New box and, well…"

He kissed my shoulder and eased the strip from my hand. At the sound of a packet being torn open, my face heated as if I'd been thrown into an oven.

How many other thirty-nine-year-old women blush at the sound of a condom wrapper tearing? I'd bet my IRA the number was a big fat zero.

Frayne's hand cupped the back of my neck. I opened my eyes and ventured a look over my shoulder at him, wondering if he'd think me as pathetic as I thought myself.

That shock of hair I was beginning to love hid his forehead and one eye. The other—thank you, Jesus— was still glowing with desire.

"Where were we?" he asked. "Oh, yeah. Right here."

In a heartbeat I was on my back again, Frayne settled above me. I'd caught a glimpse of the condom, now in glorious place, before he kissed my cheek and then moved back to my lips.

In almost no time at all, he had me panting and writhing again, silently begging for release.

Or maybe I wasn't so silent, because his shoulders

shook and he whispered in my ear, "Well, since you ask so politely."

And then he slipped inside me.

Both of us turned to stone.

In all honesty, I think I stopped breathing, too. My heart was still banging a mile a minute, though, as was Frayne's. The pulse visibly thrumming in his temple was evidence of it.

It had been a long, long, absurdly long time since my body had known the feel of a man inside me. I wasn't an eighteen-year-old virgin on her wedding night again. My body, though, thought I was.

Frayne, bless him, took his time, letting my body adjust. Gently, he pulled back, then was able to push through even farther.

"You feel...amazing." His voice burned with smoke, raspy and thick with emotion.

"You do, too."

I crossed my ankles behind his back, opening even farther for him.

Pretty soon we weren't moving slowly anymore. As we found the delicate balance and rhythm that gave us each the most pleasure, I knew I was close to coming undone again. The tense muscles of Frayne's back contracted under my hands and a low growl bayed from the back of his throat.

"Cathy, open your eyes. Look at me," he commanded.

The moment I did, and my gaze lit on those glowing crystals, my entire body exploded with release. Frayne's lips pulled back in an arrogant, triumphant gleam, and then he followed me over the cliff with a final, long, and thunderous cry.

Chapter 14

I woke when something shifted next to me. Confusion clouded my brain. When a warm, solid arm wound around my waist and cuddled me close against a heat-blasting furnace, the confusion cleared, and my mind came awake in a heartbeat.

"Mmm," Frayne nuzzled against my ear. "You feel good."

Good didn't even begin to describe how I felt.

Relaxed, peaceful, *sated* were more accurate words. I should have been exhausted. If either of us had gotten more than an hour's sleep total, it was saying something. During the night, we'd whittled the strip of five condoms down to two.

Frayne pulled me closer, and I wiggled my butt against a very impressive morning erection. His hand drifted down my belly to cup me.

It was a little embarrassing how quickly I spread my legs to give him access.

In no time at all, we shaved another condom from the strip.

Frayne kissed me and then went into the bathroom while I stretched my arms over my head and arched my back, my curled toes digging into the mattress. I'd forgotten how revitalizing sex could be, how alive it could make you feel, inside and out.

I sighed and looked over at the alarm clock on my

bedside table.

"*Oh, crap.*"

I flung back the covers and jumped out of bed, banging my shin on the bed footboard. With a loud "ouch," I stumbled toward the bathroom, and collided with Frayne as he was exiting. He grabbed my upper arms and halted me, worry creasing his brow.

"What's the matter?"

"I overslept," I said, wrenching out of his hold. "I need to be at Angelica Arms in twenty minutes to take Nanny to church," I added, switching on the shower. I secured my hair into a messy knot with a scrunchie I'd left on the counter, while he stood in the doorway, staring at me. "I don't feel like listening to a lecture if I show up late."

The water was still coming up to temperature when I stepped into the shower. Ignoring it and Frayne, I yanked the curtain, my teeth chattering from the cold spray raining down on me.

"I'll get dressed," I heard him say.

In record time, I was washed and put together for the day, my hair pulled back into a ponytail. I'd assumed Frayne had, as he'd said, dressed and gone back to the inn. I sprinted down the stairs and came to a full stop when I found him in the kitchen, his coat on, a steaming mug in his hand.

"I thought you'd left."

He shook his head. "Here." He handed me the mug.

"You made me tea?"

He shrugged. "I microwaved it since you're running late. I remember how you take it from when we were at the diner."

Could a heart sing? If so, mine did right then and there. This lovely man remembered something as trivial as how I took my tea after watching me fix it once. Danny never even remembered that, and I'd been married to him for almost twenty years.

Did I say sing? Hell, my heart belted out a chorus of hallelujahs and notes worthy of celestial cherubim.

With the mug in one hand, I slid the other up over his cheek. As he had before, he covered it with his own hand, cuddled into it, and pressed a sweet kiss to my palm.

Those angels started vocalizing again.

"Mac." There was so much I wanted to say to him, so much I needed to say. Time, though, wouldn't let me.

"I'll head back to the inn while you're at church," he said. "Can I...come over later? I know you're going to call the curator today, but can I go over a few more things before you do?"

In truth, I'd forgotten all about that.

"Of course. I have to drop Seldrine off at her meeting, but I should be home by twelve."

He nodded.

Even though I needed to leave, all I really wanted to do was to stand here with this man and forget the rest of the world and all its obligations existed.

Well, more than stand, if truth be known.

Frayne sighed and squeezed my hand. "You'd better get going. Your grandmother's waiting."

I rolled my eyes. "She hates being late. For anything. And never lets us forget it if one of us is."

The quick grin he tossed me was toe-tingling. He gave my cheek a quick kiss and said, "See you later."

Then he was gone.

****

"Are ya not feelin' well, Number One? You've been awful quiet this mornin' and ya look as if you had a fight with your pillow."

Nanny was her usual observant self this morning. There was no way, though, I could share the reason I hadn't slept much.

"Just lots of things going on up here." I swirled my finger around me head. "Nothing to worry about."

"So Olivia's event was a bust?" Colleen asked as she sipped her tea.

We were all seated in Maureen's little private alcove kitchen off the main one she cooked in for the inn, having a late breakfast. Colleen and Slade had joined Maureen, Nanny, and me after I'd brought Nanny from morning mass. My younger sister shuttled back and forth between the kitchens, assisting her helper, Sarah, serve breakfast to her guests.

I'd arrived at the nursing home with a few minutes to spare, which didn't stop Nanny from commenting on my tardiness. In the car she'd grilled me—as Colleen had assured me she would—about Olivia's event. I was truthful in my replies, even making her laugh when I described the men who'd attended. She'd patted my hand and declared, "There now, darlin', you'll meet someone. I've no doubt of it. 'Tis a catch, you are, for sure. Beauty, brains, and a bangin' bod you have, as the kids say these days."

Her faith in me warmed my heart and went a long way in boosting my ego.

"A bust for me, anyway," I told my sister. "But I didn't go there intending to meet anyone. It was more a

239

way to start. I'm having lunch with Olivia sometime this week to discuss…other alternatives."

"She's got a great track record," Maureen said while she went around the table refilling our cups. "Colleen, isn't one of your upcoming brides a match of hers?"

My sister nodded while she swallowed the forkful of pancakes she'd taken.

"Speaking of brides and weddings, we have some news," Slade said. He slid his hand into Colleen's and smiled his charming, crooked smile at her.

The entire table went silent.

"We've set a date," Colleen announced. "It's a bit sooner than we originally planned, but there are…" She waved a hand in the air.

"Mitigating circumstances," Slade, the law professor, added.

I had a pretty good idea what those circumstances were.

"Well, don't be keepin' us waitin' with bated breath, Number Two," Nanny said. "I'm not getting any younger sitting here, ya know. Tell us, lass. Tell us."

The smile Colleen gave the man she'd pledged her heart to was so filled with love, tears batted behind my eyes.

"Well, we'd thought about a September wedding because the fall colors will be beautiful around here," she said, "but we're moving it up to the beginning of April."

"That's barely three months away." Maureen's surprise mimicked my own.

"I know. I had a cancellation, though, on a weekend where I only had one wedding booked. It seemed a little…serendipitous."

"Still, it's not a lot of time to plan the shindig you've always dreamed of," Maureen said.

"Yeah, well, if we wait any longer, my dress won't fit."

"The way you've been shovelin' in those pancakes, Number Two, I've no doubt of it." Nanny's eyebrows rose as she thrust her chin toward Colleen's plate. "Eatin' like a starving' man, you are."

"Maureen's good cooking isn't the reason my dress won't fit, Nanny," Colleen said, her cheeks blooming with the rosy red hue our fair skin was tormented by. "And I'm not the one's who's starving all the time." She ran a hand over her abdomen.

"I knew it!" I jumped up from my seat and threw my arms around her, Maureen quick on my heels.

"When are you due?" I asked, reaching over and squeezing Slade's hand.

"The beginning of August," he said.

"So you'll be"—I did a quick math calculation in my head—"about four months in April."

Colleen nodded.

"I'm gonna be an auntie." Maureen's eyes filled.

"You're not the only one," I said.

They'd already spoken to our parish priest and reserved the church.

"The reception will be here," Colleen said. To Maureen she added, "Okay?"

"I'd be royally pissed if you decided on any place else."

I tossed a quick peek at the one person at the table who hadn't squealed in glee. Nanny was, for her, unnaturally quiet. The fact she hadn't scolded Maureen for her choice of words was abnormal behavior for our strict grandmother. A shaft of light flittered across her face from the bay window in the kitchen to reflect a shimmering in her eyes.

"Nanny?" Colleen said. "Are you okay?"

"Well, Colleen Sinead. How do you think I am? With news such as this?"

Uh-oh. Whenever Nanny used one of our Christian names it was usually wise to drop into a runner's stance and sprint for the wilds of the New Hampshire woods.

Colleen's bright smile dropped, a nervous grimace replacing it.

"Um, happy for us?" she offered.

Nanny's pale eyebrows tugged together. "Happy, is it? Yer informin' me I'm about to be a great-grandmother. And you without the benefit of a marriage license to your name, I'll add."

The four of us sat perfectly still, breaths held in anticipation.

"You weren't raised that way, putting the cart afore the horse, as it were. How do you think I should be feeling about that, I ask ya?"

"Fiona." Slade's tone was as hard as steel. If I'd ever had the chance to be on the opposite side of a courtroom against him, I'd be very cautious if that tone crept into his voice.

Nanny's shimmering eyes began to twinkle as a tiny crease pulled at the edge of her lips. In the next second, she let go with a full belly laugh. "Had you goin' there for a mite, didn't I?"

Four loud, collective exhales drifted through the air.

Nanny reached across the table and took Colleen's

and Slade's hands in hers. "It's more delighted than I can put to words, I am," she told them. "I love the both of ya from the moon and back. A baby of your own is about the best news you can give an old woman. It's a blessing on your lives, and to those of us who love ya dearly."

Tears waterfalled down Colleen's cheeks as she and Slade both rose and hugged Nanny.

Maureen shot me a napkin to dab my eyes.

"Hey. Why's everyone blubbering?" Lucas Alexander asked as he walked into the kitchen, his hat in one hand, a Styrofoam coffee cup in the other.

"I don't remember calling for the law," Nanny said, her back straightening as she arched her brows at him. Nanny and Lucas had a long, problematic relationship, stemming from the multiple times he'd arrested her over the years for civil disobedience. Coupled with the fact that he'd been a student in her religious education classes as a kid and then a de facto member of our family since he'd been Danny's best friend, he was a fixture in our lives, something Nanny took exception to when he'd become the police chief.

"Mrs. Scallopini." He smiled at her. "Always a pleasure. You're looking exceptionally lovely this morning."

Nanny squared her shoulders, clicked her tongue, but I swear she was fighting the urge to grin back at him. I've always suspected she cares more for him than she lets on.

"Stop flirting with my grandmother," Maureen said, taking the cup from his hand and replacing it with one of her own, filled with fresh coffee. "Why are you here?"

My sister was another one I suspected cared for our police chief more than she let on.

"Thanks." He took a long chug of the coffee, closed his eyes and sighed. "No one makes coffee like you do, Maureen. Now, answer my question first," Lucas said, looking about. "Why the communal waterworks?"

Colleen and Slade shared their news.

"I need to speak to Cathy, and I knew she'd be here after mass this morning," he told us after congratulating them. "You got a couple minutes?" he asked me.

I excused myself and walked into the hallway with him for some privacy. After we spoke about an upcoming case, we went back into the kitchen.

To my surprise, Mac Frayne was seated at the table, a look of bemusement on his face, a mug of my sister's coffee in his hand.

Where Nanny had already commented on how sleep-deprived and tired I looked, the same couldn't be said for Frayne. His pale eyes were bright and free of those tormenting shadows, the skin at the corners creased as he smiled. His color was high and robust, his body relaxed. An open smile I could only term *enigmatic* graced his face as he gazed upon my grandmother. Her hand was draped across his forearm, and her fingers squeezed it coquettishly, her tiny body leaning toward him while she spoke.

"Ah, Number One, come and sit back down. Me scribe's here."

"The last I heard he's writing Josiah's biography, Nanny. Not yours." I retook my seat opposite her. " 'Morning," I said to Frayne, then quickly picked up my mug.

"Good morning," he replied.

Two hours ago he'd left my bed after a night filled with scorching sex and mutual pleasure—given and received. Multiple times. You'd never have suspected it from the uninflected and casual tone of his greeting. We could have been two strangers, or at best, fringe acquaintances for all the animation in his voice. As he lifted his cup to his lips, though, his gaze lingered on me for a few beats.

I tossed up a silent prayer that I'd been the only one at the table to see and decipher the heated, knowing look he gave me.

From her position standing behind Lucas's chair, Maureen cocked her head and tossed me a raised-eyebrows gander. I ignored it.

"Well, me life is a much more entertainin' and fascinatin' story than that old crackpot's, to be sure," Nanny said.

"No one can argue with that," Lucas mumbled.

"Why's it not soundin' like that's a compliment, young man?"

"Oh, it is, trust me. Your life is nothing if not...entertaining."

Nanny harrumphed.

"The reverend's real story may turn out to be a surprise," Frayne told Nanny.

"What do you mean his *real* story?" Colleen asked. "We all grew up with the nauseatingly boring tale of his life drilled into us at school. I can't tell you how many papers we were all tortured to write about him. What do you know we don't?"

Frayne looked my way, his eyebrows lifting in a question.

245

"Go ahead and tell them."

He did, detailing what we'd discovered amongst Robert's stored possessions.

"Cathy is going to call the museum curator today so we can move the journals there and use their technology to read through Josiah's first-hand accounts."

"About that," I interrupted. "Leigh had her baby last night, and she's gonna be in the hospital for a few days. Father Duncan sent up a prayer of intention for her this morning at mass. It's probably better we leave things as they are until I can find out when she's coming back to work."

"So that means I can continue my research at your house?"

"Yes. With Leigh out of commission for a bit longer, I think it's appropriate."

"Well, now, isn't this an interestin' bit o' news on this morning made for announcements." Nanny's penetrating gaze shot from me, to Frayne, then settled back on me. I knew that look and the inquisitive tone partnered with it well, since I'd heard it enough times growing up. It usually preceded a thorough, intense interrogation C.I.A. officials could learn a thing or two from. "You've been conductin' your research at me granddaughter's home, have ya?"

Frayne nodded.

"Just the two o' ya, ay?"

This time his nod took a little longer coming. "Cathy has been a big help with…everything."

"Interestin'. I didn't know you were keeping all Roger's t'ings at your house, Number One."

"Oh? I didn't mention it?" I tossed her a careless

shrug and sipped my tea.

"No. You didn't. Me body may be agin', darlin' girl, but me memory's as sharp as a knife."

"Goes along with her tongue," Lucas murmured into his cup.

Nanny snuck him a heavy-lidded side eye, to which he smiled cheekily, before she turned her attention back to me.

"It made sense," I said before she could continue with her cross-examination, "since we didn't know what we were dealing with in all those boxes and containers. And there were a lot of them. A whole lot."

"I told ya from the get-go Robert was packrat, darlin'."

"Apples and trees, Nanny, because there's five lifetimes worth of stuff still crammed in your storage lockers, and it doesn't all belong to Robert. I don't think you've ever thrown anything away in your entire life. Clothes, furniture, pictures. How many holiday ornaments and decorations does one person need?"

As a diversion tactic, it proved a good one. Nanny's attention shunted away from grilling me about Frayne to plead her case and need for every item in those lockers.

My sisters tossed each other a knowing look while Nanny rambled on about how many times she'd moved and married during her lifetime, accumulating more possessions with each. They realized exactly what I was doing since they'd apprenticed in the art of Nanny-distraction at my knee.

I let her rant, mentally high-fiving myself, as I nodded in agreement with everything she said. When she stopped to take a well-deserved breath, I rose from the table.

"I need to get you back to the Arms and go pick up Seldrine," I told her.

"We can take her back," Slade offered, after getting the okay from Colleen.

"It'll give us a few more minutes to chat."

"Ah, now, that's the reason you're in the runnin' to be me favorite grandson-in-law, right there, darlin' boy."

"He's going to be your only grandson-in-law," Maureen quipped as she placed a bakery box on the table in front of her, filled with what I guessed were scones for the week.

"Well, it's not for me lack of tryin' to get you all hitched now, is it? Colleen's th' only one of ya who's managed to snag a man. And thank the good Lord above she did. After that ugly business with her previous fiancé, the scion of darkness, I was worried sick she'd never walk down a church aisle."

The reactions around the table to this comment were comical in their diversity. Colleen went beet red, Lucas laughed till he gagged on his coffee, Slade's eyes narrowed at the mention of Colleen's former fiancé (whose name was Harry, not the scion of darkness. Maureen and I called him Vlad because he was a soul-sucker, but Nanny got it confused with a character in a popular book she'd been reading at the time.) Frayne's face was sixteen shades of bewildered as he stared across the table at me.

I mouthed, *I'll explain later*. With that, I thanked Slade, then kissed Nanny's and Lucas's cheeks.

"I'll walk you out," Maureen said, taking my arm and pushing me into the hallway.

When we were out of earshot, she tossed a quick look over her shoulder and whispered, "What's going on?"

I knew what she was asking, but once a lawyer…

"*Duh.* I'm getting my coat."

"Diversion works with Nanny, sis. Not me. You know perfectly well what I mean."

Yeah, I did. Still, old habits were hard to let go of.

I shrugged into my coat and faced her, hoping the expression on my face was blank.

Hands on her hips, Maureen ran her gaze across my features. "You slept with Mac."

Okay, this perceptive talent my little sister possessed was getting annoying.

"Don't deny it." Before I could, she pointed a finger at me. "I knew it the minute he spoke to you. Plus, I saw him when he rolled into the inn this morning and tried to sneak up the stairs. Yesterday's clothes and bed head scream walk of shame."

I closed my eyes and dug deep for calm.

"Cathy?"

"Okay. Yes. Yes, I did. We did. Satisfied?"

"Are you?"

What would it have cost me to admit I was more satisfied than I'd been in a decade? Maybe even my lifetime?

Better to keep it to myself.

"Look, sis." Maureen took my free hand and covered it with both of hers. "You've forced yourself into emotional exile since Danny died. You work, take care of all of us, and do nothing for yourself."

"That's not true. I—"

"It is and you know it."

Because I did, I shrugged.

"I want you to be happy and enjoy your life again. To find a man who loves and deserves you. Who'll cherish you."

"It's not like that between us, Mo. This is just…well, I don't know what it is, really. Forced togetherness? Hormones?" I lowered my voice. "Horniness? I don't know."

Her smile was quick and filled with laughter. "There's nothing wrong with giving into a little lust, you know."

"Truth." I nodded. "I wasn't planning on sleeping with him, though. I didn't even think he liked me."

"The man feels way more than like for you, Cath. You didn't see him come into the kitchen before. When he saw us all sitting there, he tracked the table, searching for you. He looked like a lost little boy when he didn't find you sitting with us. When I told him you were talking to Lucas, his entire body relaxed and he smiled for the first time."

My heart about swelled to breaking.

"Like I said, the man feels something for you."

This time I shook my head while I buttoned my coat. "Maybe."

"No maybe about it. How do you feel about him is the question?"

"Conflicted." The word spilled out before I could prevent it.

Maureen nodded. "I get that. Can I offer a little advice?"

"Since when do you give advice? You hate getting it and never take it when it's tendered."

"True. In this instance, though, I think I can bend

my rule."

I heaved a theatrical, Nanny-worthy sigh. "Go ahead, then."

"Don't overthink what you're feeling, like you do everything else. Just...accept what is. Sleep with the man. Enjoy him, his company. Have a little grown-up fun for once. God knows, you deserve it."

Back in my car, her words echoed in my head. There was no mistaking the longing I'd seen flit by in Frayne's gaze when he saw me. And last night had proved he desired me.

Man, oh, man, had it.

But was it enough?

I wanted children and a life partner. For almost twenty years, I'd been married to a man who'd told me he wanted all those things as well, until an argument forced the truth out of him.

I could admit Mac Frayne touched a space in my heart, even before we'd slept together. I wasn't naïve enough to equate sex with love, though. What we'd shared had been wonderful and freeing, but I wanted to be loved, too. To be in love, and have my love returned.

As I pulled up to Seldrine's house, my head started to pound, and I gave myself a mental shake. Maureen was right. I needed to stop overthinking everything and live in the here and now. Enjoy the moment and the man in it.

Why that was so difficult for me was the question.

Chapter 15

After a more thorough shower than the one I'd raced through earlier, I donned warm, comfy clothes, lit the fire in the living room, and then spent an hour in my home office preparing for the week ahead. Snow started falling lightly around one, right as Frayne's car pulled up my driveway and into my garage.

Nervous anticipation bounded within me as I quick-stepped to the kitchen. Like a high school drum line practicing before a big competition, my heart was thrumming against my ribs. My fingers tingled across the doorknob as I opened the connecting kitchen door to let him in.

"Hey."

His smile stopped my heart. Open and bright, with those cheek crevices pushing in deep at the corners of his mouth, when he lit on my face he looked happy and lighthearted.

Maureen's words flew back to me.

The man has feelings for you.

Oh, how I wanted to believe it.

"Maureen sent this." He handed me a shopping bag. "She thought you might be running low on—her word—provisions."

"I love my baby sister." I sighed when I took the bag, peeked in, and saw multiple glass containers loaded with food.

Frayne laughed as he placed his briefcase down on the counter, then shrugged out of his coat. "She said to tell you the same thing."

"Give me your coat. I'll hang it up."

"I can do it." The fact he was comfortable in my home sent a warm feeling through me. "You started a fire?" he called from the hallway.

"It's cold outside, and I haven't had one in a while. I figured it was a good idea," I answered as I stacked the food containers in the refrigerator. "I love a fire in the winter, especially when it's snowing outside." This time when I found Frayne leaning against the counter, his hands crossed at his chest, I didn't jump.

"Want to get started working?" I asked. "I've got some stuff to finish up in my office for the week ahead of me, so the dining room is all yours."

"In a minute." He pushed off the counter and stepped toward me, a determined, focused glint in his eyes. "First, I need to do this."

I had a pretty good idea what the "this" was, especially when he cupped my chin in one hand and wound the other around my waist, hauling me flat up against him.

Kissing him the first time had been a mystery. Then, a revelation. Since I now knew his taste, the intoxicating feel of his lips, the way his tongue slowly and thoughtfully consumed mine, I let myself enjoy the sensations drifting through me, and freely gave up any and all control I had to him. I twined my hands around his neck, threaded my fingers through the thick, silky pelt of his hair and held on as if my life depended on it.

The hand at my chin drifted down and joined its twin around my back. Palms opened across my butt, and he lifted me even closer. So close there was no mistaking how the kiss was affecting him below his waist.

Time stopped. As did sentient thought. I stood there, encircled within the arms of a man I was rapidly losing my heart to—if I hadn't already—and simply gave myself up to his care and keeping.

After a time, Frayne broke the kiss and leaned his forehead against mine. A sigh coursed over his entire body. Eyes half closed, he kissed the tip of my nose.

"I wanted to do that the moment you walked into your sister's kitchen," he confessed. "It took every ounce of willpower in me not to jump up from my chair and pull you into my arms."

"I can only imagine the reaction it would have caused." I grinned up at him, but I wasn't kidding. Not even a smidge.

He took my face in his hands again and placed a sweet kiss across my lips.

"Cathy, last night with you was…" He shook his head, as if he couldn't find the words he wanted.

I caressed his cheek. "It was for me, too."

"You can't know how happy I am to hear that."

Oh, I had a pretty good idea. Frayne's face broke out into his charming, boyish grin, verifying I'd said the words aloud. Colleen's habit of always saying exactly what drifted into her mind had started to influence me, and I wasn't sure it was a good thing.

"Good to know." His grin was playful. Then, he turned serious. "After I left this morning, I was afraid you might have regrets about what we'd done," he said, with another kiss.

"I didn't." I shook my head and laid my hands

across his chest. "And I don't. Not one regret, Mac." A thought bloomed at my brain and took root. I bit down on my bottom lip and asked, "What about you? Doubts? Second thoughts?"

"None," he said without a beat. "And the only thought I had all morning was how long would I have to wait until I could see you again. Hold you again." He rubbed his hands up and down my back to my waist, his fingers pressing along my spine, sending tiny frissons of heat straight down to my toes. "Make love to you again."

A lump formed in the back of my throat, and when I swallowed, the action was loud in the air between us.

His mouth turned lopsided and his brows drew together when he added, "I wanted to follow you back here the minute you left the inn and continue where we left off this morning, but I figured it would make you nervous or even scare you if I did. Too intense, you know? Maybe too much too soon?"

"Why did you think I'd be scared?"

"Maybe scared is the wrong word. I don't know." He shrugged.

I wondered what he would say—or do—if he knew the utter intensity of my own feelings and thoughts about him?

Truth, I've been reared to believe, is always the best course.

Gently, I pressed my lips against his, kept my gaze attached to his own.

"If you'll remember, I was the one who kissed you first, the one who showed you what I wanted. My hope then was that you wanted the same thing."

"I did. I do."

"Good to know," I said, giving him back his words.

He smiled at me, then cuddled my head against his chest and wound his hands back down around my waist. Under his shirt, his heart thrummed with a steady, calming rhythm that soothed and stoked me at the same time. I could have stood here, held in his arms, for a lifetime. Unfortunately, life has a way of intruding on the things you want.

My cell phone blared, and with a breath crammed with regret, I pulled out of his embrace and reached for it. While I spoke with a nervous client about an upcoming legal matter, I walked back to my office and shut the door for privacy. Forty-five minutes later, I finally ended the call and found Frayne in the dining room, one of Josiah's journals in his hand, an opened laptop on the table. He'd brought his own pair of latex gloves this time and a magnifying glass with a light attached to it. Those adorable glasses were perched on the bridge of his nose, one eye shaded with his falling thatch of hair.

"Find anything interesting?" I asked.

"A few things." He laid the book and magnifier on the table and tugged off the gloves and glasses. "Remember one of the questions I posed at the luncheon was where Josiah originally hailed from?"

I settled into the chair opposite him and nodded.

"There's a brief mention, almost a throwaway line, about a trek from Richmond in the winter of 1787."

"Virginia?"

"Maybe. I did a quick search online, and there are a few cities established and named Richmond at the time. I need to read more and see if he mentions which state."

"Virginia, though, isn't far from here."

"*Now*, it isn't. In 1787, it was probably a week or two on horseback."

His eyes were bright and sparkling with intensity, exactly as they'd been the day we discovered the journals.

"If you keep searching, I'm sure you'll find the answer. I'm making a cup of tea," I told him, rising. "Do you want anything?"

His hand snaked out to grab my arm as I passed him. With a flick of his wrist and an easy yank, I was sitting in his lap.

The man had some serious hidden moves.

"Just this," he said.

Then he kissed me.

"Just you," he added, between nibbling the corners of my lips.

How was it possible to crave something as if your life depended on getting it when you hadn't even known it existed until hours beforehand?

In no time at all, the passion radiating between us had us both devouring one another. My desire to have a cup of tea was obliterated by my desire to have this man—this humble, gorgeous, and fascinating man.

Every tug and swipe of his tongue made me writhe for release. In another smooth move that took my breath away, Frayne rose from the chair in one fluid stretch, me cradled in his arms, and without ever breaking our lips apart, walked us into the living room.

The warmth flowing from the fireplace was nothing compared to the heat radiating between our bodies.

"The second I saw you'd lit a fire, I wanted you in front of it, naked, and under me," Frayne whispered as he nuzzled my cheek, "while I made love to you."

I'd never been so happy in my life I'd struck a match to the kindling.

With one hand tucked under my knees supporting me, Frayne grabbed the afghan from the rocking chair and tossed it on the rug in front of the bricks. Bent on one knee and still supporting all my weight in his arms, he sat me down next to it. Effortlessly, he spread the covering, then slid two couch pillows on top of it.

On both knees now, he pulled me flat up against him. With our arms wound around one another, our lips fused, we sank to the floor in one slow glide.

The firewood crackled and popped, the fiery orange glow of the flames dancing over the room. I've always loved the smell of a fire, and the earthy aroma of burning wood filled the room and my senses.

Frayne eased back from the kiss and trailed a finger across my cheek. It was barely three p.m., but the snow had darkened the daylight filtering through the windows. Half his face was lit from the flickering fire, half shaded. Even through the dimmed lighting, the desire in his eyes was vivid and dazzling as he stared down at me.

"Do you have any idea what you look like right now?" he asked.

I shook my head.

"Your skin is like gold, shot with the light from the fire, your eyes like two polished, freshly mined emeralds. Bright. Incandescent." His thumb stroked my bottom lip, and every nerve ending in my body fired from the sensation. "Your mouth is wet and red and swollen. I did that. My mouth on yours." His voice grew husky with the revelation. When his gaze found mine again, it took everything in me not to cry out in wonder at the fathomless cauldron of emotions swimming in his eyes. "You're the most beautiful woman I've ever seen, Cathy. And I want you. So much, I can't even find the words to tell you properly."

Exhilaration bounded and flashed through me. For him, only him, I wanted to be beautiful, inside and out.

I snaked my hands under the hem of his sweater and pulled him back down to me. His skin was smooth and soft, and my fingertips singed from his natural warmth.

"Show me, then," I commanded. "Show me."

With a simple one-handed tug, he lifted his sweater and T-shirt up and off. His hair rioted around his head, and he swiped the sides back, off his face, smoothing it down.

That done, he pulled me up to a sitting position. My sweatshirt joined his on the floor. The plain white bra I'd donned today wasn't anywhere near as sexy as the black strapless one had been, but when Frayne's eyes drifted over it, across my straining breasts, and then dilated with desire, I knew it didn't matter. He placed a sweet, wet kiss over one material-clad nipple and then sucked the tip through the fabric before moving to its twin. My back arched, allowing him better access, silently begging for more.

When his low, deep chuckle filled the space between us, I realized I hadn't been silent after all.

The fact I wasn't embarrassed by the knowledge was telling on my part.

Soon, the rest of our clothes were shed.

My hands found their true calling as they skimmed and stroked over every inch of his delectable flesh. My nails flirted with the corrugations in his abs; my fingertips teased his pebbled nipples; my palms smoothed and massaged the corded muscles in his back. And when my hand fisted over the solid, long length of him, felt him pulse and throb beneath my touch, a surge of power exploded through me again.

Before the smile blooming on my face reached fruition, Frayne had me flat on my back, the soft feel of the afghan skating against my naked skin, my wrists gently imprisoned within his hands and held over my head.

"You asked me to show you how beautiful you are to me, Cathy. Let me?"

That he'd asked, after the intimacy we'd already shared, was simply heart warming. A simple nod from me and he freed my wrists. I let them drift to my sides.

His breath was warm against my neck as he nuzzled behind my ear and then pulled the lobe between his teeth, biting down with his lips. A subtle shift and his lips dragged down my throat, over the pulse pounding in my neck.

"Your heart's racing," he whispered against the notch in my shoulder. He lifted one of my hands up to the left side of his chest. "So's mine."

He kept up his downward descent, his tongue licking across my collarbone then diving into the space between my breasts and lapping. He pushed my breasts together with his hands, then cupped and plumped each one as he drew one nipple, then the other, between his lips and suckled.

My insides coiled like a spring with each subtle tug of his tongue, tightening and spiraling dangerously close to unraveling. I threaded my fingers into his temples and clutched all that glorious, thick hair between them. Frayne smiled against my breast.

He moved down my belly, which by now had gone concave from all the air I was gulping in and gasping out, stopped to kiss my bellybutton, then moved farther downward, his lips never lifting from my skin.

That spring constricted even more as a steady, pounding pulse beat against the apex of my thighs. A nudge with his nose and my legs opened and spread wide at his silent command. My thighs quaked, my feet arched in an attempt to keep me from leaping into the air as anticipation sped through my system. When his mouth, his wet, hot, persistent mouth, tenderly kissed the folds between my thighs, my hips rose up, arching into him, pleading for…more.

Where had this demanding, insistent woman come from? I tended to think she was always inside me, biding her time for the right moment to make her presence known. And, I imagined, waiting for the right man to meet and fulfill her buried needs.

Mac Frayne, for all appearances, was that man. His generosity as a lover knew no bounds as he brought me to the pinnacle of pleasure and beyond. Tears blurred my vision as I gazed up at him after the tremors shaking through me subsided. Propped on an elbow with his free hand kneading one of my still trembling thighs, the smile he gave me was part delight, part arrogance, and all devotion.

"You're beautiful in any light," he whispered and kissed my cheek. "But by firelight, warm and satisfied, you glow."

He swiped a finger at one of the tears spilling over from the corner of my eye.

"Happy tears?" he asked.

Words wouldn't form. I pulled him down on top of me, cradled his head into the hollow of my shoulder, and, with our legs twined together, closed my eyes.

When I opened them again, I was in my own bed, the room dark. I was naked under the blankets, and I was alone.

The bedside clock told me I'd slept the afternoon away.

I had no memory of coming up to bed, nothing after the mind-blowing orgasm Frayne had given me.

Frayne.

Where was he?

I got up and took a quick look out the bedroom window. It was snowing heavily, the ground covered. From the depth of the tire tracks on the road, we'd gotten about four or six inches, and it didn't look like it was going to stop anytime soon.

Welcome to January in New Hampshire.

The clothes I'd worn after my second shower were on top of my dresser, folded. I wasn't the only thing Frayne had carried to my bedroom. I got dressed, ran a brush through my hair, then readjusted it back into a messy knot, brushed my teeth, and made my way downstairs.

The kitchen and dining room lights were lit, and the scent of burning wood told me the fire was still roaring. I found Frayne as I had earlier, seated in the dining room, typing on his laptop, totally engrossed in what he was doing. He was dressed again, but under the table, his feet were bare. My lips lifted at the chaos of his hair.

A warm, deep sense of contentment surged through

me, coupled with a feeling of such intense joy I lost my breath as I stood in the doorway staring at him.

Was it possible to fall in love with someone in such a short time span? It was barely two weeks since we'd met, been lovers for less than twenty-four hours.

Could I be in love with him?

The thought should have been alarming. It wasn't. If anything it was astonishing I could feel this much for a man after Danny's betrayal.

Frayne stopped typing to read something on the screen. I slipped into the kitchen and put the kettle on for tea.

"Cathy?"

"I'm in the kitchen."

A half second later he joined me.

"I was trying to be quiet. I didn't want to disturb you while you were reading."

"Don't worry about it. Are you okay?"

"Fine. I can't believe I slept so long. I guess I didn't realize how sleep deprived I've been lately. It finally caught up with me."

"You were pretty conked out. You never even flinched when I carried you upstairs."

I rolled my eyes and grinned as I took down two mugs. "I can't believe you were able to get me up to bed and under the covers without my knowing it. You want a cup of coffee?"

He continued to stare at me, his eyes intense and inquiring.

"What?"

"You've been having trouble sleeping?"

"Not trouble, no. It's been a little…different without George. I'm not used to being alone in the house. I guess subconsciously I realize it and don't sleep as soundly as I did when he was with me."

He came closer, relieved me of the mugs, and then slipped his arms around my waist. My hands instinctively settled on his chest and, as I burrowed into him, my eyes drifted close.

"You're so warm," I murmured, snuggling even closer.

The strong, steady beat of his heart against my ear was soothing, and I had a fleeting notion to bring him up to my bedroom where we could lie together, cuddle, and nap some more.

Or maybe do other things aside from nap.

The whistle of the teakettle shattered the thought a second later.

"What have you been doing for the past three hours while I've been imitating a sloth?" I asked while I steeped my tea and set about making him a single cup of coffee.

His grin was quick and boyish. "Never that. I discovered the Richmond Josiah alluded to is the one in Virginia. A few pages after the first mention, he clarified the location. I've been searching through online government and county records and documents from the time period to see if I can get a bead on the Heaven name."

"Any luck?"

"None so far, but not every county has digitalized their old records yet. I may need to drive down to Richmond for a few days and go through actual archives."

A tiny sense of sadness swiftly shot through me at the notion he'd be gone. What did it say about me that I wanted to go with him? Chuck my responsibilities, my clients, *Nanny*, and take off with him?

"It's too bad your schedule is so busy or we could go together."

Let's add *mind reader* to all the other attributes I'd already assigned him.

I handed him the filled coffee mug and glanced out the kitchen window at a scraping sound in my driveway.

"It's my plow girl, Hailey. She comes when we get four or more inches of snow. Looks like we've got about six right now."

"There's a job description you don't hear every day. Plow girl. As opposed to plow *guy*?"

"Her father's the guy. He owns the business, and Hailey is one of his workers. They plow me out in the winter and take care of mowing my lawn in the spring and summer. Danny was never around to do those things, and I was too busy with my practice, so I hired out."

"Two factors living in the city I never need to worry about—mowing lawns and shoveling snow."

We took our mugs and walked back to the dining room.

"I think it's time I start photographing and documenting Robert's personal things," I said after glancing at everything we'd unpacked. "The sooner it's done, the sooner I can call Leigh and have the museum take possession of it all."

"That's not a bad idea. My eyes are beginning to cross from all the reading I've done today."

For the next hour, we separated all the clothes we'd already unpacked into categories, Frayne inspecting every item, detailing the make, color, and time period of the pieces, and then dealt with the other items we'd found in the containers, while I documented them on my laptop and took pictures with my phone.

By the time we were finished, we were both hungry. The last time we'd eaten was breakfast, so I put together a simple meal of the roasted pork Maureen had sent, along with a salad.

As we sat and ate a leisurely meal together, it dawned on me how I could get used to this. Having someone at my table, enjoying one another's company, talking about everything and anything that popped into our heads. Frayne wasn't only an acute listener, he was a marvelous speaker as well. Maybe it was because he wrote for a living and loved words, but he never faltered when he was talking or stumbled, searching for a way to describe something or for a phrase. I loved listening to him as he told me about the research he'd done for the Dickinson book, or the traveling he'd had to do to discover everything he could about another of the historical figures he'd written of.

He'd have made a marvelous professor. I could imagine all the females in his class glued to the edges of their seats as he presented a living history to them.

When the dishes were done, he leaned against the kitchen counter, his hands once again crossed over his chest.

I'd been silently debating whether or not I should ask him to spend the night again. I wanted him to, but I didn't know how to ask without sounding needy. Maybe he didn't want to spend the night. Maybe he wanted to get back to his room at the inn, to his privacy.

"You look very pensive," I said after I placed the

last dried dish back in the cabinet. "Do people still say 'a penny for your thoughts?' Or is it too old-school?"

"Not in my book." He pushed off the counter and crossed to me, a question in his eyes. He slid his hands into my own and held them. The gesture was sweet and endearing. "Look, it's getting late, and the snow doesn't look like it's letting up. I should get back to the inn before it gets any worse." Something drifted by in his gaze as he spoke. Regret? Disappointment?

That daring and brazen gene kicked into high gear again.

Boldly, I wound his hands around me and stepped into the space separating us, the length of my body settling against his. His fingers dug into my hips as his brows tugged together.

"Or." I nuzzled my nose across his chin and then trailed my mouth along his jaw. "You could stay here tonight. If you did, I wouldn't worry about you driving back to the inn in this storm."

"You would worry about me?" His throat bobbed when I kissed the hollow under his chin, then down the column of his neck.

"Mmm. You're not from around here." He dipped his head toward me when I stretched up and pulled his earlobe between my lips. "During a snowstorm, the roads can be—" I bit down on it. "—treacherous to someone who's not used to them."

Frayne swallowed again. With my intent obvious, I snaked my knee between his legs and then lifted it to skim along the inside of his thigh. His breath hitched, and there was no mistaking how heavily aroused he'd grown.

"I think it's better you stay here and...ride it out.

Be safe, you know? It should be over by the morning, and Hailey will be back to plow again."

Was it terrible of me that I sent up a silent prayer asking to be snowbound for a few days?

With a groan pushing through his lips, he flattened his hands across my butt and lifted me even closer against him. "Safe?" he murmured against my temple. "I think that's…wise. To be safe. And not…sorry."

The last word died on his lips as he crushed his mouth against mine.

Pretty soon all thoughts of his leaving were forgotten.

As discussed, he rode out the storm…in my bed.

And I rode him. *Several times.*

Chapter 16

In my thirty-nine years on Earth, I'd discovered many things about myself, one of the most important being that habits, although hard for me to break, were notoriously easy to make.

Case in point: Mac Frayne.

Describing him as a habit might sound strange, but his presence in my daily life grew to be one in almost no time. The night of the storm and every night thereafter for the next week, he spent in my bed. I'd wake in the morning to the aroma of coffee brewing because Frayne was an early riser. I'd shower and be met with a mug filled with tea, a toe-curling kiss, and breakfast waiting for me when I came into the kitchen. I'd go off to the office and when I'd arrive home later in the day, Frayne'd be at the dining room table, his laptop open, surrounded by Josiah's and Robert's journals and his glasses a single inhale away from falling off his nose.

We'd spend a bit getting reacquainted—in the romantic sense—then I'd fix dinner and we'd chat about our day.

All in all, I'd spent more time with Mac in one week than I had with Danny during his last three leaves.

At night, we'd cuddle in front of the fire and talk. Mac told me all about his lonely childhood and how his parents hadn't known what to do with an inquisitive, active boy at their time in life. He'd been much of a loner all through school, quiet and intent on making a name for himself in the book world.

It came as a surprise when he revealed he'd gotten engaged in his senior year in college. His fiancée, a humanities major, had been a girl he'd been partnered with in freshman English. One thing had led to another, and soon they were dating. He proposed right before they graduated. When she was offered a chance to teach a summer course in Europe, he encouraged her to go. She had and, when she came home in August, told him she didn't want to marry him anymore because she'd met her true "soul mate" while she'd been away.

"The fact the soul mate's name was Claudia was a bit of a shock," he told me as we cuddled together on the couch.

"Oh. My. *God*." Laughter erupted from me fast and furious, and I was helpless to hold it back.

"I don't see what's so amusing."

"Oh, come on. *A bit of a shock*? Really? You had no indication the girl you were planning to marry might be batting for the opposing team?"

"No, I didn't."

"No clues? Little hints? Inklings not all was what it seemed?"

He shook his head.

"Not even during sex?"

The sudden silence was deafening.

"*Holy Hannah*, you're blushing!"

"Men don't blush." His adorable mouth twisted downward.

"Yes, they do, and yes, you are."

"Cathy." There was a warning in his tone, but like

a proverbial dog with a bone, I never back down.

In my best grill-the-defendant voice, I said, "The way your face is turning splotchy is very telling. I can't imagine the sex was very satisfying for her if she was a lesbian, was it?"

"I wouldn't know."

I stretched out on top of him, pushing him underneath me, and kissed his chin, my lower body grinding into his provocatively. I wasn't above a little seduction to get the information I wanted.

"Tell me." I licked the corner of his mouth, his frown now a thing of the past. "You knew something, didn't you? She said"—another lick on the opposite side—"maybe did something, or didn't, that niggled a little in the back of your mind, right?"

"I wouldn't know because we never slept together."

Okay, there was a surprise. Two college kids, supposedly in love and pledged to marry, and they hadn't tested the sexual waters? I grew up in a conservative Catholic home, and even I knew that was unusual and told him so.

Frayne heaved a sigh. "She wanted to wait until we were married. I respected her wishes."

"Must have been torture."

"Yeah, well…"

I slid my nose against his throat, placed a kiss behind his ear. "You really are a good guy," I told him, meaning every word of it.

"I don't want to talk anymore, Cathy." His voice had grown husky and deep and my lady parts sizzled with need. His eyes had closed, his throat working furiously as I continued moving and sliding over him.

My playful goal had been to get him to confess something he should have realized about his then-fiancée. My plan backfired, though, because with my next breath I was flipped and placed flat on my back on the couch. Frayne stared down at me, no playfulness at all in his expression.

"Me, neither," I confessed.

This time our lovemaking was frenzied and frantic, stirred—no doubt—by my actions. We didn't even shed our clothes, merely opened and rearranged them in an attempt to satisfy one another as quickly as we could.

Afterward, we lay panting, our heart rates both audible in the air around us, our clothes a disarrayed tumble between our bodies. The fleeting notion that we hadn't used a condom skimmed across my mind, forgotten when Frayne kissed the side of my neck and snuggled next to me. Within seconds, we were both asleep.

The following Saturday, he decided he needed to make a trip to Richmond for his research. He'd learned all he could online and knew he needed to go through the actual archival documents to find mention of Josiah. After a quiet dinner, we settled in front of the fire Frayne had started and made love.

I'd grown to know every little thing that brought him pleasure, as he had with me. I'd given myself—mind, body, even my soul—to him with no regrets. Firelight danced and drifted over our bodies, the warmth from the flames nothing compared to the heat we generated between us.

This time, I didn't fall asleep until we were tucked into my bed.

As soon as he backed down my driveway and onto

the road early Sunday morning, I missed him. The house was empty and the intense loneliness, exactly like after George died, seeped through me again.

This wouldn't do. I wasn't the type to mope around, sad and surly. As I started getting ready to pick Nanny up for church, she called and informed me Colleen and Slade were taking her to an earlier mass. Nanny was scheduled to play the piano while her best friend, Tilly Carlisle, sang at a post-holiday brunch for the residents and families. And, since this was Nanny, she added I could make my way to church on my own time today, but to be sure I attended in order to start my week with a spiritual checkmark next to my name.

As kids, we'd never been allowed to skip mass for any reason other than arterial blood spraying from our bodies or infectious diseases that could spread to the other parishioners. I considered Nanny's phone call as an ecclesiastical hall pass for the day and decided to do an adult skip. Father Duncan might toss me a stink eye next Sunday, but I wasn't going to lose any sleep over it.

Seldrine's mother had called me the night before to tell me they were all going to mass as a family and she would be responsible for her daughter getting to the A.A. meeting today afterward. Since I now didn't have to worry about leaving the house, I needed something to take my mind off pining for Frayne, and I decided to tackle a project I'd ignored for months: cleaning my home office. I'd left it for far too long.

Paperwork from old cases littered my desk along with opened reference books and law volumes I'd needed for case citings. Underneath a pile of briefs, I found a pair of earrings I'd misplaced a month ago.

Dozens of dried-out pens, business cards from clients, even scraps of paper with cell phone numbers I'd been given by court clerks and business people were shoved into my desk drawers, along with filled legal pads, forgotten sticky notes, and even some coupons for dog food for George.

Meticulously, because I was, after all, my OCD mother's daughter, I examined every scrap of paper to make sure it didn't contain vital information I needed before I either tossed it, filed it, or put it in a pile to be scanned into my computer.

After two hours and three rounds of rapid-fire torpedo-sneeze episodes from the dust I'd allowed to accumulate among my things, I opened the last drawer in my desk, all set to cull and clean when I stopped short. My hand froze on the drawer handle, and my spine locked. I swiped my tongue across lips that had gone desert dry, leaving a bilious, metallic taste in the aftermath.

Danny's dog tags sat in the center of the drawer draped over his official death certificate and the notification papers the army representatives had hand delivered to me. I'd forgotten I'd shoved it all into the drawer soon after his burial. I hadn't wanted to deal with the paperwork, the filing, the reading of the official reports back then. I'd put them aside, with the notion to get to them eventually.

It looked like today was that day.

My hands shook as I lifted the metallic tags. I dropped them onto the top of my now cleared desk, then did the same with the death certificate. I didn't need to read any of the information listed on it, since I knew the details by heart. The pages detailing the official report of Danny's death at the hands of an ISIS member came next. Slowly, I lowered down into my office chair and began reading. It was only when some of the ink began to run on the page from my tears, that I stopped.

Danny had never stood a chance. While my husband was out on night patrol, the insurgent had snuck into the compound during the cover of night and had shot him, killing him instantly with a bullet to the head.

I had a vague recollection of the army reps and Lucas telling me all this when they came to the house that horrible day. My mind must have shut down, though, the details too harrowing to process at the time.

Almost three years later, it was still hard, but now I had the benefit of time passed as a buffer to the hurt. I'd begged Danny not to return to duty when he'd been home on his last leave. I'd argued, cajoled, pleaded, cried, did everything I could to make him retire from the service and stay home with me for good. Nothing worked.

When I threw out the accusation that he loved the army more than the thought of being with me and making a family, I'd finally learned the truth, finally been given the reason he kept going back again and again, the reason he was never going to leave the life of a soldier.

It had all come out in a rush of run-on sentences, repeated words and phrases that wrenched and tore my heart in two.

Danny didn't want a family, and he didn't want the life with me he'd vowed to make when we were both eighteen. He already had a life he loved: with the army and with the men who served under him. The army was his life, his family. Not me.

He'd never wanted children, not even when he'd assured Father Duncan during our CANA preparation he had. He'd lied because he knew there was no way my parish priest would marry us if he knew Danny's truth.

Through sobs, I questioned why he'd ever married me in the first place, and he answered that at the time he'd loved me. He'd wanted to go overseas with the knowledge he had a place to call home with a girl waiting for him. He'd loved me, he said, and wanted to be a husband.

Until he decided he didn't. Until he took steps to ensure I never got pregnant. Or that any other woman would, either.

I threatened to divorce him. He told me he wouldn't contest it, would even hand me solid grounds. There had been lovers over the years while he was away. Women who'd help him pass the long nights. Women who'd made him realize he didn't need—or want—a wife.

I accused him of adultery. I called him a liar. I labeled him a coward.

He laughed at the first, accepted the second with a shrug, and took umbrage with the third.

And then he walked out of the home I'd made for us, the home where I'd dutifully waited for him, with his duffle in his hands and without a backward glance.

That was the last time I saw him alive.

I'd debated with myself about starting divorce proceedings for a month after he left, hopeful he'd change his mind. I cried, I railed to the empty house, cursed Danny, God, and all men. The one thing I didn't do was share what had happened with anyone in my family. Nanny was still living with my parents, and they had enough problems existing day to day and maintaining peace among the three of them; Maureen and Eileen were busy with the inn they'd recently purchased, and Colleen was still in living in New York with her then fiancé and planning her wedding. I suffered in silence, and believe me, I know how dramatic that sounds. In the end, I was glad I'd kept Danny's revelations to myself, because the day I accepted the necessity to start proceedings, the army representatives showed up at my door, Lucas in tow.

The last fight, the horrible things we'd yelled at one another, the inevitability of divorce, were all forgotten as I buried my husband, comforted his mother, and shoved my anger and grief to the side.

The anger, as I'd told Frayne, was a wasted emotion now. The grief I'd come to terms with. What was left were memories, distant and faded.

Determined to complete the task I'd set out upon, I took the tags and the reports, added them to a file folder and then placed it in the back of my metal cabinet with the label *Danny* attached to it.

Another two hours and I had a garbage bag filled with debris and an office dust-free, organized, and smelling like lemon furniture polish. Not a bad way to spend a lonely Sunday morning.

Since the cleaning bug had infected me, I set about to do as many of the rooms as I could. I tackled the kitchen and the downstairs bathroom and was able to get the living room done. At six, I was about to call it a day and grab dinner when my cell phone pinged. At the sight of Frayne's incoming text, the tips of my fingertips started to tingle, and I found myself smiling.

—Just arrived. Traffic was horrible. All checked into my motel.—

—Glad you got there safe and sound.— I hit *send.*

I put my phone back down on the counter. It pinged again within seconds.

—I miss you.—

Those three words brought unexpected tears to my eyes and sent a waterfall of emotion cascading through my system.

Other than my family, who was the last person who'd actually admitted they'd missed me?

The truth? No one.

I swiped the blurring tears away. *—I miss you, too. The house is lonely.—*

—Just the house?—

That brought the smile back.

—Well...maybe me, too. A little.—

—Just a little? Well, I miss you way more than a little.—

He added a sad face emoji and then a heart with an arrow through it.

My real heart stuttered inside my chest. Was this a declaration? I wasn't fluent in emoji-speak and had never flirted—in person or via text—so I had no yardstick to gauge what he might be telling me. Or how I should respond to it.

—Still there?— he wrote after a few seconds of silence on my end.

—Yup. Sorry. Doing 15 things at once. How long do you think you'll be there?—

—Hard to tell. Depends on what I find. Or don't.

I'm hoping only a few days.—

—Okay. Well...—

Before I hit send, I took a moment to decide how brave I was. Nanny's voice popped into my head. In her no-nonsense take-no-prisoners tone, it said, "Go for it, Number One. What have ya got to lose?"

A good question.

—A few days is too long— I typed. *—Hurry back as soon as you can.—*

Before I lost my nerve and started overthinking, I sent it.

Seconds later his return message came through.

—I'm rethinking the entire trip right now. If I leave, I can be there by early morning.—

It took everything in me not to tell him to get on the road.

—Don't— I typed. *—You've been driving all day after limited sleep, and I'd worry about you. Stay put, and I'll see you when I see you.—*

—You have no idea what hearing you'd worry about me does to me, Cathy. No idea. Okay. I'll stay put.—

I thought he was done. I was wrong.

—I wish I was there to kiss you good night.—

—Me, too.— I scrolled through my phone's emoticons, found a kissing face, and sent three of them.

—You're killing me...— he replied, and then added his own series of kiss-faces.

Who knew phone flirting could be such fun?

He signed off for good with the next text.

I missed his warmth next to me later on when I got into bed. The pillows carried a subtle trace of his scent, and I burrowed into them, inhaling, conjuring his face and body behind my closed eyes.

Both filled me with longing. It was no wonder all my dreams were filled with him. In the morning, I woke clutching his pillow.

Chapter 17

"I was starting to think you'd left town with Frayne," Maureen said when I showed up at the inn Wednesday at lunch time. I'd learned a thing or two this past year about mooching from Colleen, who was an expert on the subject, and had timed my visit perfectly in the hope my baby sister would feed me.

As I knew she would, Maureen pointed to a chair and said, "Sit." When I did, she placed a piping hot bowl of her mouthwatering New England chowder in front of me along with a hunk of bread I didn't even need to ask to know she'd baked.

"You're my favorite sister," I told her after swallowing a big spoonful of the delicious creamy soup.

"Hey," Colleen said from next to me, her own spoon of chowder in her hand.

"Sorry, sis, but you've never cooked for me."

She tossed me a pout. "My talents lie elsewhere," she said. "Did I not get you all glammed-up for speed dating?"

"One time. Maureen feeds me all the time."

Through slitted eyes, she regarded me. As kids her attempt to mimic my death stare hadn't intimidated me one whit. It still didn't.

"Just sayin'." I shoved a chunk of bread into my bowl.

"Any idea when Frayne will be back?" Maureen asked from the stove where she was filling a tray with bowls for her guests. "He kept the reservation on his room even though he's not here, which was nice of him. Unnecessary, but nice."

"He texted me last night that he'd found a mention of Josiah in a county court record. He was pursuing it today. Depending on what he finds, or doesn't, he may be back by the weekend."

"Things have gotten hot and heavy with you two, haven't they?" Colleen asked.

Ever the lawyer, instead of answering her, I asked, "What do you mean?"

"She knows Frayne's been spending nights at your house," Maureen said.

I tossed my baby sister a glare.

"She didn't tell me"—Colleen pointed her spoon at Mo—"so don't give her your lawyer face. I happened to drive by your house the other day on the way to a meeting and saw Frayne pull out of your driveway."

"So?"

"My meeting was at seven thirty. A.m.," she added for emphasis.

"We're not judging you, sis. In fact, Colleen and I are both thrilled you've met someone you're interested in, aren't we?" She peered across the table at Colleen with a Nanny-worthy don't-contradict-me glower.

Colleen nodded, then cocked an eyebrow my way. "Although, I think a little more than interested."

I've never been a huge divulger when it comes to my private life, case in point the fact I'd never told them about what happened with Danny. My sisters were nothing if not supportive and loving though, so again, the brave gene that was rapidly become a familiar facet of my personality broke through.

With as little detail as possible—because some things should be kept private—I confessed we'd become lovers and the surprise I felt about it.

"Why are you surprised?" Maureen asked. "You've both been working closely together, and anyone with eyes can see you're attracted to one another. You're both super-smart, successful people. Respected in your fields. Plus, he's hot and single, as are you. No one is surprised the two of you have hooked up."

"I'm not hot." I shook my head. "I can manage somewhat pretty with help"—I thrust my chin at Colleen—"but I'm not hot by anyone's definition."

My sisters tossed one another questioning eye rolls.

"You want to tell her?" Mo asked Colleen.

"Tell me what?"

Colleen put her spoon down on the table while Maureen continued to fill guest bowls.

"I happened to see Olivia Joyner at the grocery store Sunday morning after Slade and I dropped Nanny off from church."

"Thanks for that, by the way."

She waved her hand in the air. "Olivia asked if you'd mentioned anything about her event. I pleaded the fifth and asked her how it went."

"What did she say? Did she call me pathetic? Terrified? Not worth the effort to try and fix up?"

"Stop," Maureen said, summoning a tone remarkably similar to our mother's with a Nanny-worthy pursed lip attached to it.

"She said," Colleen continued, "the day after the event she received five—*five*—calls, one from each of the men who'd attended. Every one of them wanted a private meet with you."

"Oh, good Lord. I wasn't even a participant. I thought they all realized that."

"They did. According to Olivia, though, they told her you were—and I quote—the hottest female they've seen in years—unquote. So, who you calling *not hot*, sister dear? Independent observers disagree."

I stared at her with my mouth open.

"Just sayin'," she added with a shrug, a raised eyebrow, and a smirk.

Maureen sat down across from me and pulled one of my hands into hers. It has always amazed me how remarkably strong and warm they are.

"Look, Cath. We love you and want you to be happy—"

"I'm happy."

"—but you've been living like a nun since Danny died. You don't date, you never see anyone except us."

"I see people all the time."

"For work and as an officiant, yes." Colleen rose and carried her empty bowl to the sink. "But that's it."

"That's not true—"

"When was the last time you went out to dinner with a man?"

I wracked my brain to remember. "A few weeks ago. I had dinner with Lucas."

"A guy who's practically your brother doesn't count," Colleen said.

"You asked when the last time I was out to dinner with a man was and—"

"Don't." She stabbed a perfectly manicured index finger at me. "He doesn't count, and you know it. Stop arguing like a lawyer. I'm betting the last time you did was with Danny when he was home on leave. Am I right?"

She had me there.

"Look, sweetie…" Maureen squeezed the hand she still held. "We know you loved Danny from the first moment you laid eyes on him. We get that. But you can't live the rest of your life mooning over the man."

"I'm not."

"You have been up until now. Don't deny it. The love of your life was taken away from you, and you've shut yourself off from ever finding love again. We know Danny was your everything, your soul mate."

Silence is more telling than words in my family. Maureen cocked her head like Frayne was wont to do, and her gaze ping-ponged between my eyes, as if searching for the truth. She's not called the perceptive sister for nothing.

"He was, wasn't he?"

"Sis?" Colleen sat back down and took my free hand in hers. Together, we formed a little unbreakable triangle sitting there at Maureen's table.

For the first time, I wanted to let go of the secret I'd been carrying around inside me for three years—spit it out and be done with it. I could admit the reason why I hadn't up to now was I was fearful of what they'd think of me, married to a man who'd fallen out of love with me, who didn't want me or a family or anything to do with staying married to me.

Not an ego-boosting tale, to be sure. If I could be vulnerable with anyone, though, it was these two.

After taking a deep breath, I told them. Everything. Everything Danny'd said to me the day he'd left, everything he'd told me about how he felt, what he'd done, and what he wanted.

The first indication I had I was crying was when Maureen handed me a tissue.

"Why didn't you say something?" Colleen asked. "Why did you keep something as big as this"—she swiped her hand in the air—"all to yourself?"

"I was embarrassed. And more than a little ashamed at how blind I'd been all those years. I thought Danny loved me—"

"He did," Maureen said.

"Not enough." I shook my head, then dried my eyes. "Not enough to give up the life he'd made for himself in the army."

"Does Lucas know?" Maureen asked. "He must, right? He was Danny's best friend from the womb."

"I don't know." I blew out a breath and tissue-swiped my eyes. "We've never talked about it. I'm...well, I'm afraid to ask him. I don't want to find out he did know and condoned Danny's behavior. I don't know how I could face him and stay his friend if I knew he'd betrayed me. Or, if he didn't know and I tell him, then I've shattered the good memory he has of his friend. I'm not willing to take that chance. I'm the one Danny hurt. No one else deserves to be."

"Sucks, both ways." Colleen's ability to put into words what everyone else was thinking was a true gift.

We sat there, the three of us, lost in our own thoughts for a moment as Maureen's servers came and went with lunch service.

"Well, if it's any consolation, Mac Frayne is nothing like Danny. In looks, personality, or anything else," Maureen said. "He strikes me as a really good guy, Cath, someone you could be happy with."

"I told you, I am happy."

"You know what I mean." She let go of my hand.

I grabbed it back. With a gentle squeeze I said, "I do. I love that you want me to have a happily ever after filled with a family and a man I can adore. But I don't think there's anything long-term in Frayne and me. He's here to do a job. Being involved is a side benefit. Once he's done, he'll leave and go back to his life. Probably write a few more books."

"You're so sure of that?" my youngest sister asked.

"Of course I am. Why would he stay once he's done with his research?"

"Oh, I don't know. Maybe because you live here and he wants to be where you are?"

"What? No." I stood and carried my bowl to the sink as Colleen had. "The man has a life in New York. He's not gonna give it up to stay here with me. No man would do that."

"Slade did," Colleen said.

"Okay, well, yes. That's true. But Slade is one in a billion."

"I think Mac may be the same. You didn't see the way he looked at you when we were all here the last time. The man has feelings for you, sis."

"I told her the same thing, and she didn't believe me either." Maureen filled the sink with hot water. "You're talking to a wall, Coll. Stubborn's her Confirmation name. She won't accept the truth."

"We're gonna have to let her figure it out by herself, then."

I rolled my eyes and shrugged into my coat. Time to get back to work.

I kissed each of their cheeks. "I love the two of you beyond measure, but it can be exhausting being around you sometimes."

"Back atcha, babe," Colleen said, with a quick glance at her watch. "I've gotta get back, too. I have a new bride coming in with her mother in a half hour. The mother's texted me twice today, because as she's told me numerous times, her time is precious and she's not wasting it waiting for people." Her sigh was Nanny-worthy. "Something tells me I'm gonna need a non-alcoholic adult beverage tonight."

Maureen and I both laughed.

The rest of the week proved uneventful.

Frayne texted me Friday morning to tell me he thought he'd be able to finish up his inquiry by the end of the day and he'd probably head back to Heaven in the morning, barring any major snow delays or snags with his research. I told him Maureen had kept his room neat and ready for him whenever he arrived in town and not to hurry, but to drive safely since we'd had another storm and the roads could be icy.

He'd sent back a laughing emoji with a —*Yes, ma'am. Will do.*—

After speaking with my sisters, I'd spent a great deal of my free time ruminating on their assertion the man *felt something for me.*

I knew without a doubt what I was feeling for Mac Frayne was love.

Silly, sappy, giggly love. The toe-tapping, smile-inducing, heart-racing kind of love that, if you were lucky enough, you'd experience once in your life.

With Frayne, the giddy sensations inside me whenever I thought of him, heard his voice, felt his touch, were experiences for me as new and shiny as a freshly minted penny.

Did he feel the same?

After a while, my mind settled as I nestled under my comforter and drifted off to sleep.

The sudden blast of warmth steeping through my system filled me from shoulders to feet, and I burrowed into it.

A hand wrapped around my waist, tugged me closer to the furnace, and roused me through the thick fog of sleep. A tickle of heat at my neck had me shifting to allow better access.

That hand drifted down and slid under the hem of my T-shirt. Long, strong fingers glided over my skin in a slow, seductive dance, across my belly and up toward my breasts. My body responded before my mind could, curling my toes and flexing my knees to my chest, pushing me farther into the oven and against something hard.

Something solid and long.

Something…throbbing.

Fingers settled under my breast, cupped it, then rolled my nipple between them.

Awareness catapulted through me.

Frayne.

"You feel so…good," he whispered against my ear, then trailed tiny angel kisses along my neck.

I snuggled closer to him.

"I missed you," he whispered. "I missed holding you…like this. Kissing you. I missed…you."

"You, too. Mmm." My eyes wouldn't open, fatigue warring with arousal.

He kissed my temple. "Go back to sleep. I just

wanted you to know I'm back."

"Safe and sound," I mumbled.

"Safe and sound." His deep chuckle sent a warm wave of tranquility through me.

I threaded my fingers through the ones at my waist. "Welcome home."

Chapter 18

We woke at the same time.

I stretched, turned on my side, and then opened my eyes to find him doing the same.

The sleepy, sexy grin staring at me, coupled with the heavily lidded eyes and scruff of dark stubble lining his jaw, shot a wake-up alarm straight to my core. In less time than it takes for a heart to beat once, arousal pulled me fully awake.

"Morning." Frayne's rasp sent a shudder of want down my spine. He stretched his arms over his head, the sheet falling down low on his waist, tenting over a significant morning arousal.

I let my new bold best friend have free rein. She made me slide one leg over his thighs to straddle him.

Yup, he was as *awake* as I was.

With my hands flattened on his rock-hard chest, my naked lady parts sitting atop him, I leaned down and kissed him full on the lips, morning breath be damned. His fingers gripped my waist and held me in place.

"I missed you," I said between kisses. "So much."

"Missed you, too."

Yeah, I was sitting on top of that proof.

In one deft move, he hauled my T-shirt over my head and flipped me onto my back. "All I could think about was you." He kissed my chin. "Getting back to you." He moved down my neck, over my breasts, stopping to lick my instantly hardened nipples. "Making love to you."

He pulled up and pierced me with a look so filled with intensity and heat, it was a wonder he didn't set me ablaze. The errant thatch of unruly hair fell in front of one eye and made me smile.

I pushed it back only to have it fall forward again. Then, I cupped his cheek. As he had numerous times before, he snuggled in and kissed my palm. My heart simply swelled.

"You're here now," I whispered. "That's what counts."

Our kissing grew fevered, deeper. I couldn't touch him enough. My hands roamed and traced over every line of sinew and flesh on his body, glorifying in it. In no time at all, we were panting, moaning, frenzied.

In one effortless move, he slipped his hands under me, lifted my hips, and drove home, his breath hitching when he was fully encircled within me. My breath froze in my lungs.

"Cathy." His voice cracked, choked with need.

I pressed my lips to his, shocked to discover him trembling.

"God, I missed you," he whispered. "I want this to last, but I'm so close now I don't think I can. I need you, Cathy. Now. Right now."

I kissed him again, as the rhythm intensified with each plunge.

"Look at me," he commanded. "Don't close your eyes. I want to see you. I want to watch you."

His pace quickened, and my thighs tightened as wave after wave broke within me with no warning. I struggled to keep my eyes opened and trained on him through it. Tears erupted from the force of the orgasm. My body knew what my mind had only just started to accept about this man, this wonderful, lovely man.

A low, cavernous moan roared from deep within him as he slipped over the edge and joined me.

An hour later, after a shower together that was more sexual than cleansing, we were dressed and at my kitchen table.

"So tell me what you discovered."

"I'm not sure you're going to like it. Or if anyone in Heaven will." He cocked his head in his telltale way and took a long sip of his coffee.

"A blanket statement like that makes me want to know even more. Tell me."

He leaned an elbow on the table, his cup in his hand. "Part of how I research a person is to look for mentions in periodicals of the time, not only court documents and county records."

"What, like magazines? Newspapers?"

"Yeah. I happened to see a notation in one of the county archives about a foreclosure on a property owned by a J.E. Heaven. I couldn't find any old bank records, so I thought a search through the local weekly newspaper might have mentioned something."

"Kinda like the court and police log in our town paper."

He nodded and drank some more coffee. "The library had copies of the old newspapers on microfiche, and I spent a day going through all they had available."

"Your poor eyes."

One corner of his mouth quirked. The sight of those lips and the memory of how they'd trailed across my body recently, made me squirm in my chair. Frayne, bless him, gave no indication he knew what was going on under the table.

"Yeah. Microfiche is torture on any day. Anyway. I found a reference in the paper of the foreclosure, and it confirmed the owner was one Josiah Ephraim Heaven, occupation listed as farmer, aged thirty-two. It stated he was a widower, his wife having died in childbirth shortly before the foreclosure."

"Oh, that's sad. No mention he'd been married before was ever made in any of our archival papers."

"No. Not in his journals, either."

"So now we know he came here by way of Virginia. Why would you think I wouldn't like that news?"

"That's not the news I mean." He forked in some eggs, swallowed. "Josiah didn't leave Richmond because of the foreclosure of his farm."

"Then why?"

He paused, cocked his head, his soul-piercing stare doing all kinds of weird and wonderful things to my insides.

"Two days after the foreclosure, the newspaper reported Josiah was seen entering the home of the bank manager who'd ordered it. Witnesses stated they could hear the two of them fighting. The sheriff was called, and Josiah was escorted from the home. He wasn't arrested but told to leave the bank manager alone or he would be."

"Again, not seeing why this a problem."

"The next morning, the bank manager and his wife were found dead in their bed. Stabbed, multiple times."

"Oh, good Lord. And Josiah was a suspect?"

Frayne nodded. "I read every weekly newspaper

edition for the next year I could find. Multiple mentions of the unsolved murders. The sheriff named Josiah as a suspect. Unfortunately, he'd fled the area and couldn't be found. This happened in the late fall. Pretty soon winter erupted, and any trail or trace of him went dormant with the snow. Remember, back then the only way to track someone was by physically following behind them and interviewing folks who might be able to provide eye-witness accounts."

The nosy parker in me asked, "Did you find mention of any other Heaven descendants living in the area? Josiah's parents? Siblings?"

"None. There was no birth record for him, either. I pored through old church records but came up empty. Not unusual for the time. The only indication of his age was in the newspaper."

My lawyer DNA started devising scenarios.

Frayne's head-cock activated again. He stretched out his hand and took mine with it. "Watching your mind work is fascinating," he murmured. "What are you thinking about?"

"Alternate theories."

His eyes widened. "You don't think Josiah committed the murders." It wasn't a question.

"I'm not saying he did or didn't. But I have a very fact-based nature, and there's no actual proof, no tangible evidence, that Josiah killed those people."

"He loses his wife and baby; he loses his home. He fights with the person responsible for one of those things. That person turns up dead. Sounds plausible to me."

"Circumstantial, at best."

"Then why did he run?"

"We don't know he did. It may be as simple as he decided to leave the area since it doesn't seem there was anything to keep him there. Wife dead, home gone, no family. Maybe he wanted a fresh, new start in life."

"And the day he leaves, the person responsible for his problems turns up dead? What do you think that was? Serendipity?"

I shook my head. "Josiah might not have been the only person with a grudge against the bank manager. His leaving town around the time of the murders could be purely coincidence. He didn't change his name, which if he was guilty, you'd think he'd do so he couldn't be found."

Frayne stared at me, his expression circumspect and chary, almost disgusted. "You can't believe that, Cathy."

"I don't know what to believe since, like I've said, we have no true facts of what occurred. People are named as suspects of crimes every day. It doesn't mean they're all guilty."

His mouth turned downward.

Before he could challenge my thoughts, I added, "Or say he did commit the murders—"

"I think the facts as they've been presented assures he did."

"And I believe there's room for doubt. But say, for the sake of debate, he did. It may explain why, when he landed here, he spent the rest of his life atoning and dedicating his days to service and spirituality. He started a new life in a new place and set about doing everything in his power to do good. You know from your research about the ways he helped the community grow and prosper. There was never a hint of scandal or of any kind of wrongdoing. A tradition of service to the greater good filtered down to his family and the generations that came after him."

Frayne shook his head, and his eyes drifted down to where he held my hand. He shook out of it. "You can excuse what he did simply because he never did it again? Because he lived a blame-free life from the moment he arrived here? Because he tried, to use your word, to *atone* for it with his newfound religious fervor and dedication?"

"That's not what I'm saying—"

"It sounds like it. It sounds like you feel all his further actions of supposed service to man and God made up for the taking of two innocent lives."

"I'm not saying it's true; I'm merely offering it up as an explanation, a theory. And nothing excuses murder, Mac. I would never condone that. If the scenario is true, though, it would explain a great deal about why he set the town up the way he did, why he made the teachings of the Bible such a tenet of the town he helped build. Wasn't one of the questions you wanted answers to why the streets all had to have ecclesiastical names and meanings? Why Josiah had such a religious bent?"

"Naming streets and preaching the word of God doesn't excuse heinous crimes or behavior, Cathy."

"I didn't say excuse, I said explain."

It was as if he hadn't heard me.

"What about the families of the bank manager and his wife? How do you think they felt, knowing their loved ones were murdered with no one to take the blame, no one to prosecute for the crime? They didn't get the chance for a do-over, like Heaven did. They didn't get to run away and start over with no consequences for their past actions, wipe the slate clean. They didn't get revenge on the person who took those lives—"

"Don't you mean justice?"

He stopped, brows pulled so close together I couldn't see where one eyebrow ended and the other started.

"What?"

"You said revenge. Don't you mean they didn't get justice for what happened?"

"Christ. You argue like a lawyer—"

"I *am* a lawyer."

"A fact that's never far from my mind, believe me." His face was a mask of loathing. "I thought you might be upset your town founder, the man who supposedly gave it all to God and country, could, in reality, be a murderer who fled arrest and eluded capture. I thought, erroneously it appears, you might feel wronged your beloved town leader, a man who all believed was a paragon of the love-thy-neighbor philosophy could be nothing more than a gutless killer. I thought you'd feel, I don't know"—he swung a hand in the air—"*betrayed* that the man was a liar, a killer, maybe a psychopath. That you might feel something bordering on anger instead of this blind acceptance he'd somehow expiated himself for a great sin. I guess I was wrong on all counts."

Frayne stopped, shook his head again, and stood, cup in hand. He brought it to the sink and then placed his fists on either side of the rim, his chin dropping to his chest. Somewhere along this discussion we'd slipped out of speaking about a 1700s crime and were brought much closer to one from the more recent past.

Like the loss of his family, my despised status—I'd come to understand—was never far from his mind. His indignation, be it for an unsolved, centuries-old double homicide or a present-day tragedy, was strong, and nothing I could say or do would change it.

I should have been angry at his continued revulsion of my profession, or at best, hurt. I'd thought we'd gotten past it. I should have railed in my own defense and for Josiah, who had no one to speak for him now, or it appeared, two and a half centuries ago. The need to comfort this tortured man who'd stolen my heart was stronger than those needs though, because I went to him, pressed my body against his back, and wrapped my hands around his waist.

He stiffened.

I ignored it and pressed in closer.

The breath he expelled a moment later was sonorous in the still room. His shoulders dropped, and he cupped my clasped hands with one of his own and squeezed. His reflection in the window above the sink showed a man stark with emotions and tragically sad.

"I'm…sorry," he said after a while. "I don't know why I snapped at you."

I did, but those words were better left unsaid.

He twisted around to face me and slipped his arms around me as I had him. "It wasn't my intent to start an argument about all this. I don't want to fight with you."

"Look," I said. "As much as I love a good debate, I don't want to fight with you, either. About Josiah or anything else. We're never going to be one hundred percent sure what happened since it occurred long ago. Speculating about the info you've found is fine, but it's not a definitive answer. Maybe we should just be happy you've found a link to Josiah's past in Richmond for your research. That's more than any other biographer has ever done. The reason he came here may not ever be proven, but you've gone further, historically, than anyone else ever has, and that's something to be celebrated."

His eyes were still heated, the expression floating in them wary and concerned.

"And speaking of your research, I have some news," I said.

"What?"

"I finally called Leigh James yesterday and told her about the storage locker contents. She was wicked excited about the discoveries you've made. I invited her over this afternoon and told her how you've been instrumental in cataloging everything. She should be here about one-ish."

"I thought you wanted to wait."

"I did, but this overwhelming cleaning bug hit me last week, and I realized I wanted all that"—I cocked my head toward the dining room—"out of here so my house could look normal again. Besides, some of those pieces, the clothing and Josiah's journals, need to be in an environmentally secure space so they don't start to deteriorate from exposure."

Frayne nodded. "It's the right thing to do, I know. Look..." He slipped out of my hold and leaned back against the counter. "I'm tired, and I'm gonna head back to the inn. I've been gone for a week, and I need to get some stuff done. I'll come back a little before one to meet with Dr. James. Okay?"

"Of course. You don't need to ask permission.

You're the one who discovered the stuff was missing, after all. I'm sure Leigh will value what you've done and any further help and insights you can give her."

He slipped his hands into his front pants pockets and nodded, his gaze hidden behind the fringe of hair dropping across his forehead. If I was forced to describe him right now to a third party, I'd have to admit he looked equal parts tired, upset, and anxious.

I could understand all those emotions, because in truth, I was feeling the same way. The shock that Josiah might have been an escaped murderer was one thing. Coupled with the continued animosity Frayne had for my career and how close to the surface his feelings about it were made me a little angry and a whole lot of nervous it would ever change.

"Cathy…" He shook his head, then pulled me back into his arms. His fingers trailed up and down my back as the solid, steady beat of his heart against my ear went a long way in calming my nerves.

My only wish was I could do the same for him.

Chapter 19

I'd forgotten what a powerful force of nature Leigh James could be. I think she was made more so, postpartum.

The moment she laid eyes on the artifacts in my dining room, her eyes narrowed, and I swear I could hear her brain working and calculating while she went into command mode. Within an hour, I had a professional moving company in my house, boxing each item up with more care than Nanny had ever taken, to be sure. I'd been correct when I'd told Frayne Leigh would appreciate his help and insights with the discovery. As the workman wrapped, packed, and stored each item with infinite precision, Leigh peppered Frayne with questions about the information in the journals, each article of clothing, the timeline he'd written, even his trip to Richmond. I might have been designated the keeper of the keys by the historical society, but I was a lowly drone compared to Leigh. She was the queen bee, the high holy prefect of the entire museum and all its relics.

They worked late into the evening, the packers included, to get everything ready for removal to the museum's laboratory, where each item would be examined by a licensed archivist and antiquarian, and then by the insurance adjustors on the museum's board. While speaking with Frayne, Leigh had called a handwriting expert she'd worked with and made arrangements for him to view Robert's and Josiah's journals immediately upon arrival at the museum.

My head was spinning. I'd had no idea the extent of the legal verification necessary for the museum to claim the items were, in fact, true and actual possessions of the Heaven family. I should have known—for obvious reasons—but hadn't given it much thought, caught up in the discovery and my relationship with Frayne.

When they'd all gone and my house was empty again, my dining room resembled a tornado in the aftermath. Frayne left at the same time as Leigh to follow the truck back to the museum. He'd given my arm a squeeze before leaving and had promised to call or text me. I'll be honest, I was disappointed he'd left. Selfishly disappointed because I'd hoped he'd stay the night as he had prior to his Richmond trip.

Life the next week shunted back to what it had been prior to our becoming lovers. The house slipped into hollow emptiness again with Robert's belongings now at the museum and Frayne no longer around to do his research. I'd hoped he'd come around in the evenings, maybe join me for dinner, but he hadn't. Sporadic texts about the busy work of cataloguing and authenticating every item hit up my phone. Gone were the nightly texts telling me he missed me that I'd grown used to.

When I'd had lunch with my sisters one afternoon at the inn, Maureen shared with me Frayne had become a bit of a ghost guest. He'd leave for the museum right after breakfast every day, and when he returned, he'd sequester himself in his room, the sound of his typing on his laptop evident through the door. That he was focused and intent on the project was something I'd admired in the beginning when we'd met. I still did, but his dedication came at a cost to our budding relationship, and I couldn't help but feel ignored.

Work got me through the loneliness, though, as it had in the past. Several family court appearances and a few adoptions filled my days and my mind.

A phone call one morning had me gearing up for a court date on a day I hadn't been scheduled to appear.

I met with my young client and his grandmother before he was brought in and prepared a quick argument in my head. After the preliminaries were done, I happened to glance toward the back of the courtroom. Frayne stood, watching me. For a brief moment, I lost the train of my argument but was able to get the train back on the proverbial tracks a moment later after a deep breath and readjustment of my papers.

When Asa handed down his decision, I bid my clients a quick goodbye and told them I'd be in touch. Frayne was standing outside the courtroom, his hands in his jacket pockets, a familiar expression on his face.

"This a surprise," I said by way of greeting.

A deep breath elevated his shoulders and did nothing to wipe away his scowl.

"What's wrong? You look furious."

His eyes narrowed. "What I am is disgusted with the entire system you represent."

Oh, Lord. Not again.

Bracing myself, I asked, "Why?"

"I can't believe you even need to ask—"

"Humor me. Please."

His lips twisted, his scowl deepening. "Because the

law is geared toward protecting and coddling the criminals, the lawbreakers, not the innocent victims. That boy"—he jerked a thumb over his shoulder toward the room I'd exited—"stole something, and he's being slapped on the wrist and given a *do better the next time, son.* It's disgraceful. There's no accountability for any kind of behavior anymore in this society."

"That's not true."

"Isn't it?"

"No. How long where you in there?"

"Long enough."

"So did you hear me say Dylan is an honor student and a varsity basketball player who's never been in trouble before? For anything?"

"So what? He still broke the law. Just because he's been a good kid doesn't mean he hasn't turned into a bad one."

"Wrong." I stabbed my finger at his chest. "He's not a bad kid. Circumstances led him to do something he'd never have considered a month ago. Hell, a week ago."

"Oh please. He made a choice—a bad one—and got caught."

"Because he needed the money." My voice started to rise, and it took me a second to pull back and collect myself. "Not everything is black and white in the world, you know. Good people do bad things when faced with impossible choices. They shouldn't all be drawn and quartered as punishment."

He put a hand up to halt me. "Save it. I have no desire to hear any bleeding heart arguments right now."

For the first time in my life, I understood what the phrase *seething with anger* really meant. I literally saw a red haze form in front of my vision.

Lowering my tone to the pitch Colleen calls scary-sister-you'd-better-run voice, I ground out the words I wanted to scream at him. "Too bad, because you're gonna listen to what I have to say." He opened his mouth, but I steamrolled right over him. "His parents are opioid addicts and abandoned him last year. His grandmother, the only living relative he has who isn't drug addled is in the process of gaining legal guardianship of him, which is why they're my clients. A few weeks ago, Dylan's mother broke into her mother's home and stole a great deal of money from her, money needed to pay the rent on the small apartment she and Dylan are living in. She's sixty-seven and survives on Social Security and a minuscule pension. Money is beyond tight, and add a growing teenage boy who needs to be fed, clothed, and housed into the mix, a boy who plans to attend college to better his life, and the theft left them in a dire situation. Dylan was terrified they were going to be evicted, and he did something stupid to try to help with the rent—"

"Stupid is the right word."

"—and make sure they could stay where they were, safe and warm and not put out on the freezing sidewalk with nowhere to turn. He did it because he loves his grandmother and was afraid."

Frayne swiped his hand in the air dismissively. "Sugar coat it anyway you want. What he did was wrong—"

"And he's going to pay for it. He's being held accountable for his actions, but one mistake shouldn't be used to prevent him from attaining his future goals. He's a good kid. He's got the potential to go far in life."

It was as if I hadn't spoken.

"You said pretty much the same thing about Josiah Heaven. I don't understand why lawyers are willing to excuse heinous behavior, shove it to the side, without anyone ever having to face consequences. You all bend facts to fit scenarios, let criminals go free when they should be incarcerated because of dumb mistakes and poor police work. You make plea deals that serve no justice. The judicial system in this country is an aberration and a joke. Thieves get to steal with abandon, murderers walk free with no thought of the consequences of their actions."

People passing by stared as Frayne's voice rose with each sentence. All the aggravation lacing his words had a beginning point from the moment his wife and daughter were killed. I knew it, but I also knew I couldn't allow him to simply paint every single defendant and lawyer with a corrupt and contemptible label. In truth, I was sick of having to defend myself and my profession.

"You know," I said, "I wonder how high and mighty you'd be if you'd ever made a mistake, ever made a choice that turned out to be a wrong one. Would you really be as contemptuous of the entire judicial system if you were falsely accused of something or if you were hanging out to legally dry because of your actions? I'd bet lawyers and the system wouldn't look so abhorrent the moment you realized having them could save your ass from sitting in a jail cell."

His face turned the color of chalk as I spat the words at him. I was tired, furious, and had had enough belittling comments about my job to last me a lifetime.

I turned at a sudden presence behind me to find

Lucas, his thumbs tucked into his pants waistband. His shoulders were relaxed, and he was rocking back on his heels, a bland look on his face. A stance signaling he was calm and untroubled and which I knew meant he was anything but. Lucas was never as deadly focused and primed as when he appeared tranquil and composed.

"Everything okay here, Counselor?"

"Peachy."

He cocked his head at me while his brows rose. "Okay. I need to talk to you about something."

"Give me a few minutes, and I'll meet you downstairs," I told him.

He threw a stern warning glare at Frayne, then his gaze shot back to me. With a curt head bob, he walked away.

I waited a beat before turning my attention back to Frayne. His bare hands were fisted at his sides, his shoulders hugging his ears. The stiff posture was a good indication of how furious he was.

In a much lower, less lethal tone, but one still forged in steel, I said, "Look. There's nothing I can say that'll ever change your opinion of the legal system or lawyers. After everything you've said, I finally realize that."

His gaze raked my face, his brows drawn so tight together, it was a wonder he didn't have a headache from the tension.

"So I'm done trying. Now, why are you here?"

I don't know if he was surprised I wasn't arguing with him any longer, or if the awareness of people staring and listening to our exchange as they went about their business in the courthouse filtered through him.

Whatever the reason, he relaxed his shoulders and flexed his neck from side to side. The jagged breath he inhaled told me how much pulling for calm was costing him.

"I'm leaving," he said.

"Oh."

As far as responses went, it was about as pathetic as they come.

He was going home. Going back to his life, back to his world. I shouldn't have been surprised or upset about it. I had, after all, told my sisters he would.

Somehow, in the back corner of my mind, I'd hoped he wouldn't. I'd hoped he'd…stay. With me. For me.

"When?" I asked, thankful my voice continued to remain calm and cool.

"Right now. Something's come up at home and needs my immediate attention."

I nodded, not sure of how else to respond. I knew what I wanted to say, what my heart was begging me to say. How I wanted him to see me for the woman I was and not the profession I worked in. How he'd awakened my heart and soul again when I'd locked it away after Danny's death. I needed him to hear what he meant to me, how much I wanted to be with him, how precious he'd become to me. He needed to know he could stay with me for a night, a day, or forever if he wanted.

And I desperately wanted to tell him I loved him, but the fear that he didn't reciprocate that love stopped the words from releasing. The unemotional way he'd come to tell me he was leaving was all the proof I needed that he didn't feel for me what I did for him. Not even close. The dispassion in his voice, the cool glaze in his eyes, all confirmed it. If he'd ever felt something for me, it sure wasn't strong enough to compete with his disdain for my lawyer status.

"Everything at the museum is completed?"

"Almost. Dr. James has it under control. She doesn't need my help."

We were as stiff and awkward as two strangers meeting for the first time under less than perfect circumstances.

I swallowed the tears bubbling up from deep inside, shoved them back down, and held them there with all my will. I wouldn't cry in front of this man. He wouldn't see me break.

"Okay. Well...I guess this is goodbye, then." Ever Nanny's dutiful oldest granddaughter, I offered him my hand.

His gaze dropped to it, then dragged back up to meet mine. Those corrugations on his forehead returned, and the corners of his eyes slitted as he cocked his head.

Ignoring my hand, he took a step in closer. "Cathy, I—"

I took two back.

He stopped short, head jerking back as if I'd slapped him. The bulge at his throat bobbed as he swallowed, the color in his cheeks losing a little more shade. His gaze held mine as he lifted his hands in an I-give-up gesture and stepped back.

"I wanted to...tell you...say...thank you...for everything. I—I couldn't have done this without you. Without your help."

"My grandmother was more helpful than I was," I said. "She was the one who told you about Robert's things. She's the one you should thank."

"I already have."

Okay, this was news.

"I went to the nursing home yesterday and brought her lunch from Maureen. We talked for a couple of hours, actually. She's delighted all the stuff she kept of Robert's is actually going to be displayed in the museum. She thinks he'd be pleased to have his personal possessions added to the collection."

I'd bet cash money she was right about that.

"Thank you for that. And for visiting her. I know she appreciates the company."

He rocked back on his feet, the uncomfortable, tense silence returning.

We stood there, staring at one another.

I was the one who finally broke. "Well, I don't want to keep Lucas waiting, so I'll say good-bye again. I'm looking forward to reading the book. Get home safe and sound."

I didn't put out my hand this time.

"Cathy."

I waited. He continued to stare at me, something remarkably like regret filling his eyes.

But for what was the question.

"I don't want to leave this way."

"What way?"

"With you angry and upset. It wasn't my intention." He blew out a breath. "When I heard the case you were presenting, it, well…it brought back everything again."

"I can't and won't change what I am, what I do for a living, because it makes you uncomfortable," I said.

"No. I know that. I'm not asking you to. It…it

wouldn't be fair to you."

He shoved his hands into his bomber jacket and dropped his chin to his chest. A few minutes ago, he'd been a fierce force of anger. Right now he was ravaged by sorrow and remorse. I desperately wanted to comfort him, take him in my arms, and tell him everything was going to be okay.

But I knew it wasn't. As long as he couldn't get past his loathing of the system I'd dedicated my life to, there was no way things were ever going to be okay between us.

"For what it's worth," I said, "I'm not angry. I'm just…disappointed."

He lifted his chin, those piercing crystal eyes filled with sadness.

"Good-bye, Mr. Frayne." I turned, stalked away from him, and never looked back.

Chapter 20

"You're quiet this morning, lass," Nanny said as I drove her to Maureen's after mass. "Are ya not feelin' well?"

"Just tired. Work has been crazy busy."

I mentally crossed my fingers. Not twenty minutes after receiving communion and here I was telling a lie. There had to be a special place in purgatory for people like me.

Purgatory sounded pretty good right now because I'd spent the last three weeks in my own private version of Hell. Sleepless nights spent roaming my empty, lonely house; long, quiet evenings with no one but myself for company; mornings where sadness would cause me to burst into tears in the shower.

Pity party, table for one, rang through my head often when I found myself moping and pining.

"Ya look like you've lost a few pounds, too," Nanny said, her wise eyes scrutinizing me across the cab.

"My pants aren't complaining." My attempt at levity fell flat.

"Cathleen Anne Eleanora."

Uh-oh.

"I'm fine, Nanny. Really." I flicked my gaze her way, then cut back to the road as I pulled down the lane to Inn Heaven. "No worries. I've just been too tired to cook when I get home."

That part at least wasn't a fib. I'd had no appetite for days. In fact, a generalized queasiness and overwhelming exhaustion typically engulfed me for most of the day. Hot tea helped, as did a few antacids every now and again.

"Make sure Number Four gives ya some provisions to take home."

I didn't want to discuss why I looked like something the family cat hacked up after a night carousing, which was where this conversation was heading, so I said, "Thanks," hoping to put an end to it.

Silly me. This was Fiona Bridget Mary Darcy Sullivan O'Dowd Heaven Scallopini. Nanny was like a dog with a bone when something tickled her granny-radar.

"I've been meaning to ask ya," she said as I pulled around to the back of the inn, "have ya heard from Mac?"

Suddenly, talking about why I looked like hell didn't seem all that bad.

"Um, no." I parked and sprang out the door to help Nanny, grateful for the few moments of silence.

"Hold onto my hand," I told her as I slipped on arm around her waist. Even though Maureen's groundsman kept the walkways and stairs de-iced and snow-free, it was always in the front of my mind that a slip and fall for Nanny could be catastrophic at her age.

"I'm not feeble, Number One," she scolded but held my hand regardless.

"Not a word anyone would ever associate with you, Nanny, but it's February in New Hampshire, and I'm not taking any chances."

Once she was at the top of the stairs, she pulled out of my embrace.

"Hey." Maureen kissed Nanny's cheek and helped her from her coat. "How was mass?"

"It wouldn't kill ya to find out on your own, young lady."

My sister's grin was pure devil. "Sorry, Nanny, no can do. Guests to feed. Rooms to clean. A business to manage. Hey." She bussed my cheek and rolled her eyes behind our grandmother's back.

It was no secret Maureen's aversion to attending weekly church services began when Eileen was buried. She'd never discussed why she'd turned away from the religion she'd been raised in, but I'd always secretly suspected she was furious with God for taking her twin and needed to blame someone for the horrible loss.

"Colleen's got a wedding in Concord, so it's just us today."

The kitchen was oven warmed, the tangy sweetness of Maureen's fresh cinnamon rolls wafting about the room.

"It smells like Heaven in here," I said, shucking out of my coat.

"Aye, it does." Nanny planted herself in her usual chair at the table and said, "I'll take one o' them rolls, lass, and a cuppa."

They were in front of her before she put a period on the sentence.

She took a large sip and sighed. "There now, that's fine, 'tis."

"I've got a box of scones ready for you to take back, Nanny. I figured you were getting low."

"Aye, I am. Tilly's been sneakin' into me room at

night, pilferin' 'em. Can't seem to get enough to eat no matter how much she stuffs in her face durin' the day. Not gainin' an ounce, she isn't, either. And speakin' of not enough to eat"—she turned those wise eyes to me— "have you got some provisions for this one to take with her? She's not been eatin' right of late, and it's beginnin' to show."

Maureen peered at me across the table as she placed a tray of rolls, freshly baked bread, and a stick of butter down on it. Her beautiful blue eyes narrowed a bit at the corners, and she pressed her lips together in a very Nanny-like purse.

I flicked a quick look at Nanny, who was regarding her tea, and mouthed *Don't ask* to my sister. If Maureen was ever blessed enough to have children, I knew for certain they'd cower under the force of her questioning perusal.

"I'll put some things together."

For the next hour, the three of us sat and chatted, with Maureen rising at times to help serve.

During a lull, I told them something I'd been musing over the past week.

"I'm thinking of getting a dog."

"Are ya, now?" Nanny's eyes went on hyper-alert, the brilliant blue in them glistening as she focused her attention on me.

"I miss having a dog. George was such a part of my life for so many years, and I miss coming home to love and licks and someone to care for."

Maureen asked a string of questions about the breed I was interested in, and then had to leave to deal with a guest issue.

Alone now with Nanny, the intense, inquisitive

stare she was tossing my way was very similar to Frayne's. There was a Nanny-quisition coming.

I girded my loins.

"Is it a dog you're wanting, lass, or a man and a family of your own?"

That perception trait of Maureen's could be laid firmly at this little Irishwoman's DNA door.

"Well, George was family." I lifted my shoulder in what I hoped was a careless shrug.

"You're a smart, no-nonsense, tell-it-like-it-is woman, Cathleen Anne. But I am as well, so don't be thinkin' you can bullshit one who was raised in th' muck and mire."

To hear an epithet come from my grandmother's mouth was akin to Halley's comet lighting up the sky: a once-in-a-lifetime occurrence. Maybe that was the reason I divulged the true reason I was considering bringing a dog into my home again.

With a heavy sigh, I took a sip of my tea, swallowed and then said, "Finding a dog is a lot easier than finding a man to love and make a family with, Nanny. Especially living here. The field of available men isn't exactly wide open."

"Nonsense, lass. Two of me four husbands hailed from Heaven. There's plenty o' men you could choose from."

"Forty years ago, that may have been true. Nowadays, not so much. Getting a dog seems…simpler. There's no emotional baggage to sift through, no issues other than training them not to pee indoors. "

Nanny squinted at me, and I have to admit, I wiggled in my chair under her scrutiny. I was almost forty years old, yet my grandmother still had the

317

capability to make me revert to a naughty six-year-old, anticipating a come-to-Jesus lecture.

"I'm not blind, ya know, lass."

I bit my tongue so I wouldn't remind her of her recent cataract surgery, necessary because she'd—literally—turned as blind as a dingbat.

"Any fool could see there was somethin' goin' on between you and Mac Frayne. Had the look of a man besotted whenever you were in a room together. More than me commented on it at the home when you both came t' visit."

Heat rushed up my neck and cheeks.

"And by the look o' that flush boundin' up your face, you're equally smitten. Don't try to deny it," she added when I opened my mouth. I slammed it shut again. "Now, tell me what happened between the two of you. One minute Mac was at the home, telling me about Robert, the next, he's gone. What happened?"

So I told her. Everything. From Frayne's family tragedy, how he'd helped me with George, his distaste about my being a lawyer, and the argument we'd had in the courthouse the day he'd told me he was leaving.

And Nanny listened without saying a word, which had to be difficult for her, since she'd never shied away from interrupting, offering an opinion, or making herself heard at any time during my entire lifetime.

Maureen rejoined us as I recalled that last day. When I was done I felt…lighter, somehow.

"You're in love with him," Nanny said, nodding once I'd finished.

Since it wasn't a question, I didn't feel compelled to respond.

"Do ya' know how he feels about you, lass?"

"In all honesty, no. Yes, he was attracted to me, I can't deny that. But did he feel enough for me to get over what he thought about what I do?" I shrugged. "I think it's obvious he couldn't."

Maureen squeezed my hand.

"Men can be such dolts. And clueless, as well, to what's right in front of them." Nanny shuddered and shook her head.

I laughed. Leave it to her to speak the truth.

As I got her settled back into her room at the nursing home a while later, the box of scones from Maureen hidden in her bedside table drawer, Nanny pulled me down into a fierce hug.

"If I've learned anythin' in all me years," she said, "it's love finds ya when you're least expectin' it to show up. There's someone for ya, darlin' girl. Someone to build a family with and who'll make ya feel like a queen. I've no doubt of it.

I smiled down at her, wishing I could feel as confident as she. "Your lips to God's ears, Nanny."

"No worries, lass. I've a direct line, I have."

Those twinkling eyes pulled a smile from me. A peck on her cheek and then I left her to her latest romance novel.

****

"I think I'm coming down with something," I told Martha a few days later. "I have zero energy, and I can't shake this queasy, upchucky feeling."

"Your color's off, for sure. I'd even say you look a little green around the edges."

I'd been feeling weird for a while, but today a bone-zapping fatigue was begging me to put myself to bed.

319

"Your schedule's clear until Monday afternoon. Why don't you go on home and get some rest? I can manage everything here for the rest of the day."

A hot date with my pillow sounded like bliss, and forty minutes later, I was snuggled deep under it, about to drift off when my garage doorbell rang. I was prepared to ignore it, but it rang again.

I tugged on my ancient bulky bathrobe, and as I stumbled down the stairs, I had to hold on to the bannister for dear life to ward off the dizziness spinning in my head. On wobbly legs, I threw open the door, took one look at Mac Frayne's face, and then everything around me went black.

A man was speaking, the words muffled, like when you're trying to hear someone talk underwater.

"No...I caught her before she fell...okay. I'll be here."

Frayne.

My eyes flew open, and I found myself flat on my back on my kitchen floor, one of the cushions from a kitchen chair propped under my head.

"Cathy." Frayne tossed the cell phone on the table, dropped to his knees, and took my hand. "Are you okay?"

"What happened?" I tried to sit up, but I slammed my eyes closed again and turned to stone because the room started spinning.

"You fainted." His hand grazed over my forehead and trailed down to my cheeks. "You don't feel warm, but you look ill. Have you been?"

With my eyes closed, I told him I hadn't been feeling well for a few days. Maybe a little longer, now that I thought about it.

"This is the first time I've fainted, though." To test the dizzy-waters, I slowly opened one eye, then the other. Frayne's face above me was carved with concern. His eyebrows were a hair from touching in the center of his forehead, his lids tight at the corners. That delicious, delectable mouth I'd more than once fantasized about kissing in the past few weeks was drawn tight.

Something wasn't right about his face, though. I was able to see all of it.

"You got a haircut."

He continued to stare down at me. A tiny tug lifted one corner of his mouth. "Well, your vision's not impaired. Do you want to try and stand up? I can help you."

I nodded because my butt was uncomfortable on the floor.

Frayne slipped one arm around my waist and grabbed my hand with his other. "Go slow. I don't relish seeing your eyes roll back again. Once was enough for a lifetime."

Together, we managed to get me upright. In full disclosure, though, I have to admit I leaned against him a bit more than I needed to, relishing the feel of his chest against my side, his hand steadying mine. If I could have done it without being obvious and thereby mortifying myself, I would have snuck in a quick graze of my nose against his neck.

Once I was standing, he hooked his foot around the leg of a kitchen chair and helped lower me into it.

"Okay? Not dizzy?"

"I'm good."

He dragged a sister chair close to mine, and from the way he was scrutinizing my face, he didn't believe me.

"I'm fine. Really. I must be dehydrated or something. I've never fainted before."

He rose and took the filtered water jug from the fridge, poured me a glass, and then wrapped my fingers around it.

"Drink."

"When did you get so bossy?" I asked between sips. *And why is it so comforting?* "Who were you speaking to?"

"Maureen. I called her because I didn't know if I should call an ambulance or not. She's on her way over."

"I'd bet cash money she's bringing Colleen with her." I reached for the cell phone.

Frayne was quicker. Holding it out of my reach, he asked, "Who do you want to call?"

"My sisters. They don't need to come, fuss, and hover. I just need some sleep and I'll be fine. I'm never sick. On the random chance I am, though, it usually blows over quick if I rest. Which I was doing when you started pounding on my door." I took a big sip of the water, which tasted divine. "Why are you here?"

He put the cell back down on the table out of my reach. "I finished the book."

"Oh. Wow. Good for you."

"Thanks."

"So, you're here because…why?"

He sat back in the chair and swiped a hand through the sides of his temples, all the while keeping his attention focused on me. "I wanted you to read it before I send it off to my editor. Get your insights on what I've written."

"Okay, wow again. That's, well, an honor. I guess. Why?"

I hadn't realized I'd missed that head tilt and penetrating, quizzical stare as much as I had until he tossed both my way. I might not be feeling at my peak, health-wise, but I was still a woman and his stare fired an arrow of longing straight through to my core.

"Why what?"

"Why do you want my"—I flapped a hand in the air—"insights?"

"A number of reasons." He ticked them off on his fingers. "First, you know the history of this town more than my editor, so you'll be able to detect if I've got any inaccuracies timeline-wise. Second, you were an integral part of my research. If it weren't for you, I might never have found the link to your grandmother, which led me to Robert, who eventually pointed me to Josiah's true beginnings. And third—" He stopped, his eyebrows slamming together.

"Third?"

I wasn't sure, but I think the color in his cheeks darkened.

"Well, third is…you're one of the smartest and most honest people I've ever known. You have an uncanny ability to put into words what people are thinking and feeling. That trait is probably part of what makes you so good at what you do, and because of it I think you'd tell me the truth about whether or not the book has any merit. I'd really appreciate your opinion of it."

"Did you just compliment my being a lawyer? Or did I hallucinate that because I'm sick?"

This time both sides of his mouth pulled up. In the

next instant, it went straight again, a serious, thoughtful expression glazing his eyes.

"Cathy." He stretched a hand across the table and pulled one of mine into his. "I want to apologize for that last day. At the courthouse. I was—well, rude doesn't describe it enough. I caused a scene where you work, where people know and respect you, and I'm sorry for that."

I had a great deal I wanted to say in reply to that. Sometimes just listening is the best course, though.

"I hadn't planned on leaving that day. But—"

The kitchen door flew open, interrupting what he'd been about to tell me.

Maureen, armed with a shopping bag I instinctively knew was filled with food burst through the door, Colleen close at her heels. Both had lines of worry etched on their faces.

"Mac told us you fainted," Maureen said. She dropped the bag on the counter and shrugged out of her coat. Then, she took my face in her hands, lifting my chin and examining me with a thorough rake from eyebrows to chin. "How long have you been sick? Have you seen a doctor? Do you want me to call yours?"

I slid a hand up and over one of hers, squeezed it, and said, "Stop."

The uber-concern she was expressing could be laid directly at her twin's door. The first indication we'd had Eileen was sick was when she'd fainted one day in the inn. A quick trip to the emergency room and a complete physical by her private doctor had led to the breast-cancer diagnosis. Colleen had fainted a few months ago from stress and exhaustion. Maureen's fear another of her sisters had a life-threatening disease burst bright and harsh in front of her mind.

"I've got some kind of stomach flu or virus. That's all. It needs to run its course."

"But you fainted."

"Because I haven't been drinking and I'm dehydrated. That's all."

Her breath caught, and she was one tear away from losing control. I pressed her hand again. "Mac made me drink water, and I feel better already. Promise."

"Have you eaten anything?" Colleen asked from over Maureen's shoulder.

"Not much. I feel like I'm gonna barf most of the time."

She nodded. "I brought you a box of saltines. They've been a lifesaver with my morning sickness. If you've got a tummy bug, they might help you, too."

I thanked her.

Maureen took a breath and finally let go of my face. "I brought chicken soup."

"Nanny's recipe?"

"Of course."

"My grandmother's soup has weird healing powers," I told Frayne. "The only one she's ever shared the recipe with is Mo, so none of us knows what's in it."

"An extra dose of love," Maureen said, quoting Nanny. "Want me to heat some up?"

"Not now. I'll take a few crackers, though."

"I'll make you some tea," Mac offered.

Who of the three of us was more surprised when he rose and opened the cabinet where I stored the tea bags was debatable. Colleen's eyes narrowed as she watched him pull a bag from the box. Maureen's expression went from concerned to thoughtful in a nanosecond when he filled the kettle with water, and I was dumbfounded he remembered where I kept everything.

While the water boiled, he turned, leaned against the counter with his arms crossed over his chest, and found three pair of inquiring eyes zeroed in on him.

This time I was certain his cheeks darkened.

"The warmth from hot tea helps with nausea," he said.

"That's true." Colleen nodded. "Slade has been researching nausea cures for the past two weeks. Bland foods, like crackers, and plain tea go a long way in helping me get out of bed in the morning."

Absentmindedly, she rubbed a hand across her still flat stomach.

"I'll leave the soup in the fridge for when you want to heat it up." Maureen began unpacking the bag she'd brought. "There's some herbed bread, roasted chicken and potatoes, and a container of oatmeal for when you're up to eating solids again."

"You're still my favorite sister," I told her and then grinned when Colleen tossed me a pout.

"You might change your tune when it's time for Slade and me to choose godparents," she said.

While Mac steeped my tea, my sisters fussed.

I loved these two beyond words, but I wasn't used to this kind of attention. It made me a little uncomfortable and a whole lot of anxious.

"Don't you have an inn to run?" I asked Maureen. "And it's Friday," I tossed to Colleen. "Don't you have a wedding rehearsal or something you should be at?"

"Charity's taking care of everything."

Mac handed me a mug and said, "Drink."

"People around here have gotten wicked bossy all of a sudden." The grouse was mumbled, but everyone in the room heard it.

"It's payback for all the times you bossed us when we were kids." Maureen finished putting the provisions away and closed the refrigerator. "You know what Nanny says about payback."

" 'Tis a goddess bitch, t' be sure." Colleen's brogue was better than any actress's could ever be.

Without thinking why I shouldn't, I shook my head and immediately regretted it. A tsunami of queasiness bubbled up from my empty stomach at the movement.

"Here. Take small bites of this." Mac opened the crackers and handed me one square. "It'll help."

This time I didn't complain about being told what to do. I'd have obeyed an order to stand on my head if it would bring me relief from this bilious feeling.

They all watched me take a few bites, chew, then swallow. The notion popped into my head that this was how animals felt at feeding time in a zoo.

After a time, the nausea abated a bit, so I sipped some more of my tea.

"I feel almost human," I told them. "And I'm going back to bed, so you can all leave now."

Mac was right next to me when I stood, poised, probably, to catch me if I went down again.

I swatted his hand away. "I'm not gonna faint."

I'd forgotten how persistent he could be. Ignoring the hit, he slid an arm around my waist and said, "Humor me," while he led me back up the stairs, my sisters tagging behind us.

Once I was settled in bed, the comforter drawn up around my ears, my cell phone sitting on my bedside table courtesy of Colleen, I said, "You look like the three bears inspecting Goldilocks, standing there like that."

The three of them were at the foot of my bed. Mac had his hands shoved in his pants pockets, Maureen's hands were clasped together as if she were praying, and Colleen was rubbing her tummy again.

"Go. Please," I pleaded. "Let me sleep. I'll be fine by tomorrow."

I closed my eyes to underscore my desire for them to leave me in peace.

Two sets of lips kissed my cheeks as my sisters told me they'd check on my later.

The one set of lips I craved to do the same, hadn't.

****

It was dark when I opened my eyes again. Hunger clawed at my belly, loud and insistent noises coming from under the bed covers.

I sat up gingerly, thrilled to discover the dizziness was a mere memory. When I went down the stairs this time, I was in no danger of face planting on a riser.

The light in the kitchen was on, and an amber glow flickered from the living room. The smell of a wood fire filled my senses. Someone had lit the fireplace. From the doorway, I discovered who.

"You're still here."

Frayne was sitting on the couch, a laptop nestled on his lap, an open bottled water on the table next to him.

"And you lit a fire."

He tossed the laptop aside, rose, and wrapped his hands around my upper arms. "How are you feeling?"

"Better. Starving. Why are you still here?"

His grip tightened a hair before he released me. "Do you want some of Maureen's soup?"

"It's really Nanny's soup, and you didn't answer my question."

"Let's go into the kitchen. I'll get us both something to eat and we can...talk."

I didn't argue, mainly because I was ravenous.

"Want tea or water?" he asked as he pulled a pot from an undercounter cabinet.

"Water. I can get it," I added when he turned. After I did, I got us bowls and spoons, then pulled out the loaf of herb bread Maureen left, wrapped, on the counter.

While I set everything on the table, Mac stirred the soup. We didn't speak until our bowls were filled and we were seated at the table. I got such a profound sense of déjà vu seeing him sitting across from me. The week he'd spent with me was front and center in my mind as I asked him again, why he'd stayed.

The simple shrug he gave me wasn't as casual as I think he'd meant it to be.

"Your sisters were busy. I wasn't. It made sense for me to stay and make sure you were okay. They were very worried about the fact you'd fainted. Especially Maureen."

I gave him my theory on why.

"I can understand her concern, then. She equates the episode with something tragic."

I nodded and sipped some soup.

"This is delicious," Frayne said.

"Whenever one of us had so much as a sniffle when we were kids, Nanny would insist on feeding us this. I swear, it shortened our sick time by half."

"I envy you your grandmother. Your whole family,

in fact."

I let that sit for a minute. "You mentioned earlier you want me to read your manuscript."

He nodded. "I'd really value your opinion and any thoughts on improving or changing it you may have."

"I'm surprised to hear you say you value my opinion."

"Why?"

"You've made plain on more than one occasion what you think of me and my profession. And it hasn't been favorable."

"Not you, Cathy. Never you." He reached across and took my free hand.

I jumped in surprise but left my hand in his.

"You're nothing like any lawyer I've met before. You truly care about your clients and on more than a professional basis. You don't do what you do for riches, or commercial glory, or even public celebrity, but because you have a deep-rooted need for justice and fairness and for what's right. You want people to be the best they can be. It's an amazing trait to possess, and you do."

The soup wasn't the only thing warming me right then. His words, delivered with sincerity, meant more to me than I could ever have imagined they would.

"That's a pretty big reversal since the last time we spoke at the courthouse. What's changed in the past three weeks to make you feel this way?"

He dropped his chin to his chest for a moment, then lifted it again. "I can't begin to apologize for how horrible I was to you. I acted like a total prick, and I know it. I knew it at the time but couldn't pull back my anger. It was too…" He shook his head. "It was just impossible to."

"Why?"

When he answered me, those shadows in his eyes I'd hated seeing once again showed themselves. "I got a phone call that morning from Marci. She'd found out something and wanted to make sure I knew about it before I happened to see it online, or before a tabloid reporter called me for a sound bite."

Intrigued, I asked, "What was it?"

He pulled in a bracing breath, as if he needed it, then slowly exhaled. "The girl who killed Cheyanne and Mabel was arrested for texting while driving again. She hit a stopped school bus this time."

"Oh, good Lord." I squeezed the hand he held, then wrapped my other one around both of them, cocooning them. "Were any of the children hurt or…"

"Thankfully, no one died. Six of the kids did need hospitalization for various injuries. Concussions, one broken arm, and one broken collarbone among them. The girl texting walked away without a scratch."

"She was arrested, though, right?"

"Yeah. I wanted to head back and speak to the prosecutor, give a victim impact statement or something. Let the court know what the girl had already done, the pain she'd caused."

"That usually doesn't happen until after a trial and before sentencing."

"Yeah, the prosecutor mentioned that. I was furious, and I felt so…*useless*. Because so many children were involved in the accident though, the prosecutor had been getting calls left and right from parents who were pushing him to take her to trial and send her to jail. And he was going to do it."

"Why do I hear a *but*? Did she plead out?"

"No. The judge refused to grant bail this time because the prosecutor argued her behavior was a pattern of abuse and simply taking away her driver's license wasn't enough. He had her put in juvenile detention, which is a joke because she was just shy of eighteen."

"What do you mean, was?"

His gaze went hot, the skin dropping down around his lips crevassing into two, deep lines. "She killed herself."

"Oh, Mac."

"Apparently, she couldn't stand being incarcerated with the potential for a prison sentence for her actions. She hung herself with her bed sheet the night she was admitted."

I didn't have any words of comfort for him. Nothing I said could ever bring back his family, and saying I was happy that this girl was now dead sounded awful, in addition to being untrue.

Mac, God bless him, echoed my thoughts.

"When I found out she was dead, I waited for the feeling of elation, of vindication to come. She can't hurt anyone else, kill anyone else's family, destroy any more lives." The expression in his eyes moved from anger to sadness. "It never came. All I can feel is such a profound sense of waste and loss."

"That's because you're a good man. You're not the kind to harbor vengeance."

"I thought I was. Deep down."

"Trust me, you're not. Hate like that isn't in you. I may not know many things, but I know that."

His fingers pressed against mine. "Thank you for

believing that."

I went to stand, but he held on to my hand, keeping me in place.

"I'm disgusted with myself for how I treated you in the courthouse. I projected my anger about this girl and how the judicial system handled everything concerning her onto you, which is wrong. You had nothing to do with any of it. But I made you a target for my anger, and for that I'm so, so sorry. I can't even ask for your forgiveness because I don't deserve it."

"Yes, you do. Everyone does." When I pulled back my hand this time, he let it go. I rose and brought my now empty bowl to the sink. "Father Duncan has always taught us forgiveness benefits the person bestowing it more than the person receiving it. He's not wrong." I turned, and Frayne was standing right behind me, as I knew he would be.

I shook my head and said, "You need a bell." I took his bowl and spoon from his hands. Looking directly into his eyes, I infused my voice with as much sincerity as I could because I wanted him to believe me. "Your apology is accepted, Mac. I understand why you reacted the way you did, why you said the things you said. You were never afforded justice for what happened to your family. Anyone could understand your fury. Anyone."

"Thank you," he said, humbly.

I nodded and rinsed the dishes, handing them to him to load in the dishwasher.

"I feel like a slug," I said when I was done. "I don't want to do anything other than lie around." My nausea was gone, but I was still tired and bone weary.

"Want to relax and watch one of the movies

Colleen brought? I put them on the living room table."

"Vegging in front of a movie sounds great." I chose one, got it set up in the DVD player, and settled down on the couch. Frayne tossed the afghan over me and tucked it under my feet.

"I'm not cold or feverish," I told him. "Plus the fire's warm."

"It can't hurt" was his reply as he closed his laptop, then walked from the room with it. I thought he'd gone to pack up his things to get going. Since he knew I was feeling better and we'd made our peace, there was no reason for him to babysit me for my sisters.

The video started, and I snuggled down. Frayne returned a few minutes later with two mugs filled with something steaming.

"I thought you were heading out."

"No. I went to make us hot drinks." He placed his mug down on the table and handed me mine. Then, that adorable head tilt came my way. "Why did you think I was leaving?"

"The better question is why are you staying? I'm feeling better."

"I can see that." He sat down on the opposite side of the couch from me.

"You don't need to watch over me. Really. I'm good."

"Okay." He propped his unshod feet up on my coffee table and sipped his coffee, his attention on the television.

"You like this movie?" He nodded toward the screen.

Confused, I answered, "It's a classic romantic comedy. My favorite kind."

"Really? Romcoms are your fav? I would have guessed gritty courtroom dramas were more your speed."

"Not only is that insulting," I said as I took a sip of my delicious tea, "it's an incorrect assumption based on nothing tangible but your own prejudices."

Frayne's lips quirked as he took another sip. "You sound like a lawyer."

"With good reason."

"Granted." The smile that grew across his cheeks was heart-stopping. "Let's just watch the movie."

The next thing I knew, warmth engulfed me from shoulders to feet.

I don't know when, but sometime during the movie I'd fallen sleep. When I woke, I was stretched out on the couch, on my side, Mac pressed up against my back. One of his arms draped over my waist and pressed into my tummy, holding me close against him.

I closed my eyes again and, for the first time in weeks, slept soundly.

Chapter 21

The shower was running when I opened my eyes the next morning.

A brief memory of Mac carrying me back to my bed sometime during the night slipped into my mind.

The bed was still warm beside me, indicating not only that he'd slept next to me, but also that he hadn't been up for long. I rolled over and immediately pulled to a dead stop. The room was spinning again, and bile wormed its way up my throat. I gauged the time it would take for me to run to the guest bathroom because mine was occupied, and there was no way I could make it without a mishap. Thankfully, the shower shut off right then.

Frayne appeared in the doorway a moment later, a towel slung low on his hips. The reality I was truly sick hit home when I didn't even feel a twinge in my girlie parts at the hot, wet sight of him. All that black, swirly hair trailing down from his pecs to under the towel, his chiseled abs, those defined biceps, none of those had any effect on me.

Well, maybe a little, but it was outweighed by the queasiness.

"Morning. How are you feeling?"

"You done?" I surprised myself I was even able to get that much out.

He squinted at me and began to cross to the bed. I

shot up and sprinted past him and made it to the bathroom before mortifying myself.

There's nothing sexy or even mildly appealing about someone retching. I hadn't had the forethought—or time—to shut the door, but I was still surprised when a hand, not my own, held back the hair from my face, and another rubbed down my back as I emptied my stomach of buckets of bile.

After what seemed like eternity, I sat back on my haunches and dropped my head to my hands. Tears streamed down my face as I panted for air, a sour, metallic taste coating my tongue.

"Here." A wet washcloth appeared before me. "Wash your face, then you can rinse your mouth with cold water."

I pressed the cloth against my eyes, the coolness of it refreshing, then swiped it down my face.

"Now swish this around in your mouth but don't swallow. It might come right back up again."

The cup of cold water went a long way in killing the terrible taste in my mouth.

I handed the glass and the cloth back, but I couldn't look at him. Humiliation bolted through me. I don't do vulnerable well. "Thank you."

"Let's get you back in bed." Strong, able, comforting arms lifted me.

"I can walk," I said, secretly relishing the fact I didn't have to.

"I know. But this is easier."

Once I was settled back under the covers, Mac felt my forehead.

"No fever. That's good." He told me he was going to get dressed, then bring me some tea and the crackers

Colleen had delivered yesterday. I slipped back into sleep and woke several hours later to find the crackers at my bedside along with a bottled water and a note written in Frayne's precise block print.

If you're still nauseated when you wake up, try to eat a few of these and drink some water. It'll help.

I wasn't feeling sick, just empty and hollow. The crackers tasted like heaven.

I sat up and dangled my feet over the side of the bed. No dizzies. I felt grungy, though, so I headed for the shower. The hot water was divine.

Twenty minutes later, washed, dressed in new pjs, and feeling much better, I found Frayne once again at my dining room table, his laptop open and his glasses one nose twitch away from falling off.

My heart turned over at the sight of him. Try though I had, I couldn't fight the fact I was in love with him. Yes, his moods were mercurial, he was a bit of a loner, and he carried so much emotional baggage around with him he should have been hunchbacked. Add in the fact that he wasn't a fan of what I did for a living, and a future together didn't appear bright. But he was also kind, thoughtful, and caring. I didn't have to add sexy and gorgeous because those were evident. I wanted to tell him what was in my heart, show him how much I felt for him.

But I was still afraid.

He glanced up and smiled when he found me. "I heard the shower go on. I figured you were feeling better."

I came and sat in the chair next to him. "I am. Thanks for…before. I hate being sick, but I really hate being sick in front of someone. It's…well, mortifying doesn't seem strong enough a word."

"I had enough of my own mortifying moments when I was drinking. Believe me, I understand."

"Mac, I—" I stopped because I didn't know how to say what I wanted to.

Bless Nanny. Her voice loomed loud and clear in my head as if she was standing right beside me.

Gird your loins, Number One, and tell the darlin' man what's in your heart. You've a talent with words and such, able to convey your thoughts concisely. Use that talent now.

"Cathy? What's wrong?" He took my hand and worried the knuckles across it. "Talk to me, sweetheart."

The endearment gave me hope. "Nothing's wrong. I want to tell you something, and I'm trying to figure out how to do it the right way."

"I have a hard time believing anything you tell me would be in the wrong way."

"I hope you still feel that way when I'm done."

His eyes narrowed and he tilted his head to one side. "I'm listening."

I swallowed and then took a breath. "When you left, I was hurt. Hurt by everything you said about me being a lawyer. But more. I thought, I felt, there was…something between us. Something good. Something, well, special. But you left without a backward glance, and it had me second-guessing everything."

"Again, I'm sorry about that. I should have trusted you enough to tell you what happened, but I didn't and for that, I can't apologize enough." He reached over and took my other hand and brought both to his lips, dragging a kiss across them. "And what we had, what we *have*, *is* special, don't doubt that. Ever." His eyes were intense, the blue turning a stark, clear, crystal. "If I could have a do-over for that day, believe me, I would have done everything differently."

"How?"

"First, I would have told you why I was leaving, but then I would have explained I was going to leave anyway because when I write, I isolate myself and devote all my time and effort to getting the work done. It's easier for me, somehow." His lips pulled up. "It was always a bone of contention with Cheyanne. She called me selfish more times than I can remember."

"I don't think it's selfish." I shrugged. "It's just how you work."

His smile broadened, then he turned serious again. "I should also have told you one more thing before I left. One important thing. Well, two really."

"What?"

"One, I was coming back as soon as the book was done."

"Why?" Goodness, I was turning into some kind of monosyllabic enquirer.

"Because of the second thing I should have told you." He paused and, with a simple tug, had me in his lap. He cupped my face and held my gaze prisoner. The shadows were gone, replaced by such a well of emotion my breath caught.

"I love you, Cathy. With everything I am and everything in me."

This time, words, monosyllabic or otherwise, wouldn't form. Tears did, though, and I couldn't pull them back. Mac captured one with a soft thumb swipe across my cheek.

"I think I fell in love with you the first day at the historical society lunch. You were so strong, so commanding, so gorgeous. The way you dealt with the personalities around that table told me you were a woman who stood her ground, who didn't suffer fools. It was captivating to watch. Every time we were together after and as I came to know you better, I realized what a warm, loving, loyal, and smart woman you are. Your principles and ideals make you someone to be admired. Your love of family, of justice, of common sense, all of it, combined into a woman who's captured my heart, mind, and soul. I certainly wasn't looking to fall in love when I arrived here. But I left head over heels for you. I finished the book in record time because I wanted, I needed, to get back to you. I'm empty and lost without you. You've made me feel alive when I never thought I would be again."

He took a deep breath and laid his forehead against mine.

"I know I'm not the easiest guy to be around. I get lost in my head, I don't share what I'm feeling, and I don't take the feelings of others into consideration when I'm working. But because of you, I want to *be* better, act better. I've never thought I could before. With you, I want to."

"I think you're pretty perfect the way you are." I swiped a hand across my wet face.

"I'm not perfect, not be a long shot." He shook his head. "I know you can't possibly feel for me what I feel for you. I haven't, after all, been the most gracious and loving of men to you. But I want to be a part of your life if you'll have me. For today, tomorrow, for however many tomorrows come after that. I love you, Cathy. I can't imagine a future without you." He pulled back and trailed a finger down my jaw.

"What does that mean, Mac? The future? My life and my future are here in Heaven. Yours, in New York."

"My life is anywhere you are," he said without a pause. "I can write anywhere as long as I have a laptop. And you," he added. "All my necessary stuff is out in my car. I wasn't kidding when I said I was coming back to you. And I'm staying."

"You are?"

"I am. Know it. Now, I've just spent a ridiculous amount of time telling you what I feel and what I want. What do you want?"

The truth has always been such an important facet of my life, so that's how I answered him: truthfully.

"You. Just you. For today, for tomorrow, and for every tomorrow that comes after." I threw my arms around his neck and held on for dear life.

Mac tugged on my arms, trying to break my hold. With a laugh in his voice, he said, "I want to kiss you. Let go."

Laughing as well, I said, "I want to kiss you, too, but I don't want to give you whatever's making me sick."

"I'm willing to chance infection if it's from you," he said.

I snorted. "That's the cheesiest thing I've ever heard. You should be forced to turn in your writer's card for that."

Shifting, I looked him square in the eye.

Mac kissed my nose and grinned. "I'll come up

with something better. I've got all the time in the world as long as I have you."

Now that line wasn't cheesy at all.

****

One week later…

I was standing in the kitchen, humming, while getting dinner ready.

Goodness, when was the last time I'd actually hummed? Let's be real here: years.

I couldn't help it, though. I was happy. So gloriously happy.

Mac had become a fixture in my life, my bed, even my closets. Knowing he loved me was amazing. But the way he showed me in the little things he did each and every day was astounding. Because he was an early riser, he had tea ready for me when I got out of the shower each day. I never had to worry about mooching food from Maureen anymore because I'd forgotten to grocery shop. Mac went to the store when we needed provisions and had proven himself a more than adequate cook.

Tonight, though, I was in charge of dinner, and I wanted it to be special because I had some news to share.

The garage door sounded, and when I peeked out the window, Mac was pulling his car into the space.

He came in while I was turning the turkey, the recipe courtesy of Maureen.

"Hey," I said with a smile. "Where'd you go? I came home from the doctor's office, and you weren't here."

"Had to run out for something." He kissed my nose and then stretched over me to sniff the pot. "That smells fabulous. What is it?"

"Mo's cranberry turkey recipe." I slid my nose up along the column of his throat and did my own inhaling. He smelled way better than the turkey.

"Why don't you take your coat off? It should be ready in about fifteen minutes."

I glanced over my shoulder. His bomber jacket was a little bulky, and he was holding his arms at a funny angle, almost as if he was cradling his stomach.

"What do you have under your coat?"

He smiled.

"Mac?"

"Hear me out, okay, before you react? Promise?"

"Why don't I like the way that sounds?"

He shifted his hands a little, and a strange sound whispered up from his jacket.

"What was that?"

"I got you a present. Well, it's really for the both of us." He slowly slid the zipper on his jacket down. A furry black head popped up and out from the opening he'd made.

"Oh. My. *God*." I shoved my hands out and stroked the little head.

With a smile as wide as the Grand Canyon, Mac unzipped his jacket, and together we cradled the puppy.

"Gorgeous, isn't she?" he asked.

The black coat was shiny and thick, the face and snout typical of the Labrador breed.

"Where did you get her?"

"Shelby. I called over there a few days ago and asked for a recommendation for where I could adopt one. This little girl turned eight weeks yesterday. Perfect timing."

"She's so soft." I stroked her fur and was rewarded with a sandpaper-tongue kiss across my knuckles. With tears in my eyes and love filling my heart, I looked up into his beaming face and said, "Thank you."

He bent and kissed me, the pup wedged between us.

"We can call her Georgie since she's a girl," he said. "She's our first baby."

"Um, no."

Lord, would I ever get tired of seeing that adorable head tilt?

"You don't like the name? I thought—"

"It's not the name. You know I went to the doctor's today because I can't shake this stupid virus?"

"Yeah. I'm glad you did because I've been worried."

"No need to be."

"But you didn't feel well again this morning. If you don't have a virus or a bug, what then? An ulcer?" His eyes narrowed.

"No. But the doctor was concerned because I've been sick for so long, so she did blood work, took a urine sample, routine stuff like that." I pulled the now-squirming puppy into my arms. In a heartbeat, she calmed.

"And? What did she find out?"

"I was going to tell you this at dinner, but since you brought this little beauty home with you, you should know she's not our first baby, but our second."

His face went through about fifteen different expressions in a few moments. His eyes went wide, and he looked down at my belly, then back up to my face, and then my belly again.

"Cath—?"

"I'm pregnant."

Silence. Then, "How?"

"The usual way." I laughed and kissed Georgie's snout.

"You know what I mean." He pulled me into his arms and rested his chin on my head. "We've been careful every time."

"Not every time. There was that once by the fire…According to my dates, that's about right."

I pushed back a bit so I could read his face. "Are you…how are you about this?"

"So happy I can't think straight."

"Really?"

He kissed me long and slow as an answer.

When we came up for air, my eyes were unfocused.

"I'm due in November."

"And everything is…okay? With you? With the baby?"

"So far, so good." I rolled my eyes. "Since I'm over thirty-five, there are a few risks involved. But I'm not worried. Not in the least."

Mac kissed my nose. "I can't tell you how happy I am about this."

I could echo his sentiments. I was finally going to be a mother, and the father was the best man I'd ever known.

Mac let go of me and took a step back. "I had a big romantic scene all plotted in my head about how I'd do this and when, where. But I don't want to wait because right about now seems perfect."

"Do what?"

I almost dropped the pup when Mac took one of my hands and dipped down to one knee.

"*Mac.*" Georgie startled, opened her eyes, and licked her chops, then went right back to sleep. In a much quieter tone I said, "What are you doing?"

"I want to do this the right way, say everything I've been thinking of for the past few weeks, so let me, okay? Let me get it all out."

I cradled the pup even closer with one hand.

"Cathy, I feel like everything that's happened in my life, every good thing, every bad, every choice I've made, every decision, has led me to you, here and now, at this moment. And I'd gladly go through it all again if it ended in this exact same spot. With you. I never envisioned I'd find someone to love as much as I love you. In all honesty, I didn't think I had it in me to love anyone to the degree I love you. You gave me that. You let me see what love really is. With your honesty, your tenacity, your willingness to forgive, you opened my heart and showed me what love looks like. What it feels like."

As he pulled something from his pocket, tears streamed down my face, plopping onto the sleeping puppy.

"I told you once, for you I want to be a better man, a man worthy of your love, deserving of the kind of woman you are. And I want to show you I'm that man. My soul, my heart, everything I am and could be, belongs to you. I belong to you."

He opened his fist and held up a ring that blinded me with its brilliance.

"Cathleen Anne, will you marry me? Will you make a life with me? Walk through the good, the bad, and everything in between with me? Put up with me and all my flaws and love me, now and for the rest of our days?"

I tugged on his hand to pull him up. When we were standing toe to toe, the sleeping—now snoring—puppy wedged between us, I kissed him and said, "Yes. A million times yes. My soul, my heart, everything I am and could be, belongs to you, too. I belong to you."

After a long, thorough kiss, Mac trailed a finger across my jaw and smiled. "I love you," he said. "So much."

"I love you more."

"Impossible." He shook his head and placed a kiss on my forehead.

Georgie took that moment to open her eyes. With a quick eye flick between us, she let out a series of baby barks and then tried to lick each of us at the same time, squirming madly, her back legs pumping.

Laughing, Mac declared, "I think she loves us, too."

I let her run her tongue across my chin, then I held her up and looked straight into her soulful eyes.

"We love you, more."

A word about the author...

Peggy Jaeger writes about strong women, the families who support them, and the men who can't live without them. When she isn't writing, you can find her cooking or crafting.

She loves to hear from readers on her website:
PeggyJaeger.com
and on her Facebook page:
https://www.facebook.com/pages/Peggy-Jaeger-Author/825914814095072?ref=bookmarks

~

http://peggyjaeger.com

CPSIA information can be obtained
at www.ICGtesting.com
Printed in the USA
BVHW040905020220
571192BV00016B/379